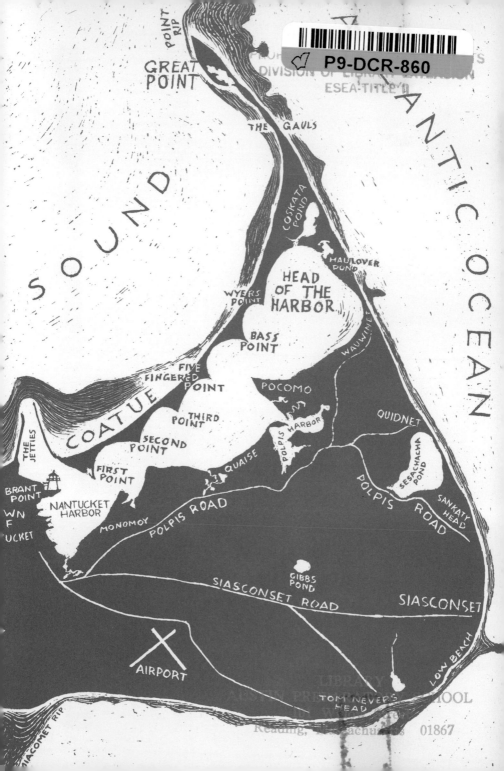

Dark
Nantucket
Noon

Books by Jane Langton

DARK NANTUCKET NOON

THE TRANSCENDENTAL MURDER

Dark
Nantucket
Noon

Jane Langton

Illustrations and endpapers by the author

HARPER & ROW, PUBLISHERS

New York   Evanston

San Francisco

London

10678

A HARPER NOVEL OF SUSPENSE

DARK NANTUCKET NOON. Copyright © 1975 by Jane Langton. All rights reserved. Printed in the United States of America. No part of this book may be used or reproduced in any manner whatsoever without written permission except in the case of brief quotations embodied in critical articles and reviews. For information address Harper & Row, Publishers, Inc., 10 East 53rd Street, New York, N.Y. 10022. Published simultaneously in Canada by Fitzhenry & Whiteside Limited, Toronto.

Designed by Dorothy Schmiderer

Library of Congress Cataloging in Publication Data

Langton, Jane.
    Dark Nantucket noon.
    I. Title.
PZ4.L288Dar3 [PS3562.A515]   813'.5'4   74-5799
ISBN 0-06-012502-0

For Maryalice Thoma

"I'd strike the sun if it insulted me. . . ."
CAPTAIN AHAB in *Moby Dick*

1

*Nantucket! Take out your map and look at
it. See what a real corner of the world it
occupies; how it stands there, away off
shore, more lonely than the Eddystone
lighthouse. Look at it—a mere hillock,
and elbow of sand . . .*
     HERMAN MELVILLE, *Moby Dick*

Below the little plane the water of Nantucket Sound slipped over
itself, the gusty wind from the east rippling the surface in an
endless rapid sparkling hastening succession of white-capped
waves, while the larger waves below them seemed motionless from
the air, a geologic mold of ocean water. But of course the larger
waves were moving too, more slowly. And, obeying a deeper
compulsion, the vast watery volume of the Atlantic Ocean was
rising in response to an urgent tide that yearned across the earth,
sending a bulge of water dragging after the moon from the old
world to the new, carrying it heaving and pulsing along the New
England coast, smashing up after last night's storm upon the
granite boulders of Penobscot Bay, running up into the tidal flats
of the Ipswich River and the clam beds of the town of Essex,
stirring the lobster pots of Gloucester and Marblehead, agitating
the scum and garbage floating around T Wharf in Boston Harbor,
pounding on the fisted forearm of Cape Cod, carrying away

1

granules of colored clay from the cliffs of Gay Head on Martha's Vineyard, washing in white breakers against the shoal that curved northeastward from the body of the island rising below the plane.

Everywhere at once the Atlantic was in motion, rocking in its bed, lifting at the summons of the massive moon, shifting the uneasy hulks of sunken vessels lying on the bottom: the *Andrea Doria*, many fathoms down, the *City of Columbus*. The tide was running in the sea; it was an ocean walking. . . .

Kitty was coming to the island only to see the total eclipse of the sun, that was all. She had taken the plane at Boston, and when it came down at the Nantucket airport she would jump into the rented car that would be waiting for her, drive to the remotest corner of the island, look up at the eclipse, and then take the next plane home.

She was coming only to see the eclipse. There was no chance at all that she would run into Joe Green. The fact that he was living on the island with his wife had nothing whatever to do with her coming. Nothing at all. She had wanted to see a total solar eclipse all her life, and here it was, only a few miles offshore. Nantucket happened to be the only place on the North Atlantic seaboard where totality would be visible, so she had had no choice. And just because she had once made a fool of herself over Joe Green, just because he had settled down on the island and married his second or third cousin or whatever it was, that was of no consequence. She would see what she had come to see, and go home.

Therefore it was odd the way the sight of the gray sickle-shaped island in the glittering sunshaft on the Atlantic Ocean alarmed her. It was positively crawling with invisible antlike Joseph Greens. They were everywhere. Kitty imagined herself aiming a powerful telescope at the island at random—at that long neck of sand ending in a little stick that must be a lighthouse, or perhaps at that stretch of red carpet in the middle of the island. She would squint one eye through the telescope and adjust the focus until the fuzzy field of view sharpened, and there before her would be Joe's face with its amiable mouth and big kindly nose and light eyes. And those eyes would be staring up at her, seeing her, identifying her through the plane window and the wrong end of the telescope, turning cold with anger at this invasion of his privacy.

At the Nantucket airport Kitty climbed out of the plane, letting the wind blow her hair like a veil over her scowling face, avoiding the eyes of the people clustered at the gate, Joe Greens, every one of them. He had multiplied, he was just at the edge of her averted gaze, he was looking through the baggage on the pavement, he was shouting greetings into the wind, he was selling her a local paper and a map of the island, he was handing her the key to her rented car, he was crowding the waiting room, he was loaded down with sleeping bags and heavy parkas and eclipse-viewing apparatus, he was talking excitedly in a loud voice. All the Joe Greens were exchanging congratulations about the brilliant day after the storm during the night, and they were swapping information about what to watch for—the solar corona, and Baily's beads, and the shadow bands, and the flash of red at the very end. But of course when any of these multitudinous Joe Greens opened his mouth Kitty knew it wasn't really Joe, because his voice had been different. She couldn't remember it exactly, but it wasn't this one or that one.

So it was a relief to find the little green car in the parking lot just where the man had said it would be, and her key worked in the lock, and she got in and slammed the door, grateful to be out of the wind, and dumped her bag on the seat beside her, and heaved a great sigh. Joe Green couldn't see her now, unless of course he was that man off vaguely to the left climbing into a station wagon—there, now he was gone.

Kitty started the engine to warm the car, and unfolded her new map. Where was that long neck of sand she had seen from the air? There had been a lighthouse at the end, but the rest of the long sandy beach had looked roadless and deserted. There it was.

3

Nantucket Memorial Airport

Great Point. She would go to Great Point. How much time did she have? She looked at her watch. Almost two hours before the partial phase of the eclipse began, three before totality. And it was the two-and-a-half minutes of totality that she had come to see, when the light of the sun would be completely blocked out by the moon, and the sky would darken, and the solar corona would appear. It was supposed to be awe-inspiring, breath-taking, wonderful. Three hours—plenty of time. Kitty picked up the Nantucket *Inquirer and Mirror* and turned the pages idly.

On page one there was a picture of Nantucket's Maria Mitchell Observatory, and an article about the expeditions from Johns Hopkins and the Oceanographic Institute at Woods Hole. They were going to photograph the eclipse at the observatory and make spectrographic studies of the solar prominences. They would all be there now, thought Kitty, the scientists, milling around, check-

4

ing their instruments, getting ready, jubilant because of the crystal sky after last night's storm.

There was an article with the headline WHAT TO LOOK FOR, and Kitty made a mental note to read it carefully later on. Then a name caught her eye—"Homer Kelly." Homer Kelly? It had a familiar ring somehow. She ran her eye down the paragraph. "Ex-Lieutenant-Detective Homer Kelly, noted scholar in the field of nineteenth-century American literature, is spending a few weeks on the island to complete his study of the men who sailed with Melville." Oh, yes, that was who Homer Kelly was. Kitty had read the biography of Thoreau he had written with his wife. What did this article mean by calling him an ex-Lieutenant-Detective? Had he been some kind of policeman?

Well, enough of that. Kitty folded the newspaper and stuck it into her bag, which was a roomy canvas carryall with a pair of leather handles. Then she looked at the map again. To get to Great Point she would have to go west first, then turn a sharp corner and head northeast on a road marked "Polpis." Good. Kitty put the map into her carryall next to the newspaper and shifted gears.

On the road she kept her eyes straight ahead, looking neither left nor right, while Joe Greens whizzed past her every now and then, going the other way. There were torn leaves and twigs on the pavement, and Kitty guessed they had been blown off in last night's storm.

SOFT TIRES ONLY BEYOND THIS POINT

The road had petered out into sand beyond the big gray shuttered hotel, and now it had come to an end altogether. Kitty pulled up, locked the car and set off with her bag over her arm. There was nothing in her ears but the noise she made cleaving the air, the slightest of slight sounds, diminishing as she picked up each foot in turn, increasing as she swung it forward. There were muddy puddles in the wheel ruts, and she skirted them. To her right a row of houses looked uninhabited, boarded up. To her left lay the wind-streaked water of the harbor. Where was the open ocean? Kitty stopped and opened out her fluttering map, then struggled to fold it up again. The sea should be just over there to the right. She plowed up a steep slope, clutching at beach grass, and came out on the open Atlantic. The water was a cold dark blue, foaming up at the bottom of the steep short beach. And there was something in the water, far out, sleek black heads and finny tails. Seals! sporting and playing, diving for fish.

Exhilarated, Kitty ran down to the sand at the water's edge and whirled around, her bag a driving force at the end of one arm, her hair swatting her neck, slapping her face. Then she walked straight ahead in big strides, the sunshine striking down upon her shoulders.

The simple facts of the seashore made her happy. Air, water, earth and fire, everything reduced to its ancient elements. She had been wanting for a long time to do something with those four things, a long funny exercise in rhymed couplets. Why didn't she just stay, abandon her students, her apartment in Cambridge, her old life, and just stay? With only these four gigantic things to think about—the salt air, the blue water, the clean sand and the fiery sun. Only three in a little while, because the sun was about to have its eye put out by the murdering moon.

The northwest wind knocked and shouldered against her. Kitty leaned into it, adapted herself to it, let it whip at her hair and at the two ends of her wrapped skirt. Suddenly she felt hungry, terribly hungry. She sank down on the sand and reached for her sandwiches. Then she had to get up and plump herself down higher up the beach, because she hadn't counted on the reach of the waves. The tide must be rising. She unwrapped a sandwich and took a lusty bite. It tasted marvelous. Then she unscrewed the top of her Thermos and poured out a little coffee. That tasted marvelous too. She felt around in her bag for the photographic plate she had wrapped up carefully in a cotton kerchief, and held it to the sun. There! A tiny nibble had been taken from the lower right-hand side. Kitty glanced around at the bluff and the sand and the sea, wondering if there would be any diminishing yet of the daylight. Not yet. Everything seemed just as before.

She stood up, let the wind carry away the crumbs from her skirt, gathered up the debris from her lunch, chased a flying sandwich wrapper, pounced on it, stuffed it into her bag and walked on. The going was hard, because the sand was mushy even at the wet edge of the water. Every now and then she rested by stopping to look up at the sun through her photographic plate. The bite that was being taken by the hungry moon was growing bigger, but still the light shining on the sea seemed as bright as ever. The shore continued to curve out of sight ahead of her as if she were walking always in the same place. Once Kitty climbed the bluff to examine a pile of shells and fragments of sponge and bits of beach glass that had been dumped there by some child. They had not come from this place, because here the shore was bare except for flotsam tossed up by the storm, pieces of broken lumber, a plastic jug. There was no other debris on the coarse golden sand, only the overlapping lines traced by the farthest-flung waves, delicate scalloped edgings the thickness of a single grain of sand, beaded with miniature pebbles and fragile tassels of seaweed and pearly fragments of sponge like crumbs of bread. Kitty scooped up some of the shells and dropped them into her bag.

The lighthouse was in sight at last, a white object far away. She looked at her watch. Only an hour before totality. Impulsively Kitty made up her mind to watch the eclipse from the lighthouse. There was no time to waste. She ran back down again to the edge of the water and began striding along, dragging her heels out of the clinging sand, feeling the pull in the small of her back. By the time the moon had effaced half of the sun's disk she was tired, but she kept her eyes fixed on the curving shore ahead of her, willing the lighthouse to come in sight. The sky was noticeably darker now, the blue deeper and more intense, the sea more forbidding, the air chillier and sharp. The crescent sun was slanting down through the beach grass on the bluff, making miraculous images of itself between the interfering blades, and the dancing sparkles on the rushing waves were crescents too. The light filtering through Kitty's hair made small crescents amid the shadow that floated beside her. But Kitty had eyes now only for the lighthouse, a faraway gleaming tower above the bluff. She hurried her heavy feet, feeling giddy, high-spirited. *I am running a race with the moon. So is the sun, which comes forth like a bridegroom leaving his chamber, and like a strong man runs its course with joy.*

Where were the birds? There had been small ones skittering along the edge of the waves, and herring gulls dipping and soaring. They were gone. *I must be moonstruck,* thought Kitty, giggling. *I'm suffering from moon madness.* She pounded on, her feet doggedly taking turns, her chest rising and falling in gasping breaths. The land had narrowed. She could see the ocean on either side. The sandy neck was all one beach. Suddenly her shoes were in water. A shock of cold went through her, and she looked down. A wave had run up the shore and spilled over on the other side. Kitty tried to dodge the next, but it caught her and dashed against her legs, soaking her shoes and woolly stockings and drenching the hem of her skirt with the freezing water of the North Atlantic. Ankle-deep, Kitty stood still and cried out with

the bitterness of the cold. The wave slipped sideways back, and the next impulse was not as high. Swiftly she pulled off her sopping shoes and stockings and stuffed them in her carryall. The sand seemed almost warm to her bare feet. The sky was darker now, the wind freshening, lifting her hair, blowing up the loose heavy edge of her skirt. Lightfooted, Kitty began to run again, glancing up at the streaking rays glaring over the rim of the moon. *Not yet, moon, don't put the sun out yet. I want to touch base first.* Gasping, she ran, shivering with cold, the wind tossing her hair in a long streamer, blowing the flap of her skirt up about her waist, exposing one pale cold leg. At first Kitty tried to push her skirt down, but it was too much trouble. And why bother? There was no one to see. Even the all-seeing eye of the sun was about to be put out. It was really dark now, quite dark. She stopped running and plodded along for another half mile. Then with a breathless laugh Kitty suddenly reached up and wrenched off her sunglasses. Sunglasses! At a time like this.

Touch base! She was nearly there. She ran across the wet sand, her hands stretched out, the stone side of the lighthouse looming up before her, and at last her fingers touched the peeling white paint of the wall. Then she turned and tottered a few steps, her heart in her mouth as a pall of darkness suddenly dropped upon her shoulders. The sand was fluttering with strange shadows. She threw her head back and looked up. The sun was going. A single piercing ray glistened at one side, and then—

Kitty screamed. The sea screamed, the sand, the sky. The sun was gone. There was a black stone in its place. A small black stone. Pearly brightness flared up around it. Two planets welled up in the midnight sky near it.

God have mercy. Kitty shuddered, struggling not to burst into hysterical tears. She should never have come out here alone. No one should behold the end of the world like this alone. Oh, God, the black stone. She should fall on her knees and pray, she should offer herself up as a sacrifice, she should wail and hammer some brazen gong. But all she could do was cry, and stare up, mesmerized, shaking, weeping—until the moon at last drifted to the left and released a blaze of sunlight to the right. Choked with relief, Kitty laughed, and wiped her face with the backs of her hands, and then stumbled around the base of the lighthouse, holding her palms out to catch a handful of sunlight, circumambulating the round tower like a pilgrim praying his way around a holy place, babbling to herself. She felt cracked, unhinged, deranged, delirious. Everything was suddenly at high pitch. And so when she saw the empty cars parked down near the beach on the other side of the dune, a pickup truck and a jeep, she whirled around and looked up at the top of the lighthouse, because she knew immediately exactly where the people were. They were up there! But she was too near, it was too dark, she couldn't see, she laughed with understanding, she was only looking up into blackness. And then her attention was caught by something at the foot of the lighthouse wall. There was a woman there. A woman was lying at the base of the wall, her head bent sideways to look at Kitty. She had been hurt. There was a red stain on her shirt. It was not surprising. Kitty did not feel shocked. The moon had thrown down a bolt like a thunderstone. She ran up to the woman. Perhaps she could help her. Perhaps the woman wasn't dead.

There was a great deal of blood. Kitty knelt down on the cold sand and pulled her kerchief out of her bag and dabbed at the brimming wound. But there was too much blood, and the kerchief was soon soaked. Puzzled, Kitty looked at it in disbelief, then wadded it into a sopping ball, dropped it back in her bag, and scrabbled around for a sweater that was rolled up in there somewhere. Had she lost it?

Impatiently Kitty upended the bag and dumped everything out on the sand. Ah, there was the sweater. She pressed it against the woman's breast. But it was no use. The woman was dead. The cage of her chest was not rising and falling. Kitty shook her head and abandoned the effort, and began picking up her possessions from the sand and dropping them back in her bag. What a mess. They were all bloody from the bloody kerchief. And there was too much stuff. She put a big shell in her skirt pocket.

There. Kitty stood up, the bag in her hand, and saw the people in the lighthouse coming out. They were looking at her, looking down at the dead woman.

There were four of them. Three men and a woman. They were staring, exclaiming. One of the men dropped to his knees beside the dead woman. It was Joe Green. Kitty was not surprised. One of the other men was looking at her, choking, saying something ridiculous. "You killed her," he said. He meant Kitty. He thought she, Kitty, had killed the woman.

"No," said Kitty. "It was the moon, you see. The moon did it."

The third man had his camera out. He was taking her picture. The woman was crying, her hand over her mouth, her horrified eyes looking at Kitty. Now the man with the camera was bending down, pointing at something in the sand. He wasn't a man, after all, not a grown man. He was a young student of Kitty's, Arthur Bird. "Hello, Arthur," said Kitty.

Arthur's face was pale. Usually it was pink, Kitty remembered, with boyish red patches on his plump fair jowls. "There's the knife," he said.

"Oh, thank you," said Kitty. "That's mine. It fell out of my bag." She picked it up. It had fallen point down and nearly buried itself in the sand.

The three men and the woman all recoiled, staring at her. Then Arthur lifted his camera and took another picture.

"No, no," Kitty said. "You don't understand. I didn't kill her." She dropped the knife back in her bag. "It was the moon, don't you see? The moon did it."

2

"Hast not been a pirate, hast thou?—Didst not rob thy last Captain, didst thou?— Dost not think of murdering the officers when thou gettest to sea?"

Moby Dick

They overpowered her then. There was nothing, really, to overpower. The man who was not Joe Green or Arthur Bird merely walked around the body of the dead woman and took Kitty's arm. He asked her politely for her bag, which she surrendered promptly, and then he asked, please, would she mind getting in the jeep? Well, certainly, she'd be glad to. She didn't really want to walk back. And now she was shivering so dreadfully, so uncontrollably, that she was glad to climb into the warm enclosed car and sit down, pulling her bare feet up under her.

The man she didn't know reached across her and took the key out of the ignition. Kitty sat alone on the front seat of the tipped jeep, her shoulders hunched high, her body canted a little to one side, and stared out to sea.

The daylight seemed almost normal now. The shore birds were pattering back and forth at the edge of the water once again, and the herring gulls were back at work—ho hum, no rest for the weary. Kitty tried to compose her mind with a mental exercise, an example of poetic imagery for her freshman class in versification. *My mind is a library, you see, class, and when I open a book, all the pages are blank.* Kitty rested her straining head for a moment on the thought of an empty page, then slammed the book shut again because there were wet red splashes of blood on the white paper.

What were those people doing? She craned her head around to look. Joe was standing away from the others, his back to them in a crooked posture of grief. The others were talking, glancing in Kitty's direction. She looked back at the water, feeling her face flood suddenly with guilt and misery. A sense of appalling disaster hung in the air. Her disordered intellect was beginning to be restored by the sunlight to the normal rational processes of commonplace reckoning. She had done something dreadful, she understood that now. Instead of running away from Joe Green, she had been drawn to him, sucked, pulled, like the tides by the moon. Running from him, yet she had raced after him, followed him, chased him, sought him out on this remote corner of the world to which he had fled, backed up against the sea. How he must have winced to see her, and what must he think now? *The dead woman had been his wife.* She, Kitty, had not been just an irritating presence from the past. She had destroyed him. Kitty beat her fist against her forehead. Why couldn't she have gone to that observatory along with everybody else? If she had, she would be on her way home right now.

She looked in the rear-view mirror. They were lifting the dead woman's body, carrying it to the pickup truck, wrapping it in somebody's coat, putting it down in the back of the truck. Joe was starting to climb in beside it, but the others were pulling him back, leading him to the cab, helping him in. Arthur Bird was getting into the driver's seat. The other man opened the driver's side of the jeep, folded the seat forward so that the woman could climb into the back, and climbed in himself behind the wheel. He waved to Arthur, and Arthur started the truck, backing and turn-

13

ing, heading along the narrow beach past the lighthouse and then driving up onto the high sand and following the churning tracks the two vehicles had left behind them on the journey out. Kitty's driver revved his engine and started after the truck. They were off, murderer safely deposited in one car, murderee in the other. Kitty grimaced and suffered, watching the wrapped body bound a little up and down with the jouncing motion of the truck, seeing the stoop of Joe's shoulders through the rear window.

She tried to talk to the man at the wheel. But he shook his head and moved his hand in a gesture that meant *Don't.* The woman in the back seat said nothing, only whimpered a little. She had Kitty's bag in her lap. She was guarding it, but when Kitty asked for her shoes, the woman groped in the bag and pulled them out, and Kitty put them on, struggling awkwardly as the jeep wallowed in the tracks that made a sort of road along the middle of the narrow neck. Before long the sea on both sides had disappeared, and they were traveling between scrub growths of trees. At last they reached the place where Kitty's car was parked, but when she said it was her car, the man beside her merely shook his head and drove around it. On the paved road Arthur Bird stopped his truck beside an air hose and got out to fill up his tires. Then Kitty's driver pulled up in front of him to take his turn. Everybody got out of the two vehicles except Kitty and Joe. Looking back at what she could see of him, Kitty was depressed to discover that the shape of Joe's bowed head still affected her in a way she didn't want.

They all climbed back in. The fields and woods and at last the outskirts of the town of Nantucket went by Kitty's window, and she looked out at them but saw nothing. One of her pockets hurt her. She pulled a big shell out of it and held it in her hand. It was a great smashed and broken whelk. The jeep slowed down and stopped. The pickup truck was stopping too, parking beside a small gray-shingled building. It was the police station, a charming little cottage.

Kitty's driver got out, walked around the front of the car and

opened Kitty's door. Silently Kitty climbed down, walked ahead of him, stood still while he opened the door of the police station, then turned at the last minute to cast one panic-stricken glance at Joe Green. For a brief second their eyes met. He dropped his instantly. How he must hate her. How he must loathe her.

The police officer at the desk was busy on the phone. Kitty's guide waited patiently. Then the redheaded young man with the fresh red face put down the phone and said, "What can I do for you, sir?"

"I'm afraid something terrible has happened. . . ."

After the hurried arrival of the Nantucket chief of police and his hurried departure, after the matron's search, after the waiting around, after the psychiatrist, after the reappearance of the chief of police, after his questioning, Kitty was led down a little corridor past a row of empty cells, and shut into the last one. The small room was windowless and lined with tin. "If you want to use the bathroom," said the young officer with the red face, "just call me. It's right across the way. My name is Sergeant Fern."

Kitty sat down on the bunk bed. After a while she could hear the men in the office changing shifts. She could hear them kidding, exchanging the time of day, their voices hushing to talk about what had happened at Great Point, about the girl in the last lockup. She could feel the vibration of their big frames moving about. She got up and stood at the barred door.

"Sergeant?" called Kitty. "Could you come here a minute?"

The voices stopped. There were heavy footsteps and then the sergeant appeared. He thought she wanted to go to the bathroom.

"Might I have a pencil and some paper?" said Kitty.

The young sergeant paused, looking at her. "Well, sure," he said. "I don't see why not." He disappeared, then came back with a pencil and a pad of lined yellow paper and a paper bag. The bag contained her shells. "I don't see why you can't have these back," he said.

16

"Thank you," said Kitty, smiling at him. He had a nice face with a high color.

She sat down again on the hard bed and emptied the bag out on the blanket. Some of the shells were sticky with dried blood. Kitty took the big broken whelk out of her pocket too, and held it up to the light of the bare bulb in the ceiling. Then swiftly but painstakingly she began scribbling a description of it on the pad of paper:

> A great shell, twisted, half smashed, turning spirally inward according to some Grecian law of harmony and proportion, the inner surface coated with a microscopic honeycomb, a colony of some infinitesimal sea animal, some form of coral, the outside crusted here and there with sandy pebbles and tiny shells in the hollow clefts of the spiral turnings. And here are some pieces of sponge called dead man's fingers, narrow thumblike growths. And fragments of sand-colored grassy seaweed, the color of hemp, the color of hair. Whose hair is just this color?

Kitty's pencil faltered. It was the color of Joe's wife's hair. And the dead man's fingers were . . .

Enough of that. Kitty tumbled everything back into the paper bag and turned her attention to the room in which she had been locked up.

Four walls of tin . . .

3

*Not by beef or by bread, are giants made or
nourished.*

Moby Dick

"Your attorney is here," said Sergeant Fern, looking in at Kitty.

"My attorney?" Kitty was surprised. She had told them she had
no attorney. She had said she was going to think about it. Now
they had assigned her one. What if she didn't like him? She stood
up and backed into one corner of the cell as an extremely tall man
ducked under the metal frame of the door and stood with his
stooped head grazing the ceiling, his big body filling the space,
crowding it.

"I'm Homer Kelly," he said. "They've been telling me about
you out there. Now you tell me."

Kitty folded her arms and stared at him, as Sergeant Fern came
back and created a moment of confusion by trying to get a chair
inside. Homer Kelly? Kitty had been reading about Homer Kelly
somewhere, ages and ages ago. She had been sitting in her rented
car reading the Nantucket paper, and there had been something
about Homer Kelly in the paper. He was here on the island for

some reason or other, he was doing something about Melville, and she had been surprised to learn that he had been a policeman. A lieutenant-detective. And he must be some kind of an attorney as well.

His face had a keen severity Kitty liked. "I just came to see the eclipse," she began slowly, watching Homer Kelly fold himself down onto the chair, which creaked under his weight.

"Why did you go to Great Point?"

"Because it looked empty. I mean from the air. And there weren't any roads leading out to it. It looked to me as if I could be all by myself."

"Why did you want to be all by yourself?" The big ugly face was hard, chill, stern.

"Because I was trying so hard not to run into Joe Green." Kitty bared herself with a conscious effort of will. "We used to be lovers." She didn't know what else to call it.

"When was that?"

"Oh, a year ago. A year and a half. Then he changed his mind. He went to Nantucket and met"—what was her name?—"Helen Boatwright. And they got married."

"They were married exactly a year ago today, I understand."

"They *were?*" Kitty was surprised.

Homer Kelly looked at her. Then he crossed one enormous leg over the other, and a chair rung clattered to the floor beneath him. Absent-mindedly he felt around for it. There was a new look on his face. Kitty breathed a little more freely and sat down on the edge of the bed.

"Look, my girl, you're in a whole lot of trouble," said Homer Kelly. "Now just let me get some things straight. Tell me what happened from the beginning."

Kitty took a deep breath and started her story all over again. Doggedly she plowed on to the end, while Homer listened, leaning forward, gazing at the floor, his hands clasped between his knees. When she finished he leaned back and looked at her sharply.

"Where did you get the map and the newspaper that were in your bag?"

"At the airport."

"And then you drove directly toward Great Point? And parked your car and walked six miles? You didn't go into town or stop anywhere else?"

"No, that's just it. Why would I go directly to Great Point to kill someone, when I didn't even know that person was going to be there?"

Homer paused. "You mean you're telling me you didn't know Joe Green and his wife would be at the Great Point light?"

"Of course I didn't! That's what I said. I thought I would be all alone on Great Point. All by myself."

Homer studied her again with his small sharp eyes. Then he took something out of his pocket. It was a copy of the Nantucket newspaper, the *Inquirer and Mirror.* "What did you see in this?" said Homer. "What do you remember?"

"Well, I saw about the people on the front page who were going to be doing things at that observatory, and I decided that was one place I wouldn't go because it would be so crowded. And then I saw the article about what you should watch for during an eclipse. And let's see—I read about you. That's all."

Homer opened his copy of the paper, folded it back and tapped an item on one of the inner pages, holding the paper up so that Kitty could see the headline: FAVORITE VIEWING SITES. "Did you read this?"

Kitty leaned forward and squinted at the headline. "No, I didn't. What—do you mean that one of the viewing sites was the Great Point light?"

"Not just that." Homer reached in his pocket for his glasses, put them on and began reading the article aloud. " 'Several parties have made plans to view Saturday's total eclipse of the sun, our island spectacle, from various vantage points. Mr. and Mrs. Harold Edgeworth will set up a six-inch reflecting telescope at the Old Mill. Professor Randolph Spitz and an astronomical party from Johns Hopkins will gather on Altar Rock with telescopic and spectrographic equipment provided by the Smithsonian. The lighthouse at Great Point will be the site of an eclipse-viewing expedition by Mr. and Mrs. Joseph Green of Nantucket.' "

Kitty sat in shocked silence. Wordlessly she leaned forward and looked at the line of type where Homer's finger was pointing. Then she looked at Homer and shook her head.

"You didn't read that? It's right under the article about that big boob Homer Kelly."

"I see it is. But I didn't read it. If I had, I wouldn't have . . ."

Homer looked at her. "You're the poet, aren't you? Katharine Clark the poet?"

"Yes," said Kitty.

"You said you heard a scream at the same instant that *you* screamed, when the sun went into total eclipse."

Kitty's face took on a stubborn look. She had been through the screaming problem several times already. She had sounded idiotic before. She would sound idiotic now. Warily she said it again, in a low voice. "It was the universe. The whole universe screamed."

Homer reflected. "Well, how many voices did the universe have? Was there just one of them? Or more than one?"

Kitty tried to remember. "One," she said. "Just one."

"Was it loud? Did it scream with a human voice? Was it a woman's scream? Was it everywhere? Far away? Nearby?"

Kitty thought about it soberly. Then she leaned back against the wall, feeling very tired. "It was a woman's scream. It was her, of course, it was her. It was Mrs. Green. It was near me; quite near, I think."

"Good." Homer tested his footing in another fragile place. "What did you mean when you said, 'The moon did it'?"

"Well—did you see the eclipse?"

"Yes, I saw it."

"Well, then, I guess you know. Or you should know." Kitty stopped and bit her lip.

22

"Oh, come off it. Well—all right, I guess I see what you mean. It was really something, wasn't it?" He reached over and patted her arm. "Now let's talk about the knife. Why do you carry a knife?"

"Self-protection. I'd carry a gun, except that I'm scared of guns. A knife can't go off by mistake."

"They think it's not like a woman. I mean, you had an oilstone to sharpen it with, and everything."

"What's wrong with that?"

"Nothing, nothing." Homer waved his hand. "Why was the knife out of its sheath?"

"The snap must have been undone. It falls out. I've cut myself on it sometimes."

Homer shook his head. "Oh, Katharine Clark."

"Kitty. You don't believe me."

"Yes, I believe you, Kitty."

There was a pause. Homer looked at his shoe. "Let's be sure we know everything they have. What did they take from your bag? Try to remember everything."

"Well, there was a cotton bandanna and a red wool sweater, both of them soaked with blood, and a small purse with about fifty dollars in it. And a hairbrush. And the newspaper and the map. And an exposed photographic plate for looking at the sun. A pair of woolen stockings. And—the remains of my lunch, a small Thermos. My knife, the oilstone, the sheath of the knife. My airplane ticket. A key ring."

"Any papers? Identification? Letters?"

"Oh, just the cards I carry around: driver's license, Social Security, a university card so that I can park at B.U., a couple of—"

"That's where you teach? Boston University?"

"Yes. And some credit cards." Kitty clenched her fists. "I'm afraid there may have been a picture. It was down among the cards. I never took it out and threw it away."

"Whose picture? Joe's?"

"Yes." Kitty felt strangled. She stood up and waved her arms. "Look, this is all so silly. I didn't kill the damned woman. I just saw her there after she was dead. When can I go home?"

Homer Kelly looked at her, his face expressionless. Her heart sank. "You'll be out on bail shortly," he said. "Now, one more thing. Have you any history of mental illness?"

"Mental illness? Oh, of course, I see. They think I'm crazy. No. No, I haven't."

"You've never been institutionalized for mental illness? Have you seen a psychiatrist? During the last year?"

"No. Not last year nor ever. Except for that jerk this afternoon."

"Well, all right. I don't know if that's good or bad." Homer turned his head and bellowed for Sergeant Fern with a huge roar that startled and pleased Kitty. It was a kind of primitive force, that roar. So was the strange violent event that had picked her up so ruthlessly and set her down in this place. Perhaps one primitive force could overcome the other.

Homer stood up. "Look, Kitty Clark, here's what's going to happen. You'll be arraigned, probably Monday. That's a formality. Then you'll be out on bail. I'll see to that. Later on there'll be a probable-cause hearing, and then the grand jury will deliver an indictment, and then we'll have to get ready for a trial before the superior court in May. Except that I'll make them postpone it till September, when the court sits again. So don't worry. I'll be back tomorrow morning. Good-bye."

He was gone.

"Could I go across the hall?" whispered Kitty, as Sergeant Fern reached in the door for the chair.

"Certainly," said Sergeant Fern, blushing, picking up the chair. It came apart in his hand and fell with an echoing crash that rattled off the tin walls of the cell. He collected the pieces of chair, hugged them to his chest and stood back to let Kitty out, his blush deepening because she was making noises in her throat and he thought she was laughing at him. But she was having all she could do not to start crying until she had closed the door of the bathroom behind her and turned on the water in the sink full force. Then she sobbed as quietly as she could, leaning up against the wall with her hands over her face. Feeling better at last, she washed her face and emerged from the small room.

Sergeant Fern was waiting for her, his face redder than ever. Had he heard her crying? Kitty followed him across the hall, glancing hungrily at the sky through the window of the door at the end of the corridor. "Oh, wait! Stop, stop," she said. Something extraordinary was happening. Sergeant Fern looked where she was pointing.

"What is it?" he asked cautiously.

"Don't you see it?" said Kitty. "The sun. It's doing something again. It's a double rainbow. Oh, please, may I look?"

"I don't see anything," said Sergeant Fern. But he let her stand at the door and look out. He stood beside her and looked too. The sun, as if to make up for having its eye put out, was making itself a twin. Above it in the western sky, beyond the brick building at the rear of the jail, glowed another, fainter sun, and passing through the second sun there was a rainbow, and above the rainbow there was another rainbow. *I'm still here with bells on,* the sun seemed to be saying.

Sergeant Fern smiled. "What do you know about that?" he said, and Kitty went back to her cell feeling comforted.

4

*. . . if I shall spread a rainbow over his
disastrous set of sun . . .*

Moby Dick

Joe Green beheld the double bow around the sun from the front
porch of a house belonging to Mrs. Donald Wilkinson on the
North Bluff at Siasconset. He was still gaping at it when Mrs.
Wilkinson opened the door.

"The sun," he said, gesturing at it.

Mrs. Wilkinson studied her visitor coldly. She did not look at
the sun.

Joe pulled himself away from the splendor in the sky. "I've lost
something," he said. "Last night. I wonder if anyone found a
piece of paper around here anywhere?"

"Around here? This is private property."

She was rich, Mrs. Wilkinson. Joe knew her well, although he
had never met her before. She was one of a breed of rich arrogant
old women whose husbands had retired to Nantucket. He opened
his clenched fists with an effort of will. "Yes, I know," he said.

"That is, I thought the footpath was open to the public. I was just walking along the footpath."

"There's a sign—'No trespassing.' " Mrs. Wilkinson dragged on her cigarette with thin orange lips. "It's hard to see how you could have missed the no-trespassing sign."

God damn the woman. "I'm sorry. It was dark. And I guess I dropped the piece of paper and it blew away. It might be in your garage. I slept for a while in your garage."

"My toolshed. You went to sleep in my toolshed?"

"Yes. Did anyone find any paper there? A single folded sheet of paper, eight and a half by eleven?"

"No."

Enraged, polite, Joe turned away. But then by some trick of light from the fading spectacle in the sky, Mrs. Wilkinson suddenly recognized him as Nantucket's famous young novelist, Joseph Green, and she immediately became another woman. Hail, fellow, well met! Wouldn't he come in?

He would not. He was ducking out from under the porch lattice and climbing into his car. Mrs. Wilkinson watched him drive away, and then she turned slowly and walked to the fireplace in her living room. With a brass fire tongs she probed in the neat pile of kindling and bundled newspapers her maid, Millie, had laid on the hearth. Somewhere in the pile there should be a crumpled piece of paper she had herself found wedged under a clutter of driftwood on the beach that morning. She had picked it up and brought it inside and dropped it on the logs behind the gold fan. Mrs. Wilkinson stooped over the fireplace opening and poked and poked. Ah, there it was. She lifted the tongs, grasped the piece of paper and began to read.

5

Napoleon was a great man, a great soldier, and a great statesman; but he was an off-islander.

NANTUCKET SCHOOLBOY

Next day, Homer Kelly sat down in his accustomed chair in the library of the Whaling Museum on Broad Street and looked over the letter he had started to his wife on Friday—an eon ago, a couple of eons ago now.

Dearest Mary,

By the time you get this I will have beheld the eclipse, which is supposed to begin throwing its shadow over the island tomorrow around noon. I'll write you a flabbergasted letter tomorrow night.

In the meantime I'm spending my days here in the library of the Whaling Museum, where I sit in monkish solitude, looking up the men who sailed with young Melville in 1841 on the whaler *Acushnet*. This is a grand place. After a couple of hours in the company of these seamen's logs the floor of the library begins to feel like a quarterdeck. It tips beneath my feet. The winds of the Horn whistle around my chair. I can hear the creaking of the masts, and there's old Daggoo in the mainmasthead, crying, "There! there again! there she breaches! right ahead! The White Whale, the White Whale!"

For an abominably lonely and wifeless man, I'm feeling fairly settled in at last. Do you remember those comic maps of the United States with a few little states squeezed in around Texas? Well, a Nantucketer's view of this continent is pretty much like that. I now see North America as a large but rather vague and somewhat hostile island over there across Nantucket Sound somewhere, a place called "America" or "away," absolutely chock-full of ignorant off-islanders. I only wish I were a Boatwright or a Roper or a Coffin or a Macy or a Folger or a Starbuck—then I wouldn't feel like such an oafish outsider. But of course everybody has been enormously kind to me, especially Mrs. Deerborn here in the library of the museum, and Miss Abernathy at the Atheneum, which is what they call the public library, and of course Alice and Alden Dove, who are renting

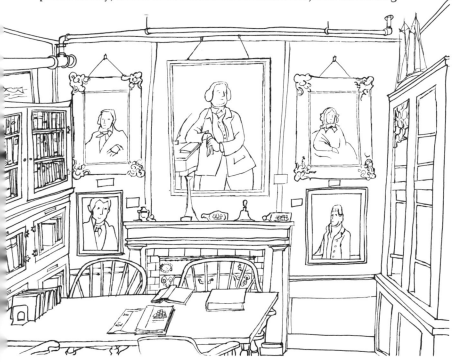

me a room in their place out on the moors. Alice works part time in the bank, and Alden is a scalloper during this season of the year, but they also tend a bunch of chickens and goats and dogs and a crippled swan and I don't know what-all. Reminds me of your sister's place back home in Concord, sort of a messy busy place, things happening all the time, work going on. You'd like it.

God damn it, I wish you were here right now. Do you really think those British feminists are going to keep you there so long, waving their brollies and stamping their feet? I know, I *know* that marvelous fellowship is supposed to last all summer, but I worry whether or not your life can be sustained that long in the desert wastes of the British Museum.

As for me, I expect I will have exhausted the records here on the island in about a week's time. Then I'll go over to New Bedford and see what I can dig up there, and then I'll go home to Concord and write up my little piece. But when you come home again at last, Mary, darling, here's what we're going to do. We're going to have a holiday on this island. I want to show you around. I want to gesture grandly like an Indian sachem or a First Purchaser or a Proprietor. I want to say, "Lo! see where the boat comes in! Avast! here's where my tire went flat! Behold! a place to buy fried clams!"

Good-bye for now, my sweeting. The library's closing. (It's starting to pour. Maybe we won't see the eclipse after all.)

Your loving husband,
Homer

. . . Maybe we won't see the eclipse after all. Good God, thought Homer, it would have been better for Katharine Clark if the storm had gone right on howling, because then maybe she would never have come to the island. He thrust his letter aside, jerked another sheet of paper out of his briefcase and began again.

Mary, the world has turned upside down, the veil of the temple has been rent in twain, all hell has broken loose. The sky was clear and we saw the eclipse, all right, and it was all you said it would be, spectacular, astounding—but unfortunately it was a lot more than that. The two minutes of darkness turned out to be a period of wicked grace for somebody who used that little interval of blackest midnight in the middle of the day to murder a woman. I've been called in by the poor girl who was found hanging over the body. Remember those verses we liked by someone named Katharine Clark? It's her. The accused, I mean, not the victim. It's a ghastly business. The grieving husband is Joseph Green, who wrote that novel that was all over the place for a while. We didn't read it, I remember, because we were on our honeymoon at the time and indifferent to other people's passions. At any rate, Katharine Clark is supposed to have killed Green's wife because she was in love with Green. Kitty is a downy-cheeked child who reminds me sadly of Melville's Billy Budd, who was strung up on the yardarm for killing somebody in a moment of fury and frustration. Not that I think Kitty killed anybody. I'm positive she didn't. It's her helpless sort of innocence that reminds me of Billy. She's in the jelly of youth, to use a Melvillean expression. And of course unless I can save her she's going to get the yardarm treatment.

But me they'll lash me in hammock, drop me deep.
Fathoms down, fathoms down, how I'll dream fast asleep.

Oh, they won't hang her, naturally; they'll just drop her fathoms down, fathoms down, in Framingham Women's Reformatory.

I went off this morning to rent a four-wheel-drive vehicle, so that I could go out to the lighthouse where this disaster took place, because it's just a long sandy neck out there and our old Chrysler would never make it. Picture your lordly husband sitting high above the world wrestling masterfully with the wheel of a great lumbering object called an International Harvester Scout. I spent the rest of the morning in it, out there on the sandy wastes at the northeastern tip of this island. Didn't learn much. It's a wild lonely place, worthy of a Captain Ahab, that neck of sand, with a rip shoal running off the end of it highly suitable for violent deaths and spectacular shipwrecks, like the ghastly sinking of the *Pequod* at the end of *Moby Dick.*

But I must say there's not much else that's reminiscent of *Moby Dick* here on this island anymore. Except for the Whaling Museum and a few other antiquarian places, there's nothing much left of the life of the old Nantucket, unless it's the scallopers dredging along the shore of the harbor, making miniature voyages in feeble imitation of the whaling men. And of course instead of a bunch of healthy young Quakers setting sail across the world, all we've got here is a lot of Unitarians and Methodists and neo-Buddhists selling crewelwork and perfumed candles to the tourists. It's rather sad.

Homer tipped back in his chair and stared up at the portrait over the mantelpiece, seeing the serene face of Mary Kelly instead of master mariner Timothy Folger. Then he bent forward over his letter again and finished it with a tender paragraph. He could have spent the whole afternoon writing to his wife, because as long as his pen was moving across the paper she seemed present in the room, an effusion given off by the ink on the page, a vapor in the air, but as soon as he put down the pen she withdrew, sucked back across the Atlantic to the dim island of England, where she was studying the women's suffrage movement, writing a book. Ah, well, it was high time he got back to work anyway.

Homer put his letter away, shuffled through his notes, shoved his chair back heavily, stood up, smiled at Mrs. Deerborn, and consulted the shipping file behind her desk. In his hand was his list of vessels, the Nantucket whalers encountered by Melville's ship on the Pacific Ocean in 1842—the *Henry Astor*, the *Columbus*, the *Congress*, the *Enterprise*, the *Ganges*, the *Richard Mitchell*, the *Ontario*, the *Phenix*, the *Potomac*. Were the logs of any of those ships in this library? If they were, then surely they would contain some mention of their meetings on the high seas with the *Acushnet.*

Homer fumbled through the file, looking for the first ship on his list. There was a whole big folder of *A*'s. He took it out of the drawer and glanced through it at the table. To his surprise, most of the material in the folder had to do with another kind of ship altogether, the Italian luxury liner *Andrea Doria*. Good God, it had sunk, he remembered that now. It had been an immense seagoing hotel, and it had gone down off the coast of Nantucket some time back. What had happened to it? Inquisitive in spite of himself, Homer was soon lost in clippings from the *Inquirer and Mirror*, and *Life* magazine, and *The New York Times*. There were accounts of the collision with the Swedish-American liner *Stockholm*, stories of the various adventures of the passengers, details of the air-sea rescue, articles about a number of unsuccessful attempts at salvaging the thirty-million-dollar vessel. . . .

Jesus. Everybody and his brother had gone down there to take a look at the sunken hulk. Even Jacques Cousteau. Some of them were just curious, but most of them had been greedy for the riches that were supposed to be on board, the gold bullion and the jewels and the works of art and the two tons of provolone cheese and the millions of dollars that were reputed to be locked up in vaults and safes.

And dangerous! Christ, how many fools had gone down into those abysmal depths in that gruesome cold and darkness? And there had been sharks, good God. Well, he shouldn't be surprised at what people were willing to endure for the sake of some crazy dream of sunken treasure. Greed was a pretty powerful incentive for all sorts of violent and perilous adventure. Take murder, for example. Homer found himself staring at a fuzzy photograph of a poor wretch of a diver, his mask thrust up over his grease-blackened forehead, his features twisted, agonized, because he had just witnessed the accidental drowning of his diving partner. God, what a tortured face! Homer scrabbled at the clippings, shoveled them back into the file and wished he had never examined it. Pictures like that could stick in your mind and ruin your digestion the rest of your life. And anyway he was just wasting his time. He bent over to pick up a last clipping from the floor, glanced at it as he put it back in the folder, took a second look, and then decided he hadn't been wasting his time after all.

The clipping was from the *Inquirer and Mirror*, and it was a long account about the death of a Nantucket couple in the disaster, Chambers and Dorothy Boatwright. Jesus Christ, they were the parents of Helen Green. She had been Helen Boatwright. She was listed as their only child.

The poor kid. Unnatural death certainly seemed to run in her family. She must have been born under some malign astrological influence, some accursed conjunction of planets, some god-damned unlucky star.

6

I would up heart, were it not like lead.
Moby Dick

It happened just the way Homer had said it would. By eleven-thirty on Monday morning Kitty was free. She hobbled out of the Town and County Building on Broad Street with Homer's hand on her elbow, her legs and back stiff from the hard bed in the lockup, her skin trying to grow a rind of toughness, a horny carapace, to protect it from the looks on the faces that stared at her. A flash exploded in her eyes as she stepped outside, and Kitty put out one hand as if to ward off a blow. For the first time it dawned on her that she was public property. She dropped the hand into her pocket, which was lumpy with a talisman, the broken shell of the whelk.

In the front seat of Homer's Scout she fingered the sharp edges of the shell and watched him struggle with the truck's unfamiliar mechanism, cursing the obscenity gears and the obscenity fools on the sidewalk. Chief Augustus Pike was knocking on the window of the truck. Kitty rolled the window down, and he looked

past her and spoke to Homer. "You understand about the dates, Mr. Kelly? The hearing is next Monday, the grand jury probably a week or so after that. And unless I miss my guess, you must be sure to have her back here on the island for trial on September second. Fifty thousand dollars bail is no joke."

"I understand," said Kitty. But Chief Pike ignored her and waited for Homer's reply. The chief was an honest man of action, and he was leery of Kitty. The strange whims and tumultuous passions of errant womankind alarmed and puzzled him. He preferred to deal with her attorney as man to man.

"Well, of course I know it's no joke," said Homer angrily.

"I think you've got your emergency brake on," said Chief Pike kindly.

"Well, of course I know I've got it on," snarled Homer. He released the brake and the truck bucked forward, plunged down

Broad Street and squealed around the corner.

"Where are we going now?" shouted Kitty.

"Airport. I'm going to see you safely home to Cambridge. And I want to take a look at that apartment of yours and see what they've turned up."

"Turned up? You mean they will have been there?"

"Oh, sure."

Kitty thought about the top of her desk, the contents of her drawers, certain boxes of papers and letters and pictures. She looked at the broken shell in her hand. *I am like the shell,* she thought. *Smashed and broken into.* But then she ran her fingers over the microscopic honeycomb that coated the inner surface, and smiled with grim vanity. Yes, she was like the shell, broken and exposed, but she was still coded, still secret in some ways and unreadable.

Her car was parked at Logan Airport. Kitty picked out its friendly shape from far away. "Here," said Homer. "They gave me back your keys." Inside the small car he loomed up gigantically. "Listen. Suppose I asked you what the prosecutor will ask you. 'At the time of Mrs. Green's death, were you still in love with her husband?' What would you say?"

"What would I say?" The car descended into the dirty melancholy of the tunnel under Boston Harbor, and Kitty thought it over. It was easy enough to decide to speak the truth. But the trouble was, it got lost in the telling. There it would be, flowing forward from the mind, an urgent incoherent mass, carried swiftly into the mouth by the eager breath—but look what happened to it there, on the very brim of expression. It had to be chopped up into words and offered up bite-size, and somehow it was no longer altogether true, but dangerously misshapen, if not actually false. Kitty glanced cautiously at Homer. "I would lie," she said.

"Well, all right. But do you think you left anything lying around in your apartment that might indicate you still had any feeling for Joe Green?"

"Oh—yes. Yes, I did. A sort of ballad. I've been worrying about it. It wasn't even any good." Kitty laughed unhappily. "If they're going to convict me I'd rather the evidence against me scanned."

Homer laughed too, and Kitty felt again that rude aboriginal power that had comforted her before, as if sheer physical strength could pull and jerk and haul and lift her out of this hole she had fallen into. "You mean you don't mind being convicted for being a murderer," said Homer, "as long as nobody calls you a bad poet. Christ, how vain these scribblers are."

Kitty's apartment house was a sunny building on Cambridge Street with small rocks set in among the bricks. Her basement room was a funny mixture of heavy old Morgan Memorial furniture and new wicker chairs, with a lot of fire-engine red scattered here and there. It amused her the way it always did, and she was surprised how happy she felt to be back in it again. She went straight to the long table against the wall. "It's gone," she said. "That poem." She opened a drawer. "Picture's gone too."

"A picture of Joe Green?"

"Yes. I don't know what I kept it for. Damn-fool thing to do."

"Did you have a picture of Helen Green?"

"No." Kitty's face brightened. "So how could I have known who that woman was?"

"Oh, they can get around that. Her picture was probably in the *Boston Globe*. Maybe *The New York Times*. 'Bride of rising young novelist.' "

"It was. I saw it in the *Globe.* "

"There, you see. What else did they get?"

Kitty ran her finger along a shelf. "I think they may have taken one of my books. I had six or seven copies left. I'm not sure exactly how many."

Homer drew out one copy of Kitty's book of poetry and stroked the raised letters of the gold prize seal on the glossy purple cover. "Pretty good for a kid like you," he said. "Joe got one of these prizes too, didn't he?"

"Yes, that's right. For his first novel. Oh—look. That's gone too. My copy. And there was something written on the flyleaf."

"You mean your own personal copy of his first novel? Humpf. Did you read the second one? The one he wrote on the island?"

"No. The reviews said it was inspired by his wife. It was supposed to be a sort of epithalamium, a celebration of a wedding. I just didn't ever get around to—well, I didn't want to read it."

"I didn't read it either, matter of fact. Say, you haven't got a drop of something around this place, have you?"

Kitty took a bottle of bourbon out of the cupboard under the sink and a couple of glasses from a shelf. She banged some ice out of a refrigerator tray. She handed Homer a glass and got some cheese out of the refrigerator. They sat down in her wicker chairs. Solemnly Kitty sliced through the red wax of the cheese with a paring knife, watching the serrated edge bury itself cleanly over and over again in the plump flesh. "Homer," she said, her voice sepulchral, "are you sure I didn't do it? Sometimes I wonder if I did it and didn't know it."

"Well, you know, Kitty Clark, when I walked into that police station and talked to Pike, I'll have to admit I wondered what in God's name had got into that clever young woman whose work Mary and I had been running into lately, here and there. But when I talked to you—well, I don't know what happened to Mrs. Green, but I've decided in my heart and brain that you didn't do it, if that's any comfort to you."

"But unless all those people are lying—Mr. and Mrs. Roper and Arthur Bird and Joe—then it couldn't have been any of them. They were all up at the top of the lighthouse together the whole time. And they didn't see another soul."

"It was dark, don't forget. For two or three minutes it was almost as dark as a moonless night. That's a long time. Anything could have happened. And the people up at the top of the lighthouse were further blinded because the light turned on. That little room up there was flooded with light."

"The light turned on?" said Kitty. "You mean the *lighthouse* light?"

"Yes. It's operated by an electric eye, and turns on automatically when the sky gets dark. So naturally at the instant of totality it turned on. The people in the same room with the light had a poor view of the eclipse, because the pupils of their eyes were suddenly so constricted."

"But I should think a tremendous light like that would have blinded them! Wasn't it dangerous?"

"Oh, no. There's a lot of candlepower in the thing, but it's concentrated by the lens system to throw a narrow beam way out to sea. Up close it doesn't seem bright. That's what they tell me."

"It's funny I didn't notice it was on."

"Well, you were looking the other way. And immediately afterward there was enough light in the sky so the light turned off."

"Homer," said Kitty, hit by a sudden stroke of genius. "You don't suppose she killed herself?"

"Killed herself? Stabbed herself somehow? Well, how did she stab herself and then hide the knife while she was expiring? For God's sake, girl, don't cringe like that. What did you say?"

"I said it was the moon."

"Well," said Homer gloomily, rolling a piece of red wax in his fingers, "that's as good an explanation as any of the others that come to mind. By the time I got there yesterday the place was one mess of sand, as if an army of little children had been digging with giant buckets and shovels. But Chief Pike made two things very clear, getting there as quickly as he did in that amphibious vehicle of the Coast Guard's before the tide came up again. Nobody—*nobody* walked up out of the water anywhere around that point, because the marks of their feet in the wet sand would have been distinctly visible, and there weren't any around that whole end of Great Point above the Gauls—that's what they call that long narrow place where it's all one beach, you know, that place where the water was rolling over and you got wet. The sand was undisturbed. Except for the car tracks and your little tootsies, naturally. They've got pictures of your footprints galloping up. And the other thing Pike said was that Helen's movements were plain. She came a couple of steps out of the lighthouse and dropped in her tracks. Died almost immediately. Couldn't have bled for more than four or five minutes before her heart stopped pumping."

Kitty was sinking deeper and deeper into despair, her head drooping in her hand. Homer looked at her, then thumped his glass down on the table and picked up a quarterly review. "Say," he said, "isn't this the one with your thing in it? The one with all the *q*'s? Yes, here it is—'Quit me no quits.' And all those queries and quixoticisms and querulousnesses. That's the one."

"Oh, did you like that?" Kitty smiled. "I had fun with all those *q*'s." She sat up suddenly. "Two things, Homer. First. I've got a lot of my salary saved up, and I can pay you more money anytime. How about right now?"

"Oh, Jesus, no. I've been well enough paid already. If I want more, I'll tell you. For God's sake, shut up."

"Well, all right, but I'm not a charity case. I'm going to pay you what's right and proper. Second. I'm going back to Nantucket. I'll miss my classes for the rest of the year, but I know Dr. Winter will take over for me, and the university would probably be better off without an embarrassing person like me on its hands anyway."

"But Jesus Christ, what are you going back there *for?*"

"I've got to find out what really happened to Helen Green."

"You don't trust me." Homer stood up, offended. "My God, you get hired and fired pretty damned fast by some people."

"No, no, Homer, it isn't that." Kitty stood up too and grinned at him. "I just have this feeling that it's not just a matter of finding blood on things, and so on. If I knew a little more about the island, maybe I could help you."

"I see. You might discover that the moon makes a habit of falling on Great Point once a week. Okay, girl, I know what you mean. And I'd be grateful for that kind of help. Every police department ought to have an officer in charge of spiritual investigation. Serious deficiency in law enforcement and citizen protection throughout the land. I wish you could stay with the Doves, where I am, but they've only got the one spare room. I'm crowded in with old scallop dredges and fishing rods and lobster pots and boat hooks and rubber boots and nautical charts and coils of rope, and sometimes I even expect to feel the tide rising around my bed. But you won't have any trouble finding a place to stay. It'll be easy. After all, it's off season."

7

"All hands bury the dead, ahoy!"
MELVILLE, *White Jacket*

Homer was wrong. Off season or not, Nantucket did not open
hospitable arms to take an indicted murderer to its breast.

Kitty came over on Thursday on the boat from Woods Hole,
the back seat of her car loaded with clothes and books. She drove
straight up Main Street, looking right and left, hunting for a place
to spend the night, and stopped in front of a house where a sign,
GUESTS, hung on the railing of the front porch. Yes, the old lady
had a room to rent. Just sign the guest book, please. But when
Kitty signed her name the old woman sucked in her breath and
looked at her queerly. "Oh, you're the one that's in today's paper," she said, nodding her head at a copy of the *Inquirer and
Mirror*, which was lying open beside the guest book. For a moment Kitty was afraid the woman would ask her to leave. But
instead the old lady handed her a key with trembling fingers.
"Number twenty-one," she said. "At the top of the stairs."

"May I borrow the newspaper?" said Kitty.

Main Street

"Help yourself," said the woman. Then she scuttled sideways, her eyes round and frightened, and disappeared into her parlor, slamming the door and rattling a key in the lock on the other side.

Kitty had an impulse to kneel in front of the door and scream boo through the keyhole. But instead she picked up her suitcase and the newspaper and walked upstairs. She sat down on the bed and looked at the front page.

It made her wince. At the top there was a blurred photograph of someone she faintly recognized, the face washed out and staring, one hand up as if in self-defense. Behind this dim person was

Homer Kelly, large and solid in the doorway. Cheek by jowl with this picture there was another photograph of another couple in another doorway, a church doorway this time, and it was all broad smiles, radiant bride, grinning bridegroom, Mr. and Mrs. Joseph Green on their wedding day. It was Helen and Joe, and Joe was like a bridegroom leaving his chamber, like a strong man running his course with joy. . . .

Triangle, shrieked the pictures, so crudely juxtaposed. *Triangle,* shrieked some accuser in Kitty's head. Of course the newspaper was too refined to use such a word, but the inference was clear that this off-island madwoman, insane with jealousy, this obscene person of "a voluptuous appearance"—incredulous, Kitty read the words again: "a voluptuous appearance"—had apparently committed first-degree murder, killing with malice aforethought the island's most precious citizen, Helen Boatwright Green, beloved bride of . . .

There was another photograph of Helen on page two, with a tearful obituary. "Distinguished island ancestry . . . a marriage that seemed predestined by a happy fate . . . the last survivors of this historic Nantucket family joined in wedlock . . . Helen Boatwright Green . . . youth, beauty . . . selfless devotion to the Nantucket Protection Society . . . inspiration of her life to all who knew her . . . grief of her bereaved husband, whose book about their marriage is still a best seller . . . hundreds turned away at the church." *Shock, despair, horror,* exclaimed the *Inquirer and Mirror.*

Well, don't look at me, said Kitty to herself. *It isn't my fault. And so it isn't a triangle at all, you see. After all, it was Helen and Joe who were the children of destiny, not me. I was just a random episode in the distant past.* The paper drooped in Kitty's hand. With a deliberate effort she slapped it open and looked for advertisements for real estate. There was a big one on page four. She picked up the telephone beside the bed and dialed the number.

"Magee Realty," said the telephone. "Mrs. Wilhelmina Magee speaking."

"Hello, Mrs. Magee. I'm looking for a house or an apartment to rent. Do you handle rentals?"

"Yes, we do. I'm sure we can do something for you, Miss . . . ?"

"Clark. Katharine Clark. And I'd just as soon not be right in the town. Would there be anything a little farther out?"

The telephone fell silent. Then Mrs. Magee said, "I'm *terribly* sorry, Miss Clark, but, would you believe it, every single one of our rentals has been taken. You might try the Miller cottages. You'll find them in the phone book. *Good*-bye."

Doggedly Kitty worked her way through the ads in the paper. At last she ran across a man who didn't boggle at her name, and he drove over to the guesthouse on Main Street and took her to see a couple of places on the north side of town.

"They're very nice," said Kitty. "But I really would like to be farther out, where I could be a little more private."

"Well, zheesh, it's too bad. I don't have a thing out of town right now, except for one listing. But it wouldn't be right for you at all. Old Mr. Biddle's place. Old chap didn't keep the place up."

Kitty was interested at once. "Where is it?" she said. "Is it cheaper than the others? That would be great."

"It's out the Polpis Road. It's not anywhere near the beach. Way down a dirt road. Doesn't even have an inside toilet. You wouldn't—"

"Really, I don't mind. It sounds fine."

The realtor, whose name was Flakeley, shrugged his shoulders and looked significantly at his watch. What he meant was, customers like Kitty should accept his professional opinion and shut up—after all, he had been twenty-five years in the business. But Kitty insisted. "Okay, sister, it's your funeral," said Mr. Flakeley. Grumpily he eased his expensive car away from the curb, drove through town and turned out on the Polpis Road.

It was a gray day. Kitty found herself looking at the Nantucket landscape as if she had never seen it before. She had been this way twice, that day last week. But she hadn't seen it at all—the wind-swept trees, the colored fields, the thick silvery undergrowth. "Why, it's beautiful," she said, turning to Mr. Flakeley.

"Beautiful?" said Mr. Flakeley, "Oh, sure. Beautiful." The word seemed to offend him. "That's what *they* always say. After a while it makes you puke."

"They?"

"Conservation types. Holier than thou. That Nantucket Protection Society. Creeps." Mr. Flakeley began to talk, almost to himself, slumbering resentments whining in his voice: partly at Kitty, who was wasting his time this way, partly at the damn-fool snobs in the Nantucket Protection Society, who were trying to ruin his livelihood by keeping people out. "That's what they're really saying, that bunch: 'Stay out. This island is our personal property. You can't have it.' Or they gas away about the goddamn birds, as if birds were more important than people. What difference does it make to a bird if it lands on this tree or that tree? I ask you. It's still got about a million trees to land on, on this island."

Kitty was curious. "You mean people are trying to keep Nantucket from being built on anymore? And that's not good for real estate?"

"You can say that again. Got a new bylaw." Mr. Flakeley glanced at Kitty balefully. "Here we have all these nice potential buyers, would like to live here, build a house. They've got the money too. They'd like to put up a nice home in a high-class neighborhood. You know as well as I do that people like that aren't about to clutter up the island with cheap jerry-built cottages. They're well-to-do. Nice people. Probably spend half their time feeding the goddamn birds. But no, those snobs with their Nantucket Protection Society won't let an honest man pick up one square acre of their precious sacred holy soil. You'd think Jesus Christ had personally peed on every square inch of it. Excuse me."

Kitty felt herself warming to this big crass brute. "This new bylaw—it will really make a difference?"

"A difference! Christ! We had it all set. The whole deal was set, all the signatures on the dotted line. One hundred acres of nice land over near Madaket. A million dollars it was worth. We were going to build really high-class hundred-thousand-dollar homes. And then that Nantucket Protection Society and that whole self-righteous bunch of people, they had to come along and put the kibosh on the whole thing. Got up a petition for the new bylaw, squeaked through Town Meeting with it. Left us holding the bag. There was Holworthy, the owner, out of his million. He was hopping mad. From now on all that hundred acres of his is good for is a place for the fucking birds. Excuse me. He can't build a doghouse on it. Oh, he could sell it to the town for part of their conservation district, but a fat lot of good that'll do him. They'd never pay what we were going to pay. No, his best bet is to sit tight and keep working to get the zoning back the way it was before. Outfox that woman Helen Green and her fucking Nantucket Protection Society. Excuse me."

Kitty turned color. She asked a bold question. "Helen Green? Did you know she was dead?"

"*Dead?*" Mr. Flakeley nearly went off the road. "Mrs. Green? Dead? Christ! No. I've been away. What happened?"

"They think—they think she was killed."

"*Killed?* You mean *murdered?* My God. Mrs. Green, dead! She was a beautiful young woman! . . . Here, this is the turnoff. Jesus, some people are so damn thoughtless, don't even keep their goddamn bushes cut back so a car can get through without getting scraped all to hell. . . ."

"I'll take it," said Kitty, the moment the house came in sight. It was a shambling gray saltbox, swaybacked along the ridgepole, leaning a little outward on all sides, disintegrating into the tall golden grass around it. A bittersweet vine was strangling the downspouts and there were lilac suckers sprouting out of the foundation. The privy stood high and conspicuous on a little knoll.

"Well," said Mr. Flakeley, smiling, cheering up at once. "Day goostibus, that's all I have to say. Each to his own poison."

8

*The Good Man pouring from his pitcher
clear,
But brims the poisoned well.*
                    MELVILLE, translation of a
                    twelfth-century poem

Dear Mr. Green,

I am Katharine Clark's attorney. I am convinced of her innocence. I feel sure you would not like to see her convicted for a crime she did not do. I can understand why you might not wish to talk to me, but I hope, in the interest of discovering the truth about your wife's death, that you will permit me to see you for an hour or so. I can be reached at Alden Dove's house.

Homer Kelly

Homer read his letter over, cursed himself for an egocentric bastard because every sentence began with "I," stuffed the letter back in its envelope and dropped it in the mailbox. Then he crossed the cobblestoned street in the direction of the Pacific National Bank.

He was thinking of his sailors again, the men who had shipped

with Melville. The ones who came back to Nantucket from the ship *Acushnet* might have brought their shares of her profits to the Pacific National Bank, their three-hundredth lay, perchance, like Ishmael's on the *Pequod*. And the backers of those voyages would have had dealings with this bank too, at the rate of so much gain for a barrel of sperm oil or seal oil or a firkin of ambergris rumbling over these very cobblestones on a horse-drawn dray— or so much loss for drowned barrels, drowned seamen, at the bottom of the Strait of Magellan.

Homer climbed the seven granite steps to the classical portico, right on time for his appointment with the bank's cashier, Richard Roper. He had to step aside for some lady depositors who were coming out the door, because the Pacific National Bank was still very much in business, conducting the transactions of the resort trade, carrying the accounts of the shops and services that waited upon the tourists, handling the mortgages of the residents and the loans and deposits of the clammers and scallopers who made a living out of local waters, and of course cashing the traveler's checks of the tourists who flooded in and out in the summertime.

Inside the bank he stood for a minute looking up at the handsome Greek Revival proportions of the lofty room and at the murals on the wall and the old scales for weighing gold, and then he looked around for his landlady, Alice Dove.

Alice had her eye on him already. She was standing behind one of the tellers' windows, frowning at him. But that was just Alice's way. Homer walked up to her window and shook the bars playfully. "Good morning, Alice, dear," he said, his genial bass voice echoing around the bank. "How's the old Federal Reserve System this morning? Fattening on the widow's mite just as usual? Could I see Mr. Roper?"

"Ssshhh," said Alice calmly. She walked around to the tellers' barred door, and the custodian let him in. Then she tapped on another door, stuck her head in, pronounced Homer's name, stood back to let him go by, and pulled the door shut behind him.

Richard Roper had his hand out. He was walking around his

desk. He had a ruddy youthful face, a high shining bald forehead, thinning blond hair, a cheery blue eye. He started off the interview with cordial courtesy by talking about the ship's portrait on the wall between the high windows. It was a happy childish painting, with a fair breeze blowing the chubby sails, whipping the blue water into choppy little waves.

"My great-great-grandfather owned that ship with his brother, and their cousin was the captain. They were all Ropers. She made four voyages from Nantucket, and she was gone three, four, five years at a time, bringing back thousands of barrels of sperm oil from the Pacific, and thousands of pounds of whalebone from the baleen whale. These pieces of scrimshaw in the glass case over here were made aboard her by one of the sailors. The one on the left is a whale's tooth, of course, and if you look closely, Mr. Kelly, you'll see the picture engraved on it, with the ship in the background behind the whaleboat. Can you read what it says on the side?"

Homer craned his head sideways. " 'A dead whale or a stove boat.' Yes, of course, that's in *Moby Dick*, a whaling man's profession of faith, like the Apostles' Creed."

Richard Roper was bringing up a chair. The formalities were over. "You're representing Miss Clark, I understand," he said. He sat down on the other side of his desk, behind a pile of *Wall Street Journals*.

"Yes. Would you mind repeating for me what you told Chief Pike last week?"

"Certainly. Glad to oblige. Where shall I start?"

"Well, first of all," said Homer, "you might tell me anything you know about Helen Green's physical condition. I saw the autopsy report yesterday. It mentioned some old black-and-blue marks on her arms and legs. Do you know anything about that? According to her husband's statement she had fallen downstairs earlier in the week. Is that accurate?"

Richard Roper smiled. "Well, if he said so, I presume that's what happened. If you're thinking he beat her, or something absurd like that, you're off on the wrong track. As for her health, I would say she was a woman in splendid physical condition. I admit I have an eye for feminine pulchritude, and Helen Green was one of the most purely beautiful women I've ever encountered. Classic features, golden hair. A real goddess. You know, tall and strong, like whooseywhatsis. Diana, the goddess of the hunt."

Homer felt a pang on behalf of Kitty Clark's dark hair and brooding face, which had been set aside for the sake of this goddess. "I only saw the corpse," he mumbled crudely. "Tell me, Mr. Roper, why did you and your wife decide to go to Great Point?"

"Well, Letty told me the Greens were planning to see the eclipse from Great Point. She writes for the paper, you see, and she was the one who wrote that story about what people were planning to do that day. So I suggested we go out there too, and then we could see the eclipse from the top of the lighthouse. Seemed a good place. The Chief Officer of the Nantucket Coast Guard is an old buddy of mine and I knew we could get the key from him. He and I often go out there in my old Chris-Craft to do a little fishing off Great Point Rip. Blues, mostly. Best fishing around the island. Helen knew that. She used to go out there too, and we'd see her surf casting plenty of times. She used to take that jeep all over the place. Of course she wasn't like some of those fools who tear up the grass that holds the dunes in place and drive over the nests of the terns in June. She was a real sportswoman, all right. Powerful golf and tennis player too. Anyway, I called her up and we arranged to go out to Great Point as a foursome to see the eclipse."

"Then there were the five of you out there, right? You and your wife, and Joe and Helen Green, and Arthur Bird?"

"That's right. Bird was already there when we got to the lighthouse. He's sort of a friend of Joe's. Although I gather Joe didn't much like the way he hung around all the time. Kind of a pain in the neck—you could see that."

"What time did you leave home to go out to Great Point?"

"At noon. We set off in Joe's jeep from his house at twelve o'clock. We had arranged to leave half an hour earlier but Helen was late. She'd been shopping. But we still had plenty of time to get there before the interesting part of the eclipse began. Must have been about twelve-thirty when we got to the lighthouse. The partial phase of the eclipse was just beginning. We all sat down on the west side of the lighthouse, eating our picnic lunch. And then a few minutes before totality we picked up our stuff and went upstairs. Helen saw a snake. I forgot about that. It was kind of a funny thing. She'd forgotten her bag, so after starting up the stairs she ran back down to get it, and when she started up again after us she said she'd seen a snake slithering away in the sand. Must have been that weird sort of darkness that had us all seeing things. Well, you know what it was like."

"A snake? In the sand?"

"Probably just some optical effect. Maybe those interference bands they talked about, just before totality."

Homer pondered, looking out the window at the Methodist Church across the street. "According to your statements, you all stayed together at the top of the lighthouse, shoulder to shoulder, during the eclipse, and none of you except Helen went down until the whole thing was over. How could you be sure everyone was under your eye the whole time?"

"Well, there wasn't much room to stand in up there. We were all jammed together. And besides it wasn't even dark in there during totality, because that blasted light went on behind us. There we were all flooded with light, trying to squint out the window at the eclipse. The whole thing was a big flop." Dick Roper laughed and slapped the top of his desk. "Somebody should have thought of that, but none of us did."

"You saw Miss Clark approaching the lighthouse? But you saw no one else, either coming or going?"

"No, *I* didn't see anybody else. As soon as we got up there and looked out, we saw her coming, and then of course we all kept staring at her. It was just before totality. There was a kind of—

oh—a weird sort of feeling in the air. You know what I mean, don't you? You saw the thing too, didn't you?"

"I did," said Homer gravely. "I know what you mean."

"So when this girl came in sight it was—it was—well, 'magic' is the only word I can think of. It was as if she came up out of the sea, like a mermaid or something. I mean, she was *beautiful*. She looked an awful lot like that picture of Venus on the half shell, you know the one? Half naked, that's the way she looked, with bare legs and bare feet and her skirt blowing off her and soaking wet. It looked like she'd been in the water. I can remember saying 'Wow,' or something like that. And when she got close to us she suddenly reached up and took off her sunglasses—and there was this glowing face, and she was running toward us, stretching out her arms. I mean, it was all I could do to hold myself back, and I'm an old married man. I tell you, it was like a goddess coming up from the sea."

"Another goddess," murmured Homer, feeling oddly satisfied that Kitty was still in the running with Helen Green in the goddess department. "And then Helen went down to meet her?"

"Yes. When the girl took off her sunglasses Arthur Bird recognized her and said her name, and then Helen suddenly started ducking down the trap door. 'I'm going to bring her up here,' she said, or something like that."

"Did anyone try to stop Helen from going down? Those stairs are tricky, aren't they? Kind of dangerous?"

"Well, yes, they are. Letty said, 'Now be careful on those stairs,' or something of the sort. Of course the lights were on down there, because we turned them on when we came up."

"Did you hear screams from down below when the sun went into total eclipse?"

"Well, no, we were making too much noise ourselves, I guess. I was cursing because the light had turned on behind our backs, and Letty was squealing, and so was Arthur Bird."

Homer leaned forward and glared fiercely at Richard Roper.

"Can you think of any reason why anybody—*anybody*—would have wanted to kill Helen Green?"

"Oh, heck, no. I mean, she was very much admired. Respected. After all, she was an island girl. The last of the Boatwrights."

"That's right, she was an orphan, wasn't she? Her parents died in the *Andrea Doria* disaster."

"Yes. And the Boatwrights were a really old family, one of the first to settle on the island. Proprietors. We Ropers went right on increasing and increasing, but the Boatwrights kept their family within bounds, somehow or other, and finally they started dwindling away until nobody was left in this generation but Helen. Oh, of course, Joe is a Boatwright too, in a way. At least, one of his four sets of great-grandparents was. But I keep forgetting about him, because he didn't grow up here. He never even came to the island until that time when he met Helen at her grandfather's funeral. And of course he doesn't even carry the Boatwright name. I mean, like the man says, some of my best friends are Jews, but it's strange to think of the blood of an old Nantucket family flowing in Jewish veins. Poor Helen." Dick Roper shook his head sorrowfully. "Known her all my life. Can't see how anybody could have had it in for her. Why, you know she was the leader of a whole lot of people who were working for the good of the island. She was really heroic, the way she went to bat to save it. She even gave up five hundred acres of her own land, gave it to a conservation trust, the Boatwright Trust. And she was the president—I guess you know that—of the Nantucket Protection Society, and I guess it would be fair to say that she was responsible for the new town bylaw to protect the future of the moors. A real crusader, that was Helen."

"That was at the Special Town Meeting in February? I've heard people talk about it. Was anybody against the bylaw?"

"Against it! Oh, sure. It just barely passed. After all, it took a two-thirds vote because it was a change in zoning. Oh, I see what you mean. Yes, I guess she did make some enemies with that bylaw. Some of the real estate dealers didn't like it, of course. Hated to see all that land pass out of the pool of future development. Although I must say some of the more enlightened realtors voted for it, Mr. Hinckley, for instance, and Mrs. Pettigrew. Of course a lot of other people were against it because they had wanted to make money off their extra land. Matter of fact, I voted against it myself."

"You did? Why? Do you own land on the island?"

"Well, yes, I guess you could say I own quite a lot of land. Came down in my family. But I was just as glad when the bylaw passed. I never intended to develop it anyway. Not like some of those landowners. They were really angry. Especially that guy Holworthy out at Madaket. Lost a million dollars he was trying to make through a deal with that crummy character Flakeley, the real estate developer. Did you read his letter in the paper? Says he's going to take that bylaw to a higher court."

"So the point is, I guess," said Homer, "Helen still had some enemies."

"Well, if you want to call those people enemies. But I'd say that was a pretty strong word. And anyway, how could any of those people have killed Helen at the lighthouse? Nobody else was there."

"Could anybody have been in the water nearby? Were there any boats offshore?"

"Oh, well, yes. I could see that classy fishing yacht of Cresswell's, away out in Nantucket Sound."

"Cresswell? Who's he?"

"Oh, he's that big moneybags who's a boyfriend of Mrs. Magee's. She's in real estate. Excuse me, I shouldn't talk about a big depositor that way. He's in oil, I think, or maybe it's wheat futures. I don't know what the heck it is. Wish I had his kind of money. What I wouldn't give for a forty-five-foot sport-fishing boat like that! I'd take it to the Virgin Islands. You just get in and drive the thing like a bus."

Homer stared dreamily at the white sails and bright pennants of the whaling vessel that had belonged to Richard Roper's great-great-grandfather. "How far out in the Sound would you say Cresswell's boat was?"

"Oh, *way* out. And I remember seeing a little sailboat, it was a Rainbow, and a red cabin cruiser in the Sound while it was growing dark. And there were some others, I think. Fishing boat from New Bedford, way out, although it was pretty early in the year for that."

"How could I find out what boats went out from Nantucket that day?"

"Why don't you ask Charley Piper? Shellfish warden. He's out there every day at Straight Wharf. Sees everything. Never forgets anything. He'd know. At least he'd know who went in and out of the harbor. He might not know about boats from the mainland that were just cruising by the island to see the eclipse."

"Charley Piper." Homer took a small notebook out of his coat pocket and scribbled in it. Then he asked another question, looking once again at the portrait of the ship on the wall. It was a cautious question, and Homer felt as if he were putting the tip of his toe very delicately below the surface of the painted waves. "As far as you could see, Joe and Helen Green were happy together? They seemed to get along all right?"

"Oh, well, sure. Of course. That goes without saying. Joe worshiped her, anybody could see that. How could he help it? Ye gods, she was so splendid. Oh, he didn't say much, or make a fuss over her in public. He isn't that sort. He was quiet. She always did most of the talking. But—well, I tell you, this death of hers, it's a tragedy. That young woman Katharine Clark ought to be— well, she's your client, but I must tell you there's a good deal of feeling about her being let out on bail. She was obviously insane. People are worried about her, walking around among their wives and children on the streets of Nantucket. Afraid of what she might do."

Homer's response was serene but savage. "You had a knife of your own, I understand, Mr. Roper?"

"Oh, that." Richard Roper's cheerfulness was unshaken, and he laughed, showing a perfect set of teeth. "My fish knife? Chief Pike took that. Exhibit B. I've bought myself another one just like it. Can't get along without it. Comes from Finland." He took a slender silver object out of his coat pocket and showed it to Homer. "See? Good and sharp. So was the other one. But good God, man, why in blazes would I want to kill Helen Green? Known her all my life. And we were all together, I tell you, and when we came down Helen was dead, and that girl was standing over her, covered with blood. Besides, if any of us had wanted to kill Helen Green, there was a much easier way. Just a little nudge on that crazy iron staircase and she'd have gone down. Why should we have bothered with a weapon at all?"

9

*. . . all that stirs up the lees of things; all
truth with malice in it; all that cracks the
sinews and cakes the brain . . .*

Moby Dick

The old Portuguese bell in the tower of the Unitarian church was
striking its traditional fifty-two hollow strokes when Homer came
out of the Pacific National Bank. The bell was rung three times
a day, and since it wasn't dawn and it wasn't curfew, it must be
noon, and that meant that he was late for his appointment with
Arthur Bird.

Arthur had a corner bedroom in a seedy big house on India
Street.

"I'm sorry we can't meet in pleasanter surroundings," he said.
"I'm a person who is physically upset by ugliness, I mean *physically*. This sort of thing almost makes me sick to my stomach."
He waved his hand around the room at the furniture, a bijou
bedroom suite dating from the 1890s.

"Whassamatter with it?" said Homer. "Lookit the carving."

"Oh, well, if you like that sort of thing. Actually, I'm about to
move out of here. I've found a *charming* place. Melville Estates

61

at Monomoy. Lovely cottages. Belongs to Mrs. Magee, a woman of *perfect* taste. Of course it's much more expensive, but I'll be delighted to pay anything to get out of *this* revolting atmosphere."

Pay anything . . . Homer had heard that Arthur Bird was the heir to Bird's Mercerized Thread. Some clever inventive ancestor had piled up a fortune, and then the family had dwindled down to this pantywaist. "You're going to stay on the island? What for?" said Homer bluntly.

"Well, you see, I feel so close to this case. I want to be right here, so that if I am needed I will be available. Of course if there's anything I can do to help Miss Clark . . . You know, Mr. Kelly, in every lifetime there are just one or two people who stand out from the rest like beacons, who point the way, do you know what I mean? Well, Miss Clark has been one of those shining lights for me."

"Well, good. Tell me why you came to the island." Disgusting loathsome ass that you are.

"Why, I came to see the eclipse, of course."

"But according to your statement you were two weeks early for that, weren't you?"

"Well, actually, since I am a student of American literature, naturally I am interested in the work of Joseph Green, the novelist. I called on him, and we became acquainted."

"Then that's why you came to Nantucket—to meet Joe Green?"

"You might say it was, in a way." Arthur's cherubic face turned solemn. "I will tell you something in strictest confidence, Mr. Kelly. I am writing a book. The personal life history of Joseph Green." He pointed a plump finger at a pile of papers on the bureau. "Since I feel already so deeply involved, knowing Miss Clark as well as I do, since, as I am sure you are aware, Miss Clark and Mr. Green were once extremely *close*, since I was present at the climactic event of last week, I feel I have a natural intimacy upon which I can base further study, and, having been schooled in the field in which they are both engaged, I know of no other single individual who might undertake a study of this kind with a better right, a work, that is, of this peculiarly delicate nature, a task—"

There seemed no way to turn the blithering idiot off but by breaking in. "What about Joe?" said Homer. "Did he agree to talk to you about Kitty?"

"Well, when I knocked on his door and reminded him that I was a student of Miss Clark's, he invited me in, and I must say I expected more of the interview than what took place. When I explained my project to him he became rather cool and unresponsive. Genius, you see, Mr. Kelly, is often shy. A great man of a creative temperament often becomes a recluse. But by patience, by constant effort, by gentle insistence, by simply being *there*, over and over again, I hoped to break down the wall of his reserve. Although, after this *spectacular* event, I must say I have a great deal to go on even if I learn nothing more."

Homer looked with suppressed fury at the stack of papers on the dresser. He could almost see the leeches crawling all over it. "Tell me, Arthur, did you arrange ahead of time with Joe to meet him at Great Point on the day of the eclipse, or did you just happen to . . . ?" Horn in, he wanted to say.

"Why, I just thought that the lighthouse at Great Point would be an excellent place. It was so out in the open, and all."

"You mean, you read in the local paper that the Greens were going to be there," said Homer ruthlessly.

"Why, yes. Yes, I did. Of course I assumed that the place would be crowded. I didn't think one more person would make any difference. And then, of course, I was surprised to find myself one of a select group."

"Did you rent that pickup truck? And what time did you get out there?"

"Yes. I rented it the day before from Mr. Woodrow. And I was there early. I went to the Greens' house first, around ten-thirty, but there was no one there, so I assumed they had already gone, and I set out at once. But when I got to the lighthouse around eleven-thirty, they weren't there yet. So I was all alone for about an hour before they came along."

"You took pictures out there, I understand. What happened to the roll of film?"

"Oh, I turned it over to the police instantly. I knew it would be of the utmost importance in reconstructing the event." Arthur's brown eyes grew big. "It was in *color.*"

Think of the blood, he meant. Think of the blood in color. Homer wanted to kick him. He gathered himself together and asked another question. "When did you realize that the girl approaching the lighthouse was Kitty Clark?"

"Well! We had all been watching this girl come across the sand, looking so *sexy* with her dress blowing up that way—I mean, it was a whole new *facet* of Miss Clark's personality—so when she took off her sunglasses and I saw who it was, I must say I was surprised! Of course it's true that I did know she was coming to the island to see the eclipse, because she told our class about it at the beginning of the semester when she was making up the schedule for the year. But I'd never seen her look like this! Afterwards, well, naturally, it was plain that she had been out of her mind, that she was in some sort of sexual delirium."

"When you recognized her you said her name, I gather. What happened then?"

"Well, when we knew who she was, Helen Green so *kindly* said she would go down and tell her to come up. I was just flabbergasted. I knew I was watching history in the making! And then I took a picture of Joe, waiting for her. His face was *etched* with suffering! And then the eclipse began, and the light turned on behind us, and we pressed up against the glass, and I found myself actually shouting."

"Could you see anything that was going on down below?"

"Oh, no, it was much too dark. And we were watching the sun, of course. And then when the sun came out again we all started downstairs, and that's when we discovered Helen's body, and there was Miss Clark standing over it, her hands all *blood,* and I saw her knife in the sand. And she seemed so *cheerful.* It was so out of keeping with the solemnity of the occasion. I took a picture of her right away, and I hope I caught the expression on her face. She was quite, quite mad."

"Did you ever notice any evidence of psychosis in her before?"

"Why, no, and that's why it's so strange. She always seemed quite sane. Sensible! Oh, she got excited about her subject, but it was well within the range of . . ." Arthur shook his head philosophically. "Still waters," he said. "Still waters run deepest of all."

"And garrulous ones run shallowest," growled Homer.

"Pardon me?"

"Tell me what you think she meant when she said, 'The moon did it.' "

Arthur brightened. He jumped up. "That's what's so absolutely fascinating," he said. "That's why I feel I can be of some use to the police in this case. This is Miss Clark's book of verse. Here, let me show you. This poem is about the moon. But the moon is the poet *herself,* do you see? Listen.

> I shine upon the house
> in which she sleeps.
> I send one ray of light
> within the window of her room.
> I the moon go where I will.
> Poor Sappho lies alone.

The moon is the *poet,* do you see? Kitty Clark *is* the moon!"

"So you think when she said, 'The moon did it,' she was confessing to the murder?"

"Of course!"

Homer leaned over and looked at the poem. Then he smiled at Arthur and tapped the poem with his finger. "It's nice. Obviously inspired by that famous poem attributed to Sappho."

Arthur's jaw dropped. "Sappho? Oh, of course. You know, something has just occurred to me. Sappho was a Lesbian, wasn't she? You don't suppose *Miss Clark* . . . ?"

"Oh, for *Christ's* sake."

10

*The Town hath granted unto John Savidge
two Acres of land to build upon and Com-
monage for three Cowes, twenty sheep and
one horse. . . .*
    Records of the Town of Nantucket,
                                    1672

Homer stood on the sidewalk on India Street, looking at his
tourist map of the town. The Ropers' house was on Fair Street.
Where the hell was that? Oh, there it was, on the other side of
Main. Wistfully Homer resigned himself to an empty stomach,
folded up the map, stuck it in his pocket and set off, stalking down
Centre Street, swinging around the Pacific National Bank to the
intersection with Fair Street, walking more slowly along Fair
Street, looking for the Ropers' house.

They were all much alike, these simple wooden dwellings, close
to the street on high foundations. It was impossible to tell new
ones from old ones. According to the map, this part of town was
in the Historic District, which meant that any new building
would have to conform to certain standards: it would have to look
like the old ones, with clapboard siding or white cedar shingles,
and a gable roof of a certain pitch, and chimneys and foundations
of select common brick, and so on and so on. There was a move

67

Fair Street
and Old South Tower

afoot to spread the Historic District over the entire island. Homer
wondered whether he would vote for such a measure or not, if he
were a citizen of Nantucket, and on sober reflection, looking left
and right, decided that he would. It would mean conformity,
academic and controlled, and any architect with a gleam of genius
in his eye would have to stay the hell off the island. But so much
of the mainland was ugly as sin. Here at least the tortured eye
could rest. There was little that was not simple, modest and spare,
the gray houses lying pleasantly on the low rolling landscape, or
starting up along the street like these, erect as maiden aunts in
tall straight chairs.

Here, this was the house. It was one of the old ones, surely, unless someone had artfully manufactured the tilt of the old roof line along with the roof walk and the row of glass panes above the front door. No, it was really old, all right. No one could manufacture the look of those weatherworn boards.

Homer banged on the brass knocker, and in a minute Letty Roper opened the door and invited him in. Letty was constructed according to a set of guidelines too, decided Homer, following her into the living room. Her nose was the right width relative to its height, her eyes were the proper degree of blue, and when she smiled her teeth protruded below her upper lip a distance that might have been ordained by statute, like the width of the shingles on the houses or the space between the pickets in the fences along the street. But something was missing. Homer thought tenderly of the dishevelment he loved in his wife. And Kitty Clark too had a skewed kind of charm.

"Just sit right down," said Letty, "while I get us some coffee in the kitchen." She disappeared. Homer sat down carefully on an antique chair beside a big television set and brooded some more. It wasn't so much what Mary Kelly and Kitty Clark had been born with, he decided, as what they had done to themselves. It was what their looking and listening and speaking had done to the delicate muscles around the eyesockets so that by some ephemeral optics light struck the watery film over the eye in a different way, displaying the opposite shore of the brain. In Letty Roper's case only a benevolent nature had so far been at work. (What had Helen Green's face been like? Homer wondered. When he had seen her stretched out on a marble table her features had been cleansed of everything but the pure pallor of death. The radiant beauty everyone spoke of had been dimmed, shadowed, eclipsed by death, by one piercing blow. Whose, whose, if not Kitty Clark's?)

Gloomily Homer slipped down in his fragile chair, telling himself it was just the low level of his blood sugar at the moment that was responsible for his melancholy, and therefore when Letty

Roper handed him a cup of coffee with two cookies on the saucer he could have kissed her. He tried not to gobble the cookies too fast, but fortunately Letty was an easy talker like her husband, and she began immediately to talk about Joe Green. Homer munched and gulped.

"That poor man. He's absolutely prostrated. I've never seen him so unreachable, so just *not there.* He won't let any of us come near. It's heartbreaking. I don't know what to do. I was afraid he might not even be eating, so I've been taking some meals over to him, but he just calls out from that little room of his to leave them on the hall table. And the last time I came, he told me not to bring any more. But I'm just afraid he might starve, there all alone, or even *do something to himself.*"

Homer swallowed his last piece of cookie and smiled at Letty. She was a sweet wholesome girl, sound and healthy like her husband, but somehow the two of them weren't quite what he would have expected in the close friends of a writer of the stature of Joseph Green. "How long have you known Mr. Green?" he said.

"Oh, just since he married Helen. Of course Dick and I have known Helen Boatwright all our lives." Letty laughed charmingly. "You know, Dick wanted to marry Helen, but she wouldn't have him, so he married me instead."

"I understand you write for the newspaper, Mrs. Roper."

"Oh, yes. I do things for the *Friends Newsletter* and the *Inquirer and Mirror.* I wrote about where people were going to go to see the eclipse—the article that's so important in this case— and I wrote the obituary for Helen Green. And I wrote about you! Marjorie Abernathy in the Atheneum looked you up and told me all about you—how you wrote that Thoreau book with your wife, and how you were a detective, and all about that famous Concord case you solved, and everything. And now here you are, working on another dreadful case! Although I must say, Mr. Kelly, I don't see how your client has a leg to stand on, that Katharine Clark. She was obviously out of her mind. You weren't there. You didn't see. It was really dreadful. The way she kept talking about the moon. Anyway, I'm certainly glad she wasn't in love with *my* husband. When we saw her coming across the sand she was like a vision. I mean, I was surprised when I saw her in court the other day. She wasn't nearly so good-looking." (Ah, poor Kitty, thought Homer. She had been wearing her somber face that day. To Letty Roper beauty had only one kind of face.)

"Well, as a reporter, could you tell me if you noticed any sort of vessel there offshore while you were at Great Point?"

"Oh, no, I'm sorry," said Letty, shaking her head. "You'd think the descendant of a whaling family would have inherited a tendency to look out to sea. That's what the roof walk was for, on the top of this house. My great-great-grandmother and her mother and grandmother before her used to go *up scuttle*, as we say in Nantucket, to see if their men were coming home. But I'm afraid I didn't. And on the way back from Great Point I just couldn't take my eyes off Joe. He was ahead of us in the truck. I could see his head through the back window, and I was feeling so *sorry* for him."

Homer felt dizzy with hunger in spite of the cookies and muddleheaded from listening to Letty. There was something else he had meant to talk about—something about the new zoning bylaw; that was it. He pulled himself together and asked whether or not Helen Green might have made some enemies with her new bylaw.

Letty widened her eyes and shook her head, and the sunlight pouring through the old glass of the window bounced off her shiny hair. "Well, yes, I suppose she did. A lot of people were pretty angry about it. Of course we had decided to vote against it, Dick and I, not because we wanted to make a lot of money from Dick's share of the sheep commons; we just voted against it on principle."

"Sheep commons," said Homer. "I read about sheep commons. Tell me about your husband's sheep commons."

"Oh, I know I really shouldn't call it sheep commons anymore.

71

You see, the original Proprietors wanted to raise sheep, and they set aside large pieces of grazing land to be held in common. So a sheep common was just like a share of stock. Though all it amounted to was the right to graze a certain number of sheep on the common land. And then later on, when people didn't have sheep anymore, some of the land was divided up for farming, and then a sheep common gave you the right to farm a certain piece of land. And then later on the whole thing broke down, and people were able to claim a certain amount of land for themselves in exchange for their sheep commons. Dick inherited about one hundred and fifty acres near Shawkemo."

"One hundred and fifty acres? I suppose that's pretty valuable land on the island of Nantucket?"

"Oh, yes! We've been told it's worth—well, one or two million dollars!"

"One or two *million?* Holy cow." Homer stared at Letty. "No wonder you voted against the new bylaw."

"No, no, you don't understand. You're just like all the rest. Don't you see? We're old Nantucketers. We want to keep the land always, we want it to stay just the way it has always been. We don't want to sell it."

"But some of the other landowners aren't as idealistic as you are, I gather?"

"No, they aren't, I'm afraid," said Letty. "They're greedy, that's what they are."

"Well, after all," said Homer, waving his hand, wondering how to explain the wicked world to this innocent child, "perhaps they were holding their land for investment, and then their right to realize on the investment was taken away. It's not greedy exactly. It's the good old American way."

"That's what they said! They kept talking about the sacred rights of private property, and so on! Well, actually, of course, Dick and I voted with them, as I said. We just felt it was wrong to force people to do the right thing. They ought to do it *because* it's right, out of deep moral conviction." Letty's little round breasts swelled with sanctimonious air. "That's the way we felt. We were willing to spend the rest of our lives persuading other property owners to preserve their land. We had such plans!"

She was charming in her enthusiasm. Homer's cynicism was almost won over. He laughed. "But now you don't need to persuade anybody. They can't do anything with their land anyway now."

"No. Unless the superior court or the state supreme court or the legislature reverses the bylaw. Helen was afraid that might happen, but she was ready to fight for it all the way to the Supreme Court in Washington, D.C. But now, without her, I don't know what will happen to it."

"Aren't there other people to carry on the fight? Was she so indispensable?"

"Well, of course there are plenty of other people in the Nantucket Protection Society who feel strongly about it, just as she did. But nobody, *nobody*, Mr. Kelly, had the kind of *dazzling* effect on people that Helen had. She was *radiant.* There was a sort of glitter about her, like—like the sun up in the sky."

11

"Struck dead by an angel of God! Yet the angel must hang!"

MELVILLE, *Billy Budd*

Homer laughed when he drove up to Kitty's door. The place was so—well, it was nice. He got out of the car and knocked on her ruined door.

Kitty looked out cautiously, then smiled broadly and let him in. "How do you like it?" she said.

"Makes me seasick," said Homer, looking around. "Not a straight line anywhere. Which way is up?"

"Well, I love it. Mr. Flakeley tells me it belongs to an old man named Obed Biddle. He got too old to go on living in it by himself, so he had to go and live with his married daughter. He used to be a fisherman, and according to Mr. Flakeley he remembers the last days of whaling on Nantucket, and after that he went whaling in the Azores, where they used to do it the same way, and then he came back home. Look, aren't the trees wonderful? And there was a deer! A deer in my front yard this morning. I wish

I had some cracked corn. I want him to come back. What do deer eat anyway?"

"Damned if I know. I know what I like, though. Lunch. How about it? I could eat a horse."

"Well, I'm sorry, Homer. I've just moved in. I went out to get some groceries this morning, but when I started around that First National things got pretty bad, and I just abandoned the cart half full of food and ran. I've got to go back and try again. I'll just have to get used to it."

"Used to what? What did they do—stare at you?"

"Well, if it was just that I wouldn't mind. It was the way they pulled their children aside, as if I might pick up a jar of pickles and bash their baby with it. But what really undid me was the lady who called me a slut. My first impulse was to stop and explain myself and say I was just an innocent bystander, and my second impulse was to cry, so I obeyed my third impulse, which was to run. Oh, here, look what I found in the cupboard—a tin of sardines. And there's a can opener in the drawer. Sit down."

There was one backless chair and a cracked table in Kitty's kitchen. Homer sat down on the chair and looked at the warped surface of the table. "Kitty Clark," he said, "it's time you told me about the dog."

Kitty started violently. The can opener in her hand clattered to the floor. "What dog?"

"The dog you killed." Homer reached for the can opener and gave it back to her.

"Oh, that dog." Kitty punctured the sardine tin and wrenched her way around the edge. "Who told you about that?"

"I got a complete report on you from my old friends in the East Cambridge Courthouse, so we'd know what the prosecution might be thinking of holding against you. All they had was this dog. The Humane Society had heard about it and filed a complaint. I gather you explained it to their satisfaction."

Kitty dumped the sardines on a cracked plate, found a fork with one broken tine, and handed plate and fork to Homer. "Yes, I did kill a dog. It was trying to kill me. It attacked me." She went back to the sink, where her collection of shells was soaking in a dishpan of water, and began scrubbing sand out of the crevices of the big whelk.

"You killed it with a knife. Was it the same knife? I'm told you thought your life was threatened?"

"Yes, it was the same knife. Yes, I thought my life was threatened. What do you think these scars on my neck are?"

"You still haven't explained why you were carrying a knife in the first place."

"I've told you. I just feel a lot safer."

"You've told me and told me. But most girls don't carry a knife to make themselves feel safe. Why should you? What makes you so different? Anyone would think you'd been raped or something."

To Homer's astonishment, Kitty's shoulders suddenly began heaving. She was crying into the sink.

"You don't mean," he said, "that you—you mean you *were* raped?"

Kitty nodded. She was bawling so hard she couldn't speak. Homer stood up and put his arm around her. "My God," he said. "You poor kid. My God."

Kitty's crumpled face began to straighten out. She wiped her sleeve over her eyes and let herself be pushed down into the backless chair. "I've never told anybody before," she said.

"You mean, you didn't even report it to the police?"

"Oh, Homer, I don't know why not. It wasn't that I felt my virtue had been stained or anything like that. I just didn't want people feeling sorry for me. I knew I wasn't pregnant because I'd just had my period. I just wanted to forget it." Kitty had the big shell in her hand. She was wiping it dry with her skirt.

"But seriously, honeybunch, getting raped is a perfectly sound reason for carrying a knife around afterwards. And it would arouse the sympathy of the court, whereas now a girl like you carrying a knife and an oilstone and all that crap—she looks like some kind of a nut."

Kitty jumped up, and the shell fell to the floor with a jarring crash. "You can't use it, Homer. I won't let you. It's some kind of primitive sense of privacy or something."

"Look, you dumb girl, would your sense of privacy feel less hoity-toity being convicted as a murderer?" Homer turned melancholy. "Well, if the worst comes to the worst we can always plead insanity. Everybody keeps telling me you must have been out of your mind. Temporary insanity. Your special lunacy stormed your general sanity, like Ahab's."

Kitty picked up the shell and thumped it on the table, shouting, "Never!"

"Look, it would be easy. Everybody expects poets to be off their rocker anyhow. And say, speaking of poetry, tell me about that Sappho piece of yours, the one about the moon. Somebody told me it means you think of yourself as the moon, and therefore when you said, 'The moon did it,' what you meant was that *you*—"

"Arthur! Arthur Bird! That *idiot!*" Kitty burst out laughing. "It was his idea, wasn't it? He's talked with me about that poem before. He's such an absolute *nincompoop!*"

"Well, maybe he's a blessing. Maybe I can make a fool out of him on the witness stand."

"Oh, Homer, could you? What a lovely thought. Now look, Homer, you're not going to have to talk about rape, or plead insanity, when you've got witnesses like Arthur Bird, and when" —Kitty stood up and waved both arms over her head—"when I'm innocent! After all! I'm innocent! I only came to this damned island to see the total eclipse of the sun!"

"My dear girl . . ." Homer paused a moment, then plunged ahead savagely, making the case against her altogether clear. When he had finished, Kitty stood silent, her arms hanging at her sides. "Come on, girl," said Homer, getting up, clapping her clumsily on the back. "Those sardines are all very well, but all they did was whet my appetite, keep it immortal in me, as Melville says. Come on over to the place where I'm staying. Alice Dove has an icebox as big as Fort Knox."

Kitty fumbled into her coat and followed Homer out to his car. He slammed the door on her side of it, climbed into the driver's seat and started backing up.

"Wait. There's something I want to ask you, Homer. Before we get there."

"Shoot."

"What can they do to me? I mean, what's the worst thing that can happen to me?"

"Well, of course they won't kill you. Life imprisonment—that would be the worst. The trouble is, you see, it looks like first degree murder. Premeditated. If it were second degree or third degree the sentence would be less."

Kitty put her hand on the dashboard to steady herself. "Life?

You mean forever? I'd be in prison for the rest of my life?"

"Probably not. Maybe only, say, fifteen years or so. Twenty."

With an effort Homer kept his voice flat.

Kitty struggled to keep hers the same. "Twenty years. I won't go. I'd kill myself first."

Homer shifted gears and headed down the narrow lane to the Polpis Road before he glanced sideways at her. The face of the girl beside him was drained of color and her knuckles on the dashboard were a bony white. The damned girl; she meant it. The jury might think, and the judge might think, and the prosecuting attorney might think that the girl on the witness stand was receiving a merciful judgment for the crime she had committed, but now here *he* was, saddled with the knowledge that he was fighting for this infernal young woman's life. It wasn't fair. Homer felt decidedly put upon. He drove too fast in his distress. The car jounced and bounced on the rutted road.

Kitty stared out at the trees lurching past on either side, noticing in spite of herself the dense twiggy growth of the stunted oaks, silver against the sky. It was the wind that had forced them into those shapes, she knew, into those thick clusterings of branches. They were forced by circumstance into density rather than height. It struck her that she could be like that. She would choose density, having been forbidden height. How long did she have? Until September? Six months. Almost six months. She would pack it with everything she could.

"Six months," said Homer. "Don't forget, we've got six months. We can do a lot in six months."

"Yes," said Kitty, smiling at him, the color coming back into her face. "I was just thinking that."

"Good girl," said Homer.

12

*"But look, Queequeeg, ain't that a live eel
in your bowl? Where's your harpoon?"*
                                    Moby Dick

The Doves' place was only about a quarter of a mile down the Polpis Road, at the end of another long dirt driveway.

"Are they farmers or something?" said Kitty, catching a first glimpse of an untidy fenced-in barnyard, alive with chickens and ducks and a couple of brown goats. "I thought you said Mr. Dove was a scallop fisherman."

"Only part time. A lot of people on the island seem to have a couple of strings to their bow. Alden is a scalloper this time of year, and then in the summer he works for a landscape gardener and sells eggs and I don't know what else. Alice works part time too, in the Pacific National Bank. But the other part of her life is more important to her than what she does for a living. Wait till you talk to her. She knows everything about the natural history of the island, all the birds and the flora and fauna and such. There's Alice now, feeding her swan. Whoops! almost ran over

that guinea hen. Hello, Alice! Brought you a visitor! New neighbor! Meet Kitty Clark."

In a flurry of squawking hens and barking dogs, Kitty got out of the car and smiled hesitantly at Alice Dove. Alice had been leaning over a fence. She looked up, nodded her head grimly and then went on scattering scratch feed from a pan in her hand. She was a plain woman, gaunt and elongated and drawn out like a poker or a hoe, wearing a man's jacket too large for her. Her gray-streaked black hair was cut no-nonsense all around. Her face was blank and still and thin as a cleaver. Kitty, not sure what to say to her, looked over the fence too. The swan was pecking greedily at kernels of grain. It was a great cob, hideously disfigured with blackened scabs. One wing had lost half its feathers.

"What happened to it?" said Kitty.

"Somebody shot it," mumbled Alice Dove, throwing down

more feed. The swan waddled unevenly on his black feet from one grain to the next, wagging his tail, thrusting out his long neck, moving slowly around his house, which was a big box painted barn red. His pen ran down the sloping ground to enclose a swampy place at the bottom. The great bird was awkward and pigeon-toed

and his scars were blackish blots on the whiteness of his large body, but the texture of his feathers was of a complexity and perfection that made Kitty exclaim. Then Alice's still face opened all at once like a door, and she shot an eager rapid glance at Kitty. "I call him Jupiter," she said.

"Hello, Jupiter," said Kitty.

They turned and started after Homer, who was walking up to the door, shouting for Alden. The Doves' house was a low one-story shingled structure surrounded by sheds and outbuildings. There was Alden, throwing open the door, hailing them all inside. He was a big man, not as tall as Homer but broader, with a large nose and curly black hair and brown eyes snapping like firecrackers. He complained loudly when Homer introduced Kitty. "Paper said she was voluptuous. She's not voluptuous, she's just fat. Just a little fat girl. Well, I must say I'm disappointed."

An empty place inside Kitty suddenly filled with air, and she laughed.

"Fat?" said Homer, looking at Kitty. "Well, maybe you're

right. Okay, then, Alice, don't give her anything to eat. But I'm a starving man. Where's that bucket of soup you promised me?"

Silently Alice lit the gas burner under a big dented pot, while Alden let in a stream of barking dogs and a couple of cats with large donging bells around their necks. Kitty studied Alice's back. If that face had not opened up a crack a moment ago and let out that streak of light, she would have seemed angry now, and cold. But Kitty guessed it was the way she always looked. "Shall I take these things off the table?" said Kitty.

"Just shove them down to the other end," said Alice.

There were books and notebooks and charts, a dead bird in a shoebox, a heavy marble paperweight with the initials AD, a china dog with a cactus for a tail. "What kind of bird is it?" said Kitty, looking in the shoebox.

Alice's face opened up, transformed once again. "It's just a catbird. It flew against the window. But it's banded, do you see? It was one of Mrs. Lord's. She banded it eight years ago. That's a record." Alice began ladling out soup, and they all sat down.

"Were you out scalloping this morning, Alden?" said Homer.

"Oh, sure. End of the season, though. Scallops getting scarce. Lucky to get three bags a day, even though you're allowed six. Of course the Japanese moss doesn't help. Stuff that grows on them, suffocates 'em." And then from Japanese moss Alden went on to the turpentine beetle that was endangering the pine trees. His voice was high-pitched and energetic. And Alice told about seeing a dead deer, killed by a hunter out of season and abandoned to the hawks and crows.

Homer and Kitty ate her split pea soup hungrily, and had seconds and thirds, while Alice talked of mute swans and hares, of bats and turtles, of scaups and goldeneyes, of the habits of fiddler crabs. She kept getting up to run her fingers over the map of the island that was mounted on the wall, or to reach for pamphlets or books that were piled on chairs and all along the mantelpiece, books by horticulturists and ornithologists, books about Nantucket, about the life of the seashore. Homer had still another bowl of soup, and glanced at Kitty, smiling, as if to say, *You see.*

Kitty sat back, relaxed, full of soup, a little sleepy, only half listening, admiring the room they were sitting in. Two small chambers had been made into one large one, and there were Lally columns supporting the dividing beam. The room was dark with ancient wallpaper. One end of it was the kitchen, with an enormous refrigerator standing on curving legs. An old grandmother dog lay asleep in a collapsed upholstered chair beside the fireplace. The walls were crowded with glass-fronted bookcases full of Indian artifacts, seaweed mounted on sheets of wrinkled paper, shells, rocks, coral, birds on wooden stands with plastic bags tied over them, a huge dusty egg. There were seedlings in flats in front of a window and a glass jar gushing with forsythia, blooming ahead of its time indoors. A brilliantly lit toilet was visible from the table, and a bathtub and a pink bathmat. Two small bedrooms opened on either side of the bathroom. One bed had been made up, the other was a sea of tumbled blankets (Homer's, decided Kitty).

Homer was pushing his bowl away at last, rapping his fist on one of the books. "I don't know why you people give a damn what happens to your island anyhow," he said. "The sea's going to wash the whole thing away in a couple thousand years. That's what this book says."

Alice turned a fierce face upon him. "But don't you see? That makes it all the more—"

Homer patted her arm and laughed at her. "There, there, now, Alice. I know, I know."

"How big is this farm of yours, Mr. Dove?" said Kitty.

"Thanks for the compliment," said Alden. "It isn't much of a farm. All we raise around here is a bunch of good-for-nothing animals, crippled swans and so forth. We've just got a couple of acres, running down to the road. All the rest of the land around here belongs to somebody else."

"But it's safe now, isn't it?" said Kitty. "It will stay just woods and fields, won't it? I mean, with this new town bylaw?"

Alice picked up the soup plates.

"It's that Mr. Holworthy," she said, shaking her head. "He's going to try to get the superior court to upset the bylaw, so he can sell his lovely land to that terrible man Mr. Flakeley."

"I met Mr. Flakeley," said Kitty. "He was the agent for my house. He was really angry about the new law."

"It's not Flakeley and Holworthy I'm worried about," said Alden. "After all, Flakeley's been here all his life. He has some feeling for the island. And he's right out in the open, blundering around. If he's going to do something stupid he lets everybody know ahead of time by putting his big foot in his mouth, and then we can all get together and stop him. It's that other real estate agent. She's the one that worries me. That Wilhelmina Magee. She's crafty. All sweetness and light, that's what she is, and then, *wham!* you discover what she's been up to when it's too late. That salt marsh she bought at Monomoy. Said she wanted to keep it for the wildlife, and before you know it she had it all dredged out. That's against the Wetlands Act, but somehow or other she got around one of our congressmen, and now she has a marina in there and a big swimming pool and a lot of cottages. And she's after the old Biddle place at Quidnet too, there on S'achacha Pond."

"Biddle?" said Kitty. "That's not the old man who owns my house?"

"That's the one. Obed Biddle. He owns that land at Quidnet on the east side of the island and he's living there right now with his daughter. Mrs. Magee keeps hovering around the place like a vulture, waiting for him to die. Keeps sending in surveyors who pretend they're just fishing. Fortunately the old fella still seems to have a lot of spark, goes to Friends Meeting and speaks up, works at the Whaling Museum some of the time. Plenty of life in the old geezer yet, thank goodness."

"Look here, you two," said Homer. "Can you tell me how many people stood to gain by keeping things the way they were before? How many of them might have thought of Helen Green as an enemy to their own personal interests?"

Alden's face was red. "Who knows?" he said. "There's plenty of black hearts in that crowd, if you ask me. I hate them. I hate their grasping money-grubbing souls. They'd betray you. They'd betray everything they pretend to stand for."

Alice had turned around from the sink to look at Alden, her eyes flashing her agreement. They were thinking of someone real, Kitty could tell.

"What about Richard and Letty Roper?" Homer asked. "Were they like that? I understand they voted against the bylaw."

Alice turned back to the sink, and Alden shook his head. "Oh, no, they're not like that. They're just very much mistaken. They keep saying Nantucketers should trust each other to have the best interests of the island at heart, that it shouldn't take a law to make them do what was right. And of course the Ropers won't try to sell their land, I suppose. But what about the children they'll have someday? Their kids might do anything with the property thirty or forty years from now. Oh, we've argued back and forth with them about it, but we never get anywhere."

"If they feel as public-spirited about their land as they say they do," said Homer, "why don't they do what Helen Green did with hers, and give it to some kind of conservation organization?"

Alden shrugged his shoulders and said nothing, and then Homer began talking about evil. "There are two kinds," he said. "And the worst kind isn't black hearts. It's a failure of the imagination. Blandness and blindness. That's the horror of it. It's some upright Christian soul, some bumbling bureaucrat who refuses to see the truth, who washes his dainty hands of the poverty and misery around him, who signs his name routinely to some damnable bland blind piece of paper, ten copies, please, Miss Blah. That's the worst kind."

There was a pause. Then Alden spoke up softly. "But what about crimes of violence?" he said. "Like murder. Premeditated murder. That's not bland and blind."

He was not looking at Kitty, but she flushed just the same, and felt the hollow place in her chest draining empty again.

"Well, of course there is such a thing as a crime of passion," said Homer. "That's something else again."

"Passion?" said Alice Dove dreamily. Kitty looked up. Alice was standing at the window, looking out. The word "passion" had sounded so strange, coming out of her prim expressionless face.

"Passion," said Homer. "Crimes of passion. Premeditated as well as not. After all, what is that great endless tormented journey of Ahab's but his long-premeditated crime of passion? 'I'll chase him around Good Hope, and round the Horn, and round the Norway maelstrom, and round perdition's flame before I give him up,' he said, and then he carried a whole ship full of men along with him to doom and death and destruction. Now I admit that may not be your ordinary garden-variety crime of passion, but it's typical of its single-minded all-encompassing overwhelming power."

They're thinking of me, said Kitty to herself. *They think I was insane with some fit of passion like that.*

And then suddenly the discussion was over. "Quick, quick," said Alice, "come outside. Mute swans. Right over the house." She was pushing Kitty out of her chair, they were all getting up and hurrying out, looking at the sky. "There, there," said Alice, pointing up over her head. "Hush, hush now, keep quiet. Listen."

There they were. Kitty saw them, two great white birds, pumping strongly over the roof of the house. Their long necks were extended, their black legs were folded under them, the afternoon sun was turning their bellies gold. Then she heard the sound of their wings, a hushed feathery beating of the air, a rhythmic soft sound, *sssshhhh, sssshhhh, sssshhhh.*

And then Alice began to talk, her eyes on the tops of the trees where the swans had disappeared. "That's what I mean, you see. The swans have rights. But they can't talk, they're mute. I think a lot about the fact that they're mute swans, and what it means to be mute." Alice's hatchet face was alight, her brown eyes were shot with glints of gold. "Those Flakeleys and Holworthys, that Mrs. Magee, they don't care about things like that. They don't see that the *land* has rights. Who will speak for the land? For the bearberry and the pitch pines and the scrub oak? For the dunes and the shore birds? For the wild swans? They're property owners too, and much more rightfully than the people who own those terrible pieces of paper that say, *mine, mine, mine*. Don't you see?"

Homer clapped her on the shoulder. "Attagirl, Alice," he said. "Talk about passion: that's what I call passion. Alden, why don't you get Alice over there in Barnstable to argue before the superior court? You don't need legal advice. You don't need Helen Green. An ounce of Alice's passion is worth a thousand pounds of rational argument and wherefores and whereases. Take it from me."

"Well, look here, Homer," said Alden, "how about you? If the thing does go to the superior court, would you help us out? Even with an enthusiast like my wife, we're going to need somebody who knows the ropes. How about it?"

Homer laughed and shook his head. "No, no, I'm not doing that kind of thing anymore. Oh, a little matter of getting a knife murderess off the hook, I'll do that in my spare time, but holy cow, I'm supposed to be a Melville scholar. Except, goddamnit, I haven't done anything about that wretched article of mine for a week. Women go around stabbing people, keep you running around like a chicken with its head cut off." Homer smiled seraphically at Kitty. "How you doing, honeybunch? Want me to take you to the grocery store? I'll punch all those people in the nose."

Kitty smiled sleepily and shook her head. "No, thanks anyway, Homer. I'll just go on home. I'm going to take a nap first and then I'll go out and get some groceries by myself. They won't bother me, those people. Not this time."

Kitty's bedroom was at the top of the steep stairs in Mr. Biddle's house. She dragged herself up to the second floor and crawled between her clean sheets with all her clothes on and fell instantly asleep.

And then it was her library of blank books all over again. But this time the books had become great organic growths with strange covers of animal skin and horn. They were mossy volumes crumbling at the edges into humus and decayed vegetation, encrusted with fungi, leaning up against one another on shelves that were lined with moss and entwined with vines and hung with twisting green metallic snakes. And the rows of shelves were open to the sky above, and the floor beneath her feet was grass, and when her hand reached out and lifted one of the volumes down, she saw that it was written in hieroglyphs, the trails of snails and the chitinous chalky serpentine patterns of sea worms and the channels and runways of ants. And the paper was manufactured by wasps and hornets, or it was birch bark and green leaves bound together. Into the dim distance the bookshelves led, blue with moisture, hazy with verdure, alive with the screams and cries of the birds that were dipping and soaring among the earth-smelling corridors.

Kitty woke up suddenly with a clear head and a sharp sense that now she knew what to do. She knew how she would use her six months, how she would give the time that was left to her some kind of usefulness and meaning. She would learn to read some of those languages, like Alice Dove. That was how she would make time dense, like the bristling thickets of the island trees.

13

. . . to think's audacity. God only has that right and privilege. Thinking is, or ought to be, a coolness and a calmness; and our poor hearts throb, and our poor brains beat too much for that.

Moby Dick

Kitty got out of bed, encouraged, bounded down the stairs, ran out to her car and drove to town. First she would stop at the drugstore on Main Street for some aspirin and a toothbrush, and then it was on! on! to the supermarket.

Her mettle was tested immediately. Half of the people drifting down Main Street in the direction of Steamboat Wharf had come to Nantucket because of its recent notoriety in the news. The particular arrangement of a thousand dark and light dots that was the published version of Kitty's face was photoengraved inside their heads, so that when she parked her car on the cobblestoned hill of Main Street and got out, her presence was discovered quickly, and the discovery was passed along. *It's Kitty Clark, Kitty Clark.* The wave crested, smashing into new boulders, sending up her name in splinters of broken glass. *Clark-ark-ark-ark-ark.*

Head down, Kitty dodged into the drugstore, dodged out again and hurried downhill, the wave retreating the other way in front of her, reminding her of the day she had met Joe Green. He had said that the ocean was saying her name.

No, no, don't think about that now, said Kitty to herself, stumbling across the cobblestones. But once under way, the memory would not be quelled. Huddling behind the wheel of her car, the smashed shell in her pocket grinding into her thigh, she backed out too fast, jammed on her brakes, stalled and started up again. Then Kitty said, "Oh, the hell with it," as the sunshine of that ancient day poured down upon her bare back, and the old waves curled in and out, and the problem she had been working on rose up again in her mind.

She had been lying on the sand at Crane's Beach on the north shore, juggling a complex collection of eight lumpish pieces on a kind of mental chessboard. She had been trying to combine the four humors of the soul, melancholy, sanguinity, choler and phlegm, with the four elements, fire, water, air and earth—it was an old problem, she was still working on it, she had thought of it again there on the beach just last week—and then a shadow had fallen across her, and she had looked up to see someone kneeling beside her. "Aren't you Katharine Clark?" he had said. He was wearing a shirt and rolled-up trousers. His feet were bare. "My name is Joseph Green." Kitty had flushed with pleasure and sat up, brushing the sand from her shoulders, which were still dead white with winter classrooms and dark libraries and the thin winter sunlight of her apartment. They had known about each other before they met, their heads were swimming already in clouds of common understanding, and then with one stride they went the rest of the way. Before long he was telling her the surf was saying her name. "Listen to it," he said. "That's *Claaaaaaaaaaaaaark.*"

"No, no, the ocean doesn't make those *k* sounds. It's more like *Greeeeeeeeeen.* Hear that? *Greeeeeeeeeen.*"

"Greenberg. It would have to be Greenberg. Except for a

couple of Nantucket Quakers, my great-grandparents were all German Jews. The waves aren't saying Greenberg. The ocean isn't Jewish."

"Yes, it is. Those waves have come straight across the ocean from the Mediterranean, from Tel Aviv and Jaffa, from—"

"The ocean is a woman. It's always been a woman."

He had taken her hand, and then on the way home in the back of somebody else's car, sun and water and mouth and eyes and hair and sunburned arms and legs had become rapturously entangled, and at the door of her apartment building Kitty had tumbled out of the car, gasping, desiring not to be cheap, but the next morning Joe had come back, and they had walked together the whole day, except for an hour Kitty had been forced to spend in class.

Part of the time they had lived in his apartment, part of the time in hers. They had been planning a wedding with wine flowing like water. Each could not believe in the good fortune that the other existed.

It had lasted through Christmas. But with the new year it had suddenly come to an end. An old Nantucket relative of Joe's had died and he had gone to the funeral. It was the first time he had ever been to Nantucket, and he had never come back. She had not seen him again. He had sent a letter at last, explaining about his third cousin Helen Boatwright, and how it had all seemed destined to happen, the union of two branches of an old family. But of course the letter hadn't explained anything. The stroke of the headsman's ax does not explain.

14

*And let me . . . admonish you, ye shipown-
ers of Nantucket! Beware of enlisting in
your vigilant fisheries any lad with lean
brow and hollow eye; given to unseason-
able meditativeness. . . .*

Moby Dick

Homer stood leaning on the counter in the police station on
Chestnut Street, where Kitty had been locked up. He was waiting
for Chief Pike to come in. Sergeant Fern was at his desk, occupy-
ing himself with this and that, moving his rolling chair nervously
from desk to typewriter table with the heels of his shiny black
shoes. Every now and then he glanced at Homer as if he were on
the verge of saying something, and Homer would look at him
expectantly, but then Sergeant Fern would turn away, his ears and
the back of his neck bright pink. Homer moved away from the
counter and studied the drug paraphernalia on the wall, and
looked at the signed photograph of John F. Kennedy, the cer-
tificate of appreciation from the Boy Scouts, and the Miranda
warning with its drawing of a handcuffed policeman and its
legend, ATTENTION, ALL CRIMINALS!

By the time Chief Pike came in at last, Homer was desperate
for reading matter, and he greeted the chief joyfully. "I'd like to

see Bird's pictures, please, if you don't mind," he said.

"You mean those color snapshots he took? Oh, no. Sergeant Fern here, he developed the roll of film and made some prints, but they were all sent over to Barnstable to the district attorney's office. Everything's in their hands now. When they want to know something we try to find out for them. But otherwise we're not involved anymore."

"Well, goddamnit, I suppose they'll be stuffy in Barnstable about letting me see those pictures. Ah, well. Thanks, anyway. Oh, excuse me, Sergeant. I didn't know you were going out."

The two men had been trying to crowd out the door at the same time. "Going off duty now," mumbled Sergeant Fern.

Homer held the door open to let Sergeant Fern go out first, and then he followed him down the walk to the street, but Sergeant Fern seemed hesitant, and he kept dropping back as if he weren't going anyplace in particular. Homer's car was parked around the corner. He ambled along the sidewalk, climbed into the car and turned the key. Suddenly Sergeant Fern's boyish face was bending down beside him, looking in the window.

"Lieutenant Kelly?" whispered Sergeant Fern. "If you'd like to see those pictures, I printed up an extra set."

"You did?" Homer was flabbergasted.

Sergeant Fern gazed at the front fender of Homer's car. "So if you'd like to see them, I could, like, bring them over."

"Well, sure, that would be great."

Sergeant Fern turned his head and looked at the rear fender of Homer's car. "Would tonight be okay?"

"Well, sure. Do you know where I'm staying?" Sergeant Fern nodded. "But you know, of course," said Homer sternly, "that I can't pay you anything."

"Oh, gee, I didn't mean that." Sergeant Fern's pink face blushed redder, all the way up into the roots of his orange hair. His blue eyes looked at Homer in distress.

Homer smiled at him and patted his sleeve. "I'll see you tonight," he said.

The kid must be sweet on Kitty. It was plain as the nose on his face. Well, he might be a big help. But he was going to get himself in trouble, giving information to the defense when he was supposed to be working for the Commonwealth of Massachusetts in its righteous prosecution of dangerous homicidal criminals.

15

He sleeps with clenched hands; and wakes
with his own bloody nails in his palms.
                                    Moby Dick

Alden was shouting something at Homer from the door of the house as Homer parked his car in the muddy driveway. "Telephone," bawled Alden. "I said, you're wanted on the phone."

"Oh, thanks." Homer jumped across the wallowing tire tracks and made his way inside, as Alden pulled his coat down from a hook beside the door and went out, whistling for his old dog Fly.

"Hello?" said Homer.

"Mr. Kelly? This is Joseph Green. Would you like to come on over now?"

"Sure."

"You know where I live?"

"Yes, I do."

"All right, then. Good."

Joe Green lived at Quaise, not far back up the Polpis Road on the side toward Nantucket Harbor. The dirt drive dipped down

The harbor at Quaise

and up through a field still rich with winter reds and browns, still dotted with last year's milkweed pods, which were perched on their old stalks in birdlike attitudes. It was a rough tumbling landscape, majestic with red cedars rising here and there. Homer parked his car near the big gray-shingled house, and sat for a moment looking past the house at the harbor. The water was a cold blue, ending in the sandy strip that was called Coatue. Between house and harbor there was a pond and a salt-water marsh of amber-colored grass. Water fowl floated in the intermittent streams. A beautiful place, by God. The property had been Helen's, of course. What would Joe do with it now?

Homer walked to the door slowly, trying to picture Joe Green, expecting a tweedy young fool, somebody he wouldn't like. When the door opened, the man inside was older than Homer had expected, his face broader, bluffer, more candid. And yet there was something odd and undecipherable in it. Melvillean phrases flickered through Homer's head. He dismissed them promptly and stepped inside.

"This way," said Joe. Walking ahead, he led Homer through the living room, a large chamber full of sunlight, yellow with paint and cloth of a color that might have been chosen to match the picture over the mantel, obviously Helen, a child with yellow pigtails and a yellow dress. Joe opened a door at one side of the room and said, "In here."

The second room was small and dark and blank. Roller shades were drawn down over the windows. There were a lot of books and papers piled on a card table. There was a cot badly made up, a standing lamp, two folding chairs. That was all.

"You did understand my letter?" said Homer. "I'm trying to help Katharine Clark."

"I understand," said Joe. He had settled down in one of the chairs and was leaning back, his arms folded, a muscle spasm ticking in one arm.

"Good," said Homer. "Let's start at the beginning, with the morning of March seventh."

"Well, I met my wife's plane at seven."

"She'd been on Martha's Vineyard for several days, is that right?"

"Yes. She'd been visiting a friend she went to school with."

"So you got up about six-thirty to go to the airport?"

"No. As a matter of fact I didn't. I hadn't been able to sleep the night before, so I'd spent a good part of the night walking around. There was a lot of wind. But it had stopped raining early in the evening."

"Where did you walk?"

"Oh—all over." Joe gestured with his head and waved his hand. "I cut across to the 'Sconset Road. Walked to 'Sconset. Walked along the footpath on the North Bluff there. Came back the same way." Joe supplied these short sentences slowly, with pauses in between. "I got back just as the sun was coming up, about six o'clock. And then I drove to the airport to pick up my wife. We had breakfast here. And then later on Helen had some errands she wanted to do. She went off in the car about ten o'clock. No, that's wrong. She came back in the house again and asked for the keys to the jeep, because she said the other car had been stalling so much. She'd been complaining about that. It was a new car. She wasn't used to it."

"And you stayed here while she was gone."

"No. I had discovered that I had lost something while I was

98

out walking, so I went back part of the way, looking for it. I took the car."

"You had lost something?"

"A piece of paper." Joe gestured deprecatingly with one hand. "I didn't find it and I turned around and drove back after a while. It must have blown away in the wind. I gave up. The Ropers came along shortly after I got home again, and we waited awhile for Helen to get back, maybe twenty minutes. She was late. We had intended to start for Great Point around eleven-thirty. She had been driving all over the island looking for a store that was open, but they were all closed because of the eclipse."

"Closed? The stores were all closed? I know some people had to work that day." Homer thought of Alice Dove in the Pacific National Bank and Alden out in his scalloping boat in the harbor. "So you set off with Richard and Letty Roper in your jeep around noon, is that right? I suppose they're your closest friends on the island?"

There was a pause. (Ah, what is a friend, reflected Homer philosophically.) "Closest friends—well, yes, I guess so. They were both born here, like Helen. They had all known each other for a long time."

"And when you got to Great Point you found Arthur Bird there waiting for you?"

Joe grimaced in mocking self-pity. "Yes, Bird was there."

Homer abandoned his official grimness and smiled. "Ass of a fellow."

Joe said nothing, but the muscles around his mouth twitched a little, as though he might smile himself.

"When did the four of you start up the stairs?"

"Just a little while before the total part of the eclipse began. There was some kind of effect Dick wanted to see from up there."

"The shadow bands," murmured Homer. "Some people at Altar Rock, where I was, put a sheet down on the ground. We saw them, flickering shadows across the sheet, just before totality. Did you see them from the lighthouse?"

"I don't know whether the others did or not. I—I forgot to look for them."

(Because you were watching Kitty.) "You saw Katharine Clark approaching across the sand. Did you recognize her?"

"I—I thought I did. Then when she took off her sunglasses I was sure." Joe had turned his face away. He was studying the blank surface of the roller shade. "And then Bird spoke up. He said her name."

"Did the name mean anything to your wife?"

Again there was a pause. "No, I don't think so."

"Did you have any pictures of Kitty in the house?"

Joe flushed. "No."

Homer stared at the roller shade too, where a vision of Kitty running across the sand was as clear as if it had been projected on a screen. "At any rate," he said, "your wife started downstairs. It was a dangerous staircase, wasn't it?"

Joe turned wretchedly to Homer. "Don't you think I know that? I should never have let her go."

"You loved your wife?" Homer's voice was flat.

A wave passed over Joe's face, and he seemed about to burst out, but then with obvious difficulty he mastered himself and said almost inaudibly, "What do *you* think?"

But Homer was ruthless. "You had been in love with Kitty Clark before."

Joe had recovered. Now he retreated behind a barrier of reserve. "Yes, until I met Helen."

"You were surprised to see Kitty coming? Did you think what you would say to her?"

Joe's voice was under careful control. "It would have been difficult. Embarrassing."

Homer shifted in his chair, leaned forward, looked down at his shoes. "The medical examiner found a number of bruises on your wife's body. Do you know how they came to be there?"

"She had fallen downstairs, here in the house."

Homer looked up to find Joe looking intently back at him, as though he were eager for the next question, seeking it, directing it. "How did she happen to fall downstairs?" said Homer slowly.

"It was the stair carpet. The tacks had come loose. It slipped out from under her one day. About two weeks ago."

"May I see where it happened?"

"Certainly." Joe led the way back to the front hall and gestured at the carpeted stairs to the second floor. "The carpet on the two top steps was loose and slipped out as she was starting down."

Homer walked up the steps and looked at the carpet. There were shiny new nails holding it fast at the top. "Had you noticed that it was loose?"

"No, neither of us had noticed anything like that."

"Mmmm." Homer stared at the bright heads of the small tacks and thought about it. A fall downstairs was seldom fatal, not for someone as young and strong as Helen Green had been. But it was odd, just the same. He shrugged his shoulders and descended the stairs. They went back to the small room with the lowered shades and sat down again in the folding chairs.

Homer changed the subject. "Were you as much involved in that new bylaw as Helen was? I understand she spent a great deal of time organizing support for it."

"Yes, she did. No, I didn't do anything. I had nothing to do with it."

"A lot of Helen's own land went to a conservation trust, I'm told?"

"Yes. The Boatwright Trust."

"Did you help with that? Or was it just Helen?"

"It was Helen's project. She took care of it."

There was another silence. Joe looked back at the window shade.

Homer changed the subject. "Are you writing anything now?" he said.

"No. I haven't . . . felt much like writing. I'm reading a good bit." Joe's eyes glanced involuntarily at the books piled on the card table. Homer looked at them too, wondering suddenly whether or not Kitty's was among them. He ran his eyes up and down the stack of books, looking for a narrow one with a purple cover, trying to think of another inconsequential question. There was a thin book at the very bottom of the stack. He couldn't see what color it was. "Do you—ah—use this room to write in?"

"This room? No, I don't write here. I have to get out of the house."

The rest of the books were all too big, too thick. The only one that could possibly be Kitty's was the skinny one on the bottom. "You've got a room outside somewhere? In the garage maybe?"

"No. I've got a little shack on the beach. I bought it when it was advertised for sale. I go there when I'm working."

Maybe if he were to lean on the table, here on this side where the legs looked rickety, the whole thing might fall down. "Where is this shack? Is that the place Chief Pike said was broken into a few weeks before your wife's death?"

"Yes. It's up at the Head of the Harbor. Nobody took anything. All they did was throw an old first draft of mine around. Vandals, I guess."

Homer tipped his chair back dangerously until it leaned on the edge of the card table. "Did your wife use it too? I mean, did you work there together?"

Joe seemed startled at this idea. "Oh, no, she never went there at all. We had an agreement about that. That was *my* place." Joe seemed to feel he had gone too far. "It's a kind of quirk I have. I don't like anybody to look at anything I'm working on until it's all finished."

"So Helen never went there? Bluebeard's chamber, eh?" With a furtive movement of his backside, Homer slid the two supporting legs of his chair so far past his center of gravity that most of his weight came crushing down upon the weak-kneed side of the fragile overburdened card table, and at last he accomplished his object. Chair, table, books and hulking clumsy oversized Melville scholar and occasional espouser of lost impossible causes went

102

over together in a shambling disastrous collapse. Homer hit his head on the edge of the table and cursed aloud. Joe Green jumped up with an exclamation of shock and sympathy and tried to lift him out of the wreck.

"Are you all right?" he said.

"Oh, Jesus, it's just my head. Just let me get all these books off me." With a massive sweep of his arm Homer tumbled the books on the floor, riffling them apart like a cardsharp examining a deck. Aha, there it was. Skinny book, purple cover, the name "Katharine Clark." "Christ, I'm sorry," said Homer. "I'm afraid there's not much left of this chair. Or the table either. I'll get you another set. A whole set."

Joe Green was helping him up. "For God's sake, never mind. They were falling apart anyway. Are you sure you're all right?"

"Positive." Homer shook himself and passed his hand through his hair. "Thanks a lot for letting me talk to you."

"You're quite welcome." They were back at arm's length. Joe was stiffly polite again. "I'll show you out."

He opened the door of the small room and waited for Homer to go ahead of him. But in the front entry he reached past Homer, grasped the doorknob and then looked vaguely over Homer's shoulder at the view of the harbor and the distant shore of Coatue. "How is she?" he said.

"How is . . . ? Who, you mean Kitty? Oh, she's . . . all right. She's fine."

Joe pulled open the door then, his face expressionless, and Homer, with a final nod, took his leave. He knew now what those Melville phrases were that had run through his head on his first glimpse of Joe Green: "He looked like a man cut away from the stake. . . ." And: ". . . Ahab stood before them with a crucifixion in his face. . . ."

Homer drove out of the driveway slowly, grumbling Melville to himself, pulling to one side into the undergrowth to let Letty Roper's car go by. Letty waved at Homer and smiled. What was

Dick Roper's wife doing here? Well, it was obvious. She was bringing another good home-cooked meal to her bereaved friend and fellow author.

Alas for poor Kitty. As Homer turned out into the Polpis Road he found himself paying silent tribute to the power of Joseph Green. He could understand now what Kitty saw in him—the large slow reflection, the clear careful eye, the steady unselfconscious grace. Homer could see how they would hang on in a girl's mind.

16

. . . this is one of those disheartening instances where truth requires full as much bolstering as error.

Moby Dick

"Come in, Sergeant," said Homer, leaning against the doorframe, stroking a full stomach. "You got those pictures?"

Sergeant Fern walked into the house and took off his coat. "Yes, sir," he said.

"Well, good for you," said Homer, trying not to smile. Sergeant Fern was wearing the kind of suit that used to be worn on Sundays, and the sort of shirt that wasn't supposed to be worn with a tie, but he was wearing a tie. He was a funny kid. Why had he gone to so much trouble? He must have thought Kitty would be here. He must have dressed up for Kitty.

Sergeant Fern looked around the room nervously, and nodded at Alden Dove, who was scooping dishes off the table, slapping them into the sink. "Hello, there, Bob," said Alden, splashing water into the dishpan. "There you are again. Fella can't turn around without running into Bob Fern. How was your catch today?"

"Not so good," said Bob. "How was yours?"

"Bag and a half. Pretty bad."

"You mean police officers go scalloping too?" Homer looked at Sergeant Fern in surprise.

"Bob's a boy of many parts," said Alden. "If he isn't giving you a parking ticket, he's dredging scallops off the bottom of the harbor right in front of you, and if he isn't doing that he's planting heather in your front yard, or putting a mustard plaster on your crippled swan." Alden grinned at Bob Fern. "Bob's an officer in the Nantucket Protection Society. He really knows his stuff."

"Well, I'll be damned." Homer looked at Sergeant Fern with new respect. The kid looked like a baby, too young to know anything yet.

"Here they are, Mr. Kelly," said Sergeant Fern, taking an envelope out of his pocket. He took out a set of color prints and laid them on the table side by side. Homer bent down to look at them, his eyes darting over the whole row. Then he swore and began picking them up in turn, holding them under the lamp.

Arthur Bird was a poor photographer. Most of his pictures were either out of focus or underexposed in the poor light before and after the eclipse. But what Homer could see in them in spite of all these failings made him shake his head with dismay. He could imagine them blown up to giant size on a screen in the courtroom. They would be damaging, very damaging. He could hear the shocked exclamations of the judge, the jury, the people crowded into the chamber. One of the worst was a picture of Helen, dead, her face distorted and staring, her blood too black in the underexposed shot, blood everywhere, an awful lot of blood. But good God, the worst of all was a picture of Kitty. There she was, in the only clear bright picture, gesturing with the bloody knife in her hand, explaining, her face all sweet reasonableness (and of course it was her reasonableness they had thought insane; reason at such an unreasonable time had struck them as madness)—and the color film had somehow exaggerated the redness of the blood upon her hands. It shone wetly, it fairly sparkled, it was running in dribbles down her arm. Good lord. Homer wrenched himself away from that one and looked at the next, a wild shot apparently taken by mistake of several people's legs against the sea horizon. Then there was a harrowing blurry picture of Joe Green with his head in his hands. Then a dark underexposed shot of Joe's profile in the lighthouse. Then another mistake, a view of the sea horizon tipped up at a forty-five-degree angle. And then a set of cheery normal shots of the picnic, taken in strong sunlight before the eclipse began.

"What do you think?" said Bob Fern, standing respectfully at Homer's elbow.

"What do I think?" Homer glanced at Bob and shook his head. "Jesus Christ. We can talk all we're worth, and produce character witnesses for Kitty by the carload, but with these pictures on the other side, good lord, I don't know. Goddamn that Arthur Bird."

"Take a look at these two," said Bob Fern. He picked up the picture of the tipped sea horizon and set it down beside the view of several pairs of legs. "This one with the legs—I think it shows the horizon to the northeast, the water off there on the open Atlantic side of the point. There's nothing out there, you see. No craft of any kind. But the other one has some spots on it that must be something. Here, compare it with this picture of Mr. Green. He's up on the slope there. Went off to be by himself for a minute, that's what everybody said, and that Bird went after him and took this picture, and then I think he took this one of the water by mistake, which is why it's all tipped. That's not the Atlantic side, that's the Nantucket Sound side of Great Point. And there are those spots out there. See, the picture of Mr. Green shows one of the spots too, this big blotch. It's in both pictures. It might be Cresswell's big sport-fishing yacht. These little spots are too blurry; you can't tell what they are. But they *must* be something."

Homer stared at the two pictures. "Good boy," he said.

Sergeant Fern flushed with pleasure. "The trouble is, they're on the wrong side of Great Point. The lighthouse is down near the water on the other side, the Atlantic side."

"That's right. Dick Roper saw them out in the Sound too, while the sky was getting dark."

"But then it got almost like the middle of the night," said Sergeant Fern. "What if one of them went across Point Rip in the dark and down the Atlantic side to the lighthouse, and then somebody threw a knife at Mrs. Green, and then the boat turned around and crossed the Rip again into the Sound, where it was when Bird took those pictures? I've been thinking a lot about that."

"But my God, man," protested Homer, "that's where the shoal is. Nobody could get across there, could they?"

"Oh, sure," said Bob Fern. "They do it all the time at high tide. They just rock up and down a little bit, and then they're over. You have to go pretty slow and easy. I've done it. Alden has done it, haven't you, Alden?"

Alden shook his head. "Not me. That plywood bottom of mine, I don't trust it in a place like that."

"Well, say," said Homer, beginning to get excited, "that's pretty good. The best thing about it is that they were all looking the other way, staring at Kitty coming along the sand, stark naked the way she was. The boat could have been coming right around behind their—"

"Stark *naked?*"

Homer looked at Bob's horrified face and patted him on the shoulder. "No, no, I didn't mean naked. She's a nice girl, after all. I mean, she may be a murderer, but she's genteel and well brought up. Kitty Clark doesn't go around naked, certainly not. Her skirt was blowing up in the wind, that's all, and it seems to have provoked a small sensation up there in the top of the light-house."

"Oh. Oh, I see."

"Anyway," said Homer, "the point is, some vessel with a shallow draft might have come around that end of the point unobserved and snuck up on Helen Green. And then at the instant of totality the deed was done. Kitty screamed because of the eclipse. Helen screamed because she was being killed. And the killer just turned around and went back across Point Rip in the dark and appeared on the Sound side again when the sun came out. Of course there's the problem of time. Two-and-a-half minutes of darkness probably wasn't long enough to accomplish all of that. And then there's the weapon. What did this seagoing murderer kill her *with?*"

"A harpoon?" suggested Bob Fern brightly.

Homer burst out laughing. Alden shook his head, threw a dish towel at the sink and went outside. "There's my Nantucket boy," said Homer. "Up speaks the shade of your ancestor the whaling man! Maybe he comes back during every eclipse of the sun, this old harpooner, and stands up in the bow of his boat, and this time he sees the dim shadowy figure of a pretty blond woman, the spitting image of a white whale if ever he saw one, so *whammo!* he lets her have it. Or maybe it was the Ancient Mariner with his crossbow. Or a plaster cupid with a bow and arrow from the sunken ballroom of the *Andrea Doria*. Or the great god Neptune himself with his pitchfork. Oh, come now, Bob—the point is, you're dead right. It could have been something like that. If the thing was done from the water, there had to be some kind of sharp-pointed weapon with a string on one end. Say, maybe that's what the snake was. What Helen saw just before she went up the stairs, when it was almost dark. It might have been a first attempt, and it missed, and she saw the rope trailing away in the sand. But it couldn't have been a harpoon; no. I saw those things in the Whaling Museum. Big things with toggles on them; they'd make a huge hole. Or they'd hang on to the body and drag it into the water. Say, Bob, do you suppose Cresswell's boat could have come across the Rip? He was out there, all right. Everybody saw him. He's that real estate lady's boyfriend—you know, that Mrs. Wilhelmina Magee."

"Too big. Couldn't have taken that big tub over Point Rip."

"Well, maybe he had a skin-diver or something. I don't suppose you skin-dive, do you, Bob?"

"No, but plenty of people on the island do."

"Well, good. That'll keep me busy for a while, tracking them all down. Thanks, Bob. You've been a big help. I'll tell Kitty. She'll be pleased."

Bob's face lit up. "Tell her . . . tell her . . . "

"Tell her what?"

"Tell her I liked the rainbow."

17

"Starbuck!"

"Sir."

"Oh, Starbuck! it is a mild, mild wind, and a mild looking sky. . . . "

" . . . I think, Sir, they have some such mild blue days, even as this, in Nantucket."

Moby Dick

Jupiter woke early, and lifted his beak from under his wing. Then he waddled out of the barn-red box that was his house and headed down the muddy slope to the swampy place and pecked at the fragile ice that had formed on the water during the night. The sun was up, casting thin horizontal beams of dawnlight on the red wall of his house, turning it to glowing copper, sending slanting rays over his little pond, stroking the ice, melting it almost as quickly as he could break it into delicate transparent fragments. The warm spring sunlight awoke something like a memory in the small round cage of his brain, a dim recollection of a time when he had not poked at the sparse shoots of this same stand of sedge and reed, when he had not been all alone. There had been another, a white and splendid one, a mate, an intimate companion.

Jupiter had been thrusting his long neck under the water to probe for new shoots in the muddy bottom, but now this bright image made him lift his head uneasily, and shake it, and arch his throat, because the vision in his mind was blood-suffused, splattered and stained with red—the red of the blood on her breast, the red of his fury as he had struck at her destroyer, the red of his own pain. And deeper down and farther back in the hollow bones and pinions of his wings he was suddenly aware of a vague wild surging free desire—to rise! To rise as he had risen a thousand times before, with a tumultuous beating of his wings at the water, to throw himself in a heavy heaving thrust at the air with a mute cry choking in his throat, to lift himself from the surface of the pond, the water arching backward from his wingtips in a spray, showering in crystal plumes from his dripping feet—to lift and lift. . . .

In a burst of longing he made a sudden rush up the sloping ground, his wings flapping frantically, his long neck outthrust. But the effort hurt him in a dozen places, and one wing leaked air where the feathers had been destroyed. He was thrown off balance, and fell back to one side in puzzled despair. Then a familiar tonking sound distracted him. Alice Dove was beating a metal ladle against the side of the pot in which she had mixed his breakfast. She was whistling and crooning at him. "Come here, my beauty. Come to your breakfast. Come, my poor Jupiter. I saw you! I saw what you were trying to do just now! But it's too soon, I tell you. Wait, wait. Someday you will fly. Someday."

Another long slanting ray of the rising sun shone through the old glass of the high east window in Kitty's bedroom, a lever of light that pried her out of bed. She jumped up and walked out to the privy, her coat on over her nightgown. Reaching for the latch of the privy door, she saw in the raking light something she had not seen before. There was a rough circle scratched on the bleached boards, and the surface of the door was pitted with holes and scars. Someone must have used it for target practice. Maybe Mr. Biddle had thrown knives at it in his spare time. (Oh, she was sick of thinking about knives.) Before going back to the house, Kitty stood on the knoll and looked around at the clear windy morning.

It was like standing above a billowing silver sea of scrub oaks. They were waist high, and the sound of the light breeze in their contorted branches was like the sound of waves rustling along a shore. Behind her Mr. Biddle's house reared up like an awkward wooden ship floating in a valley between foaming hills. A bird was singing quietly, clearly, near to Kitty. *Whiddleda-whiddleda-whiddleda.* She could see its dark shape not far away, its lifted head and open beak. She clapped her hands to make it fly, but instead it dropped out of sight and reappeared farther away on a branch tip, its watery warble distant now and more tentative. A jay flew from one low hill to another, uttering a strident cry. In the direction of the rising sun a hawk banked and turned, hovering, the ends of its primaries fluttering, poising in the breeze that buoyed it above the gray sea. Off to the north the dawnlight glittered on a rooftop. *Sail ho!* Whose house was that? Could it be the Doves'? Of course it was the Doves'. They were her next-door neighbors; she hadn't realized how near they were. She would walk there! Kitty hurried back to the house, pulled on her jeans and a sweater and a down-filled parka. Then she went back to the knoll behind the house and headed across lots, keeping the sunlit roof in sight.

She should have brought a knife or a pair of pruning shears.

113

The opening in the twiggy undergrowth had looked like a path, but before long her way was barred with great arching bull briers heavy as steel cables, thorny, an entanglement of barbed wire. With her gloved hands Kitty lifted them out of the way, one at a time.

There, now the path was clear again. But not for long. The undergrowth began to close in. Soon she was entangled up to her waist in a network of interwoven bushes. How thick they were, these interpenetrating layers, each stiff bough branching, each branch dividing, each division fingering into twigs, each twig separating in thick filaments. Something about the landscape by which she was surrounded caught Kitty's fancy, pricked up her interest in its thorny surface. The silver sea in the dawnlight . . . She wanted to know the names of things.

But she was not going to get where she wanted to go. Her parka was torn in a dozen places. Reluctantly she turned back, pushing with her padded body, until at last the low trees around Mr. Biddle's house welcomed her back with a stiff swaying of their dense boughs, which blocked the rising sun with netted criss-crossed members almost as profuse and multitudinous as if they were in leaf.

Kitty looked down regretfully at her ruined parka. How did one take a walk on this part of Nantucket Island? Apparently one stuck to the road. Too bad. She went back into the house, swallowed some cold cereal and set off again, striding along her driveway beside the tracks of a deer which had bounded along the road in the same direction during the night.

At the Polpis Road she turned right and hiked along for a half mile or so, then as she reached the Doves' driveway she stopped short, because Alice's car was turning onto the road. Alice pulled over and thrust her dour face out the car window. "Want to come with me?" said Alice. "I'm going around the island, checking on the swan population. Do it every Sunday."

"Oh, sure," said Kitty. She climbed in beside Alice and they headed up the road past Kitty's driveway. Before long Alice pulled off and parked the car.

"This is the Quaise salt marsh," said Alice. "There's a pair in here. Come on. There's an old road. You'll probably get your feet wet."

"What did you say happened to Jupiter?" said Kitty. "You said somebody shot him? Why would anybody do that?"

Alice was silent, marching along the dirt road beside Kitty. Then suddenly she threw the door of her face wide open. "It was here on this road, right here. Someone came along here too fast in an open car and ran over his mate. And then Jupiter rushed out. You should see how splendid they are, the males, with their great wings threatening and their long necks stretched forward, hissing with their open beaks! But then instead of driving away, the fool picked up a gun and shot at him, point-blank. I saw it. I was over there, sitting beside those trees."

"Who was it?" said Kitty. "Who shot him?"

Alice was silent again. The door had slammed shut. "I don't know," she muttered.

Then Alice stopped walking and lifted her field glasses. "There they are," she said softly. She pulled the glasses off and handed them to Kitty.

There was something white in the edge of the marsh, there below the hill where the gray-shingled side of a large house was washed in bright morning light. Kitty aimed the glasses at the patch of white. The swans were skimming slowly, arching their long white necks to peer down into the water. Kitty thought of poor Jupiter, limping clumsily around his muddy pen. This was what he must have been before, pure grace. "How did they get here?" said Kitty. "Have there always been swans on the island?"

"Oh, no. The first pair was imported, years ago. But they migrate now, and nest in the wild. . . . What's that?" she said sharply. She reached for the field glasses.

Kitty could see something too, a double flicker of sunlight, another pair of lenses. Somebody was looking at them. She thought of the swan-destroyer. Were the swans in danger? Then the two spots of light vanished, and a man appeared, climbing the slope in the direction of the house at the top of the low hill.

"It's Joe Green," said Alice, lowering her field glasses, her face and voice noncommittal. "He lives over there. That hilly part of the shore belonged to Helen Boatwright."

Kitty turned abruptly and started back. Alice followed. In the car Kitty struggled with herself and tried to make polite conversation, asking about the swans. Were they increasing every year? *Damn, oh, goddamn.*

"I'm afraid not." Alice started the car and headed southwest along the Polpis Road. "There are accidents—disasters. Some of the cygnets don't make it. Maybe it's snapping turtles. Then again, maybe it isn't. Malicious vandalism. *Murder.* It amounts to the same thing." Alice's face was glowering. "Martha Biddle found some little ones with their necks wrung last year at S'achacha Pond. She's your landlord's daughter."

"Oh, yes, Mr. Biddle." Kitty looked at the fence-rails running along beside the road, and thought about her landlord. Living in his house, she had begun to form a picture of a rugged and simple old man. "I wish I could meet him," she said. "I'd just like to see what he looks like. But I suppose he'd be like other people. Maybe he'd tell me I couldn't stay in his house anymore."

"Oh, don't worry about Obed Biddle," said Alice. "He's deaf as a post, and most of the time he lives in the past." Her face cleared, and she glanced at Kitty. "I'll tell you what you should do if you want to meet him. You should go to Friends Meeting. He goes there every Sunday. Ten o'clock this morning. This time of year they meet in the Maria Mitchell Library on Vestal Street instead of the Quaker Meeting House, because there's no heat in the Meeting House. Unless you're afraid of a bunch of Quakers."

18

*I sat a considerable Time in the Meeting
before I could see my Way clear to say
anything, until the Lord's heavenly Power
raised me, and set me upon my Feet as if
one had lifted me up. . . .*

JOHN RICHARDSON,
Quaker evangelist in Nantucket, 1701

Kitty came in late and sat down in an empty seat in the circle of
chairs. Nobody looked at her. Good. Discreetly she examined the
Friends, who were all sitting quietly. The room was lined with
windows and bookcases. Another room opened off it, with more
bookcases, tables covered with coats, a brass telescope on a tall
stand.

Was that Mr. Biddle, that baldheaded gentleman? He didn't
look quite right somehow. Then the door opened and another old
man came in, and Kitty smiled. Surely this was Obed Biddle. She
watched him shuffle to a chair, supported by a bulky woman in
a purple sombrero. That would be his daughter Martha. The old
man had a cane, and he leaned on it heavily. Then he tried to
hook it over the back of his chair but it clattered to the floor.
"Shit!" said Mr. Biddle.

"There, there, Daddy," said his daughter, speaking right into
his ear, helping him to settle down.

117

"All right, all right," quavered the old man noisily, waving his twisted hand. There was hair in his ears and in his nose like dragon smoke, and unkempt white hair trailed over his forehead. His long scrawny neck swayed forward like a camel's, leaving his shirt collar far behind. He coughed and barked.

Kitty lowered her head and stared at her shoes, not looking up as the door opened behind her. The circle of chairs was filled. The newcomers would have to sit somewhere else. Earnestly she struggled to imitate the thoughtful calm of the Friends who were sitting beside her. But her mind had become a restless twitching sea, niggling with small detail. It pulsed and raced. She invented two-word rhymes to use in comic verse. Her stomach growled. She had not had enough breakfast. Why didn't somebody speak up? Wasn't anybody going to be moved by the spirit to say anything? Would a whole hour go by with no sound but the echoing utterances of her own digestive tract? *Oh, Lord, let my stomach be soothed,* prayed Kitty. *Hush thou the inward groanings of this Christian flesh.* Were the Quakers Christians? Maybe not. Maybe they didn't even read the Bible. Maybe they didn't need any revelation but the inner light.

But Mr. Biddle had read the Bible! He cracked all his bones erect and coughed and gathered his spit and cleared his throat and began reciting the first chapter of Genesis. Kitty listened enraptured. His voice was grating and discordant but it was dire and threatening at the same time, like that of an Old Testament prophet.

"In the beginning,"

whinnied the old man,

"God created the heaven and the earth. And the earth was without form, and void; and darkness was upon the face of the deep."

He droned on and on, his voice alternately dying away and then bursting out again in a tuneless crescendo, grand and pitiful at the same time. Kitty thought of Mrs. Magee, the real estate lady, who was trying to swindle him out of his land. Could anyone warn him? But how could you warn and caution and persuade someone who was deaf as a post? Perhaps he would have to stand up against Mrs. Magee like the monument he was, a kind of very old but natural force, all by himself in his age and isolation against the petty thrusts and pinpricks of lesser men and women. At least he seemed to have Jehovah beside him, and Noah and Moses and Jeremiah, and surely the lot of them could hold off a lady realtor. Kitty saw him as a primordial patriarch, Moses holding aloft the tablets of the law, crying aloud the commandment about covetousness:

Thou shalt not covet thy neighbor's house . . . nor anything that is thy neighbor's.

But it was not Exodus now, it was Genesis, and Mr. Biddle had arrived at the howling climax of his recitation.

"And God created great whales, and every living creature that moveth, which the waters brought forth abundantly, after their kind . . ."

His voice kept cracking, rising suddenly an octave in pitch, penetrating to the skulls and marrowbones of his listeners like the deep knockings of a shuddering radiator.

" . . . and God saw that it was good! And God blessed them, saying, Be fruitful, and multiply, and fill the waters in the seas . . . And the evening and the morning were the fifth day. . . . "

Suddenly he sat down.

Was that all? wondered Kitty sleepily. What about the sixth and seventh days? Perhaps Mr. Biddle's memory had given out. She yawned. She wished she had taken off her coat. She was too hot in the warm room. Drowsiness was overwhelming her. Her head fell forward. She jerked it back. But in a moment it fell forward again, and her eyes rolled up under her closed lids, and she slept. She was in the same room, she was here in Quaker Meeting, but the Maria Mitchell Library had become a seagoing vessel, and she was at that very moment being pitched overboard. She was plunging with great smoothness, deeper and deeper down, fathoms beyond fathoms, the waters opening before her silently and closing just as silently behind her in a silvery bubbling froth. Now she was aware of shapes moving past her, great forms hidden in their own sleek streams of water, massive enormous presences, Mr. Biddle's great whales, newly created by God but hidden in streams of silver water, until at last one of the shapes turned toward her and opened its cavernous jaw. Kitty slowly revolved and faced it, poising in the water, ready to be engulfed. It was Leviathan. The jaw was gigantic, inviting, a chamber of velvet black. But then there was a muffled clatter and a general exhalation of breath and a rustling and a rising murmur of voices, and Kitty woke up, her head jerking back. The Meeting was over. She stood up. The man next to her was standing too, nodding pleasantly, reaching out to shake her hand. He probably didn't know she was a murdering sinner, or maybe he was a good man and he forgave her for her sins.

"Was that Obed Biddle?" said Kitty. "The man who spoke?"

"Oh, yes, that was Mr. Biddle. He's quite a tradition here. He knows the Old Testament by heart. A remarkable old gentleman. Do you know what he was referring to this morning? I don't suppose you do. He was talking about the scallop fishery."

"The *scallop fishery?*"

"It's been so poor lately. He was reminding God that the seas were meant to be fruitful and multiply." The man smiled, picked up his hat and departed.

Kitty looked at Mr. Biddle. She wanted to speak to him, to pluck his sleeve, to tell him how much she liked his house. Above the murmur of polite departing Friends she could hear him cursing his daughter. She started to move forward. How could she make him hear?

And then she was suddenly face to face with Arthur Bird. "Why, Arthur," said Kitty, feeling suddenly jovial and tyrannical. "I didn't know you were a Quaker."

"Oh, Miss Clark," said Arthur, "if there's anything I can do. Anything at all."

"But, Arthur, you already have." Gaily Kitty clapped him on the shoulder, and then she saw why he was there. Following Joseph Green. Because Joe was there, he was turning his back, the sleeves of his coat were shuddering, he was wading through chairs in his anxiety to get away.

Jonah, she was Jonah. She had failed to heed the word of God. She had gone where He had not bidden her to go, and then of course the sailors had thrown her overboard, to calm the storm of which she was the cause. *She was guilty, it was true that she was guilty.* From that first moment when she had seen the look of horror and revulsion in the eyes of Letty and Richard Roper, and Arthur Bird, and Joe himself, from that instant she had felt sunken in a sea of guilt, as though it didn't matter whether she had driven a knife into Helen's heart or not; she was foul with the deed just the same. She had gone to Tarshish, or wherever it was, instead of Nineveh, like Jonah. She had come where she was not wanted, where every instinct had told her it was wrong to come. She had blundered into something of great perfection and destroyed it. Her sin had seemed to her from that first moment not simply a venial but a mortal one.

19

. . . *We sallied out to board the* Pequod,
*sauntering along, and picking our teeth
with halibut bones.*

Moby Dick

Alden woke Homer at sunrise. "If you're coming with me, you've
got to get up now," he said.

"Good God, it's the middle of the night." Homer rolled away
from the horrid sight of Alden with all his clothes on.

"No, it's not. Look out the window. The sun's up. It's late. I
got up late on purpose because the annual meeting of the Nantucket Protection Society is tonight. I have to be wide awake to
give a speech. Come on, Homer."

"Oh, Lord."

"Look, I don't give a damn if you come or not, but it's March
thirty-first, the last day of the scalloping season. You said you
wanted—"

"Oh, I was a damned fool." Homer rolled back again and sat
up, grinning sleepily at Alden, scratching his head. He got out of
bed, put on all the clothes he could find, and ate the eggs Alden
had fixed for him.

Straight Wharf

"Bring the gas can, will you?" said Alden. "We'd better take both cars."

Homer followed the pickup to Straight Wharf, parked beside it in the parking lot, and then carried the gas can along the pier to the place where Alden's boat was moored. "So that's what you go scalloping in," he said nervously, looking down at it. "What do you call that kind of a craft? Not much to it, is there?"

"Bristol power boat." Alden stepped down heavily into the bottom of his boat, which was the simplest kind of rough seagoing vessel, with a winch made of rusted pipe, a wooden platform across the bow, and a wheel like the steering wheel of a car. There were two piles of heavy netted dredges stacked in the stern.

Homer put out a gingerly foot, pulled it back, tried the other foot, and finally managed to get down into the boat without making a fool of himself.

The man in the next boat was revving his engine, hollering at Alden cheerfully. Alden hollered back.

"How come he's got a cabin on his boat?" shouted Homer. "Jesus, don't you give a damn about the comfort of your passengers?"

"You're not a passenger. I'm going to put you to work. Here, give me the can." Alden poured gasoline through a plastic funnel into the six-gallon tank of his outboard motor, his red face bent over the task, his breath coming in steam from his nose. Then he jerked on the rope with a practiced tug. The motor turned over half-heartedly, emitting blue smoke, then settled down to a solid grinding shudder. Alden unwound the yellow nylon painter from the piling and dropped it in the bottom of the boat, where it lay in a clutter of gear, burlap bags, a can of paint, a collection of miscellaneous tools, drifts of eelgrass and broken shells. Then he waited politely for his neighbor to get out into the channel, waved his orange glove at him, put his engine into reverse and backed out of the mooring. Once in the channel, he shifted gears and then stood with one hand on the outboard and the other on the wheel, adjusting the speed of the engine, steering out into the harbor.

Homer stood beside him, hanging on to the gunwale. He hoped he wouldn't be seasick. Terra firma was his domain. The outboard made a terrible racket. "Say," he said, shouting above the din, "why don't you go scalloping in that kind of thing? That's more like it." He pointed at an enormous snow-white craft tied up on the other side of the slip, an expensive-looking vessel with a cabin as big as a ballroom and a vast superstructure crowned by a sporty outflung fishing platform high above the water. The name MIN was painted in gold letters a foot high on the stern.

Alden snorted. "Cresswell's," he said, steering carefully around it. "It's too damn big." He pointed dead ahead. "There goes Bob."

"Bob Fern?" said Homer. "So he does." Sergeant Fern's boat was more or less like Alden's, except that it had a small open cabin. It was painted a tidy white from stem to stern. "Where's he heading?"

"Don't know," said Alden. "But we're going to try over there. Off First Point."

"Scalloping still bad?"

Alden nodded, his eyes on the long low line of Coatue. "Too many of us this year," he said, his voice hoarse above the noise of the engine, his words blowing back into his mouth. "Too many scallopers. Kids, a lot of them, like Fern. Oh, I don't mind 'em. They work hard. But then of course we all thought it would be a good year, because last year was bad, and there's usually two or three good years for every bad year. But what happened was, in my opinion, some people got so desperate last year they even took the little ones, so there wasn't enough seed scallop for this year. And then there's the Japanese moss." Alden frowned at Homer, his curly black hair blowing out under his knitted cap in the northwesterly breeze.

Homer leaned back jauntily against the gunwale and put his hands in his pockets, preening himself on his sea legs. He'd decided he was not going to be seasick, after all. The boat felt like a diesel truck on a paved highway. "You mean that Japanese moss you were talking about the other day?"

"Right. It smothers the scallops. There was a bounty on it, until the money ran out." Alden reached back and fiddled with his outboard. "I'm going to start dredging now."

"Let me help," said Homer. "You want me to throw one of these things over the side?" He stepped carefully over the clutter in the bottom of the boat and fumbled with the rope netting of the topmost dredge on the port side.

"Wait till I head up into the wind," said Alden. "Here, let me do it. It's kind of tricky." He abandoned the wheel, cut the speed of the outboard and began throwing the dredges over the stern one at a time. "Now we'll just go back and forth here for a while. Move over. I'll bring her around."

Back and forth, back and forth. And back again. "Now we'll see what we've got," said Alden. He reversed the engine to slacken his towlines, unhooked one of the ropes from the stern, made it fast to the winch, and then started the little donkey engine that worked the winch. The donkey engine putted noisily, and soon the dredge was up out of the water, scraping against the stern. Alden let the water stream out of it, then he guided it over the boat and dumped its contents on the culling board. He shoveled and shoveled with his orange glove, then shook his head with disappointment. "Too small. They're most of them too small. Gotta throw most of 'em back. See this one? It's got a growth ring. You keep the ones with the growth ring. Put 'em in the basket here, empty the basket into the burlap bag. Our limit is supposed to be six bags a day, but heck, I've hardly ever got my limit since last fall."

Obediently Homer fumbled with the cold wet mess on the culling board, and began tossing scallops left and right. There were other small craft out now, heading up the harbor, and he could tell which ones were scallopers by the culling boards across their bows and the stacked dredges in the stern. "Say, Alden," he shouted, "aren't those guys late? Do you come out early to get ahead of everybody?"

"No, not that so much. Early morning's just the best time. Funny thing, the way the scallops like to frolic around at night. Early in the morning they're still up and dancing. Easier to scrape up. During the day they settle back down. Another good time is right after a storm when the tide is running. Maybe because it's dark during a storm."

"Well, say, how about during the eclipse?" said Homer brightly. "When it got so dark? The scallops must have tumbled out of bed wondering why they were still so exhausted. You were out that day, weren't you, Alden? Didn't even take the day off for the end of the world?"

"Yes, I was. A lot of scallopers were out. Business as usual."

"No soul," hollered Homer. "You Nantucketers got no soul. And say, Alden, speaking of soul, isn't it about time for lunch?"

Alden's watch said eight-thirty. Homer groaned. All at once he had lost his appetite for shipboard life. Manfully, however, he lent a hand, steering and sorting, until at last Alden took pity on him and called a halt. They headed back across the harbor and nosed into Alden's mooring.

Someone was waiting for them, a small man in a duckbilled hat. "That's Charley Piper, the shellfish warden," said Alden, emptying what was left in the gas can into the tank. "Toss him the line, will you?"

"The line? Oh, sure." Homer scrabbled in the bottom of the boat for the yellow rope, struggled with it, couldn't find the free end because he was stepping on it, untangled it at last, hurled it up in the air at Charley Piper, missed, threw it again, missed again, threw it again and realized as it fell back down that since he was six and a half feet tall he was almost face to face with the small man on the wharf. He picked up the end of the rope in his fingers and handed it to the shellfish warden daintily. "Sorry," said Homer. "Drugstore sailor."

Charley Piper shook his head in disbelief, and ran the line around the piling. "Well, Alden," he said, "you don't look in any danger of going over the limit this morning. What have you got there—a couple of bags?"

"That's all so far. But I'm going back out. I was just showing this off-islander around."

Homer stepped gratefully up onto the solid wooden floor of the wharf and introduced himself to Charley Piper. Alden hopped out too, with his empty gas can. The midday sun of the last day of March shone down on the dock, and Homer took off his heavy sweater. He had his notebook out. Charley Piper's name was in there somewhere. Yes, here it was. Dick Roper had told him about Charley Piper. Charley would know who went in and out of the harbor on the day of the eclipse if anybody would. Homer wasted no time.

"Were you right here on the day of the eclipse, Mr. Piper?" he said. "What was it like in the harbor that day? Were there many boats out?"

"Oh, sure," said Charley Piper. Charley's nasal voice was high and thin, with an authoritative whine in it. "The small-craft warnings were called off at dawn, as I recall. So most of the regular scallopers were out that day, just as usual. Now, let's see—didn't see Fern go out. Oh, yes, he did. He was late, that was all. Henry and John Irving, they didn't go. Neither did a couple of them hippies. Jack Smith, he was sick. Alden was out, weren't you, Alden, working your head off. Got a good catch for this time of year, not like some of those kids, don't want to work that hard. Lazy, some of 'em."

"Can you tell me exactly what craft might have gone right out of the harbor into Nantucket Sound on that day, Mr. Piper?" said Homer, licking his pencil, flipping the pages of his little notebook. "Do you have any idea how many boats came to the island just for the occasion of the total eclipse of the sun? And could you tell me who their owners were?"

Mr. Piper looked at Homer from under his duckbilled hat with a sober eye. "What do you want to know for?" he said.

"Charley, this is Homer Kelly," said Alden. "He's the lawyer for Kitty Clark—you know, that girl who . . ."

"The one that murdered Helen Green?" Charley Piper glowered at Homer. "He ought to be ashamed of himself."

Homer made a horrible face at Alden. Alden reasoned with Charley. Charley relented and then began reeling off a list of boats and owners and lengths in feet and tonnages and home ports and previous owners and present owners and what he thought of their churchgoing habits and drinking problems and the ups and downs of their domestic lives. He knew everything.

He had forgotten nothing. Homer scribbled as fast as he could, then gave up in despair.

"I should have warned you, Homer," said Alden. "Charley's a phenomenon. How he can sort out one day from another beats me. But there it is."

Homer told himself he was going to have to come back with a tape recorder, but he flipped over another page in his notebook and tried again. "What about boats from the mainland, Mr. Piper? I suppose there were some people who came over for the day just to see the eclipse? And then never came into the harbor at all?"

"Oh, yes, you bet. It was awful early in the year, but the place was crawling with 'em. I recognized some of 'em. Junior Jacobson was out there, with that big old cabin cruiser of his, comes here during the summer. And that big schooner of Harold Galsworthy's, he had it out already. Fine sight. Then there was that one fella, I told you about him, Alden, he's still trying to get that little ketch of his home to New Jersey. Had it as far as Block Island yesterday, somebody told me. Of course our island boats were out too. Cresswell, well, naturally, he was out there, came back bumping into the wharf on both sides, it's a mercy his boat wasn't stove in. Drunk he was, dead drunk. Mrs. Magee, his girl friend, she was screaming at him like a banshee. Guests all whooping it up, they had to carry some of them off, they were out cold."

"Must have made all sorts of interesting solar observations on that expedition," murmured Homer, writing as fast as he could. Then he whipped the pages of his notebook back again to the notes he had taken in Richard Roper's office. "Mr. Roper said he saw a small sailboat of the Rainbow class off Great Point in Nantucket Sound that morning, and a red cabin cruiser, and Cresswell's boat, and a large commercial fishing boat a long way out. Do you know about any of those?"

"Well, there were five Rainbows went out of the harbor that day. I can tell you whose they were. Tillinghast's, he's the new president of the Nantucket Protection Society, his son's gone to the bad on the mainland. Young Flakeley, he's the realtor's nephew, he had a floozy with him. Three girls, cousins, all Russells, they race against each other in the summer, call themselves the Cormorants, nice young ladies. I don't recognize the cabin cruiser. That's not an island craft."

Homer stopped writing again, unable to keep up. The empty place in his stomach was gnawing at him. He felt faint with hunger. "Just one more thing, Mr. Piper. There's only one entrance to the harbor, right? If you didn't see 'em go out of the jetties here, they didn't go out from the harbor, is that right?"

"One entrance to the harbor?" Mr. Piper looked at Alden as if to ask him what kind of nitwit he had for a friend. "Of course there's only one entrance to the harbor. Wouldn't be much of a harbor, would it now, if it was full of holes?"

20

But ropes now, and let us ascend. Yet soft,
this is not so easy.

MELVILLE, *The Encantadas*

After a couple of lunches at Cy's on South Water Street, Homer felt a lot better. He called up Kitty, who now had an unlisted phone, and told her to get ready for a trip to Great Point. "You don't mind going back there, do you?" he asked a little anxiously.

"You mean right now? Well, no, I don't mind. Of course not."

She was waiting for him at the end of her driveway, wearing her parka. The rips had been mended but the parka looked terrible. "You certainly don't look voluptuous in *that*," said Homer.

"Well, I'm sorry," said Kitty. On the way to Wauwinet she sat forward on the bucket seat of Homer's rented Scout looking eagerly left and right, and soon she was telling him the names of the trees and bushes along the road. She had been learning from Alice Dove, borrowing books from Alice. "Look at that, Homer. That's broom, Scotch broom. And that gray-green stuff is reindeer moss. It's just like lichen on a tree or a stone wall, only in the field it's just like a little plant. And those wonderful gray trees are tupelo. *Look* at them."

Homer's good humor began to drain away. The more cheerful Kitty was, the worse he felt. It meant she was relying on him, thinking he had matters under control, and he knew to his sorrow that he was faulty at the core. He looked where she pointed and nodded and made assenting growls.

On the sandy track beyond Wauwinet she became intolerable. She kept exclaiming with delight. She made him stop the truck. She jumped down to take a closer look at the stunted junipers and the low gray leafless vegetation. "This is Coskata," she said. "The Coskata Woods. There's a pond here somewhere. I don't know what those twisted trees are, do you?"

"I don't know one tree from another," grumbled Homer.

"But aren't they beautiful?" demanded Kitty.

"Oh, sure. Sort of Japanese, eh?"

"Yes. I suppose the Japanese islands have the same strong winds that stunt and dwarf and shape the trees." She was pointing back along the way they had come. "I read something last night about this beach. The sea broke through there once, a long time ago. They used to haul their boats across. It was like a shortcut into the harbor from the Atlantic, so they didn't have to go way around to the mouth of the harbor. It's still called the Haulover, that part of the shore."

Homer's interest picked up. "No kidding—is that so? Well, I wasn't such a damn fool after all. So there *were* two entrances to the harbor, not just one. Could they get across there now? I mean at high tide? Looks like a pretty high bluff all the way around."

"It is. I've climbed it. No, it's all built up again with a high dune."

Homer looked back along the shore as he climbed into the truck. "Too bad about the bluff. If there were still a weak place there, it might have been a way to get out of the harbor without being seen." He started the motor and soon the Scout was whining along in second gear once again, rearing and dipping in the mushy sand.

They emerged from the wooded part of the neck and came out on the Gauls, the sandy strip that divided the open Atlantic from Nantucket Sound. The lighthouse was a small white spire far ahead of them, just as it had appeared to Kitty when she had walked along the beach. They were quiet as they wallowed and bounded along the churning track. In the shadow of the lighthouse Homer parked the truck and they climbed out.

great Point light

"It's low tide now, isn't it?" said Kitty. "The water's much farther away." She turned and looked at the lighthouse. Then she made herself walk up to it and touch the wall at the place where Helen's body had lain. The sand beneath the wall exhibited no stain. There was nothing there now but bits of stone and gravel and clumps of beach grass, bending in the wind, the tips tracing curving lines in the loose sand. There were a few chunks of broken asphalt.

Homer poked at the asphalt with his shoe. "There used to be

a house here, years ago, Alden says, with a full staff of people. And a lawn, and a golf driving course. But it's all been washed away."

"Washed away?"

"Storms tear away chunks. The south shore has lost a mile since the last ice age. The shoreline changes all the time. The sand builds up in some places, washes away from others. The whole island will be gone someday."

Everything was doomed. Gloomily Kitty followed Homer to the scarred door, and they went inside. Then to her surprise she found her interest aroused once again. There was a cast-iron stairway that wound around and around, up and up into the dark tower. No one had told her that it was fragile and delicate-looking like lace. The treads were a fretted network like iron embroidery, like old sewing machines, like the Alhambra, like the crisscrossing dense members of the island trees. Over her head the staircase curved in narrowing spirals like those of the twisting shell in the pocket of her jacket at home, and she thought sentimentally for a moment about her own death, and about convolutions and spiral turnings and twistings that narrowed down at last to some dark hidden inner chamber where one could fold and curl oneself infinitesimally small.

"Pretty," admitted Homer, "but no fun to climb. You go first. I'll catch you if you slip."

There was a rope attached to the wall, a kind of railing, but halfway up it skipped a bolt and stretched across the narrow space, getting in the way. Kitty groped with her fingers on the cold stone of the wall and thought about Helen Green hurrying down the stairs alone.

"There now, here's the first landing," said Homer. "We're almost there. One more short flight to the padlock. The Chief Officer of the Coast Guard loaned me the key."

Above the second landing there was a metal trap door that slid to the side. Kitty climbed the last ladder and stepped out into the small twelve-sided chamber at the top of the tower. "Oh," she said. "Wow," said Homer. Around them lay the sea and the blue

sky, and running away from them to the southwest, the sandy
strip by which they had come, and the whole broad island. They
could see the scalloped line of Coatue, point cusping beyond
point, and the cold blue harbor, and the stubby lighthouse at
Brant Point. Then they turned and looked northward, and Homer
pointed out the clear fan of sand spreading away like a moth's
wing under the water, lifting close to the surface here and there
where waves broke in little white crests.

"Terrible wrecks they've had around this island," said Homer.
"I've been reading about them. There are shoals everywhere, and
they keep shifting and changing. A mariner really has to know
what he's doing. They have to keep putting out new maps of the
shoal waters all the time."

136

They turned to inspect the optical system that rose up in the middle of the chamber. It was a simple device, a narrow pillar surmounted by a hexagon of six little plastic lenses above a small bulb. "Is that what makes the light?" said Kitty. "Why, there's nothing to it."

"Yes, they've made these things much more efficient now," said Homer. He put his nose against the window that faced southeast, and peered downward. "Look, you can't even see the truck from up here. Everything near the base of the lighthouse is out of sight."

Kitty looked down, and remembered something. "What happened to those pictures Arthur took? Did you ever get to see them?"

"Yes, I saw them." Homer looked uncomfortably at the black-backed gulls, which were wheeling and dropping on the other side of the point, diving for clams in the lagoon. "Well, they were gruesome, as a matter of fact," he said. "And that reminds me. I forgot to tell you about Fern. Sergeant Bob Fern from the police department has volunteered to help us out. He's the one who showed me the pictures."

"Sergeant Fern? But he's not supposed to help the defense, is he? I should think that would be—"

"No, he's not. He'll probably lose his job, if they find out. And there's something else I forgot. I was supposed to tell you he liked the rainbow."

"He did?" Kitty ruminated on this fact soberly.

"Now listen, Kitty Clark," said Homer, "let's get to work. It still seems so strange to me that you didn't see Helen until she was dead, and yet you heard her scream. What could she have been up to? Let's go through the motions again. I'll try being Helen. Do you have any idea where you were when you took off your sunglasses? That was when Arthur Bird said your name, and so that was when Helen started down. Go back to where you were when you took them off. Then I'll start down."

She didn't look much like a goddess today, thought Homer,

watching a foreshortened Kitty hurry away across the sand. In that fat parka she was a solid little lump with toothpick legs. Now she was turning around and staring up at him with her hands on her hips. He waved at her, and promptly she made a motion as if she were taking off her sunglasses, and then she began loping in the direction of the lighthouse.

Homer started down through the trap door, telling himself to use all deliberate haste. When he got to the bottom he opened the door a crack and peeked out. Kitty was there; she was just turning away. Homer stepped out silently. She was a couple of yards in front of him now, looking down at the sand. He stood still with his eyes on Kitty's back. Now she was looking up and making a dutiful squealing noise, to show that the sun had gone into total eclipse. Homer squealed too, in a horrible falsetto, and collapsed backward, trying to fall more or less naturally, but peering over his shoulder to make sure he wouldn't knock his head against the stones of the wall. Lying flat on his back, he looked up at Kitty. She was standing in the same place, her head down, counting out loud, patiently working her way through the two-and-a-half minutes of imaginary darkness. Then she lifted her head and moved out of his sight to the right. A moment later she was standing over him.

"Did you hear me open the door just after you turned your back?" he said, getting to his feet, brushing sand off his pants.

"No. Do you think she just walked right out behind me? And then somebody killed her?"

"Maybe. Or maybe she was killed on the other side of the door and then her body was thrown outside. Well, anyway, I've had enough. Let's go. I'll just gasp my way back up and lock that trap door again. Wait a minute."

They were halfway home before Homer could think of something cheerful to say to the glum girl sitting beside him. "Listen, my friend," he said, digging her puffy sleeve with his elbow. "You know what we're going to do right now? We're going to find us a nice cozy saloon and get *smashed.* Then we're going to go to some ritzy place like the whatchamacallit Coffin House and eat half a dozen lobsters apiece and drink a couple of gallons of white wine, and then we're going to stagger out into the street roaring and raging, and we're going to *bash* down the door of the Town and County Building, and we're going to *crash* the annual meeting of the Nantucket Protection Society. How about it? We'll *smash* and *bash* and *crash* our way in there and break up the meeting."

Kitty laughed. "Good," she said. "And then why don't we make some drunken motions? You make some, I'll second 'em, I'll make some, you second 'em."

Jared Coffin House

"*Sink* the island," shouted Homer. "Moved and seconded, island of Nantucket, latitude forty-one degrees north, longitude seventy degrees west of Greenwich. *Sink it! Sink it!* Sink it to the bottom of the Atlantic Ocean on Thursday next! Poor Alden Dove, he'll be embarrassed. He's supposed to be giving a talk about scallops."

21

*". . . Think not, is my eleventh command-
ment; and sleep when you can, is my
twelfth. . . ."*

Moby Dick

They were late. They crept in the door of the selectmen's room,
all tiptoe gentility, and sat down in the back row. Heads turned
to look at them, turned front, turned back a second time, then
reluctantly faced front again in the direction of Mr. Tillinghast,
the new president of the Nantucket Protection Society, who was
trying to forward the business of the evening. Alden Dove got up
from the front row and joined Homer and Kitty in the back. So
did somebody else, a skinny young man in his Sunday suit, his face
flaming: Bob Fern. Alden sat down beside Homer. Bob sat down
beside Kitty. Kitty smiled at Bob.

"We are gathered here this evening," said Mr. Tillinghast, a
mild-looking man in a tweed jacket, "as I said, in tribute to the
memory of Helen Green. Now that the business part of the
evening is over, I believe we have a final motion from our secretary, Anna Vickers. Anna?"

The president sat down and the secretary, a plump middle-aged woman, stood up and began reading. "Moved, that the name of this organization, the Nantucket Protection Society, Inc., be changed to the Helen Green Society, Inc., in recognition of the inspiration and leadership provided by our beloved friend and former president, Mrs. Helen Boatwright Green. Whereas she was a lifelong member of this organization from the age of sixteen to her early tragic death in the flower of her youth; whereas she was devoted to the history of the island of Nantucket, and through her family was an honored participant in its whaling tradition; whereas she was a leader in the crusade for the new Nantucket bylaw preserving much of the island from further development and consequent destruction; whereas the depth of her commitment to the preservation of our beloved island was demonstrated by her sacrifice of untold financial gain in the formation of the Boatwright Land Trust, which will preserve as open land the greater portion of her ancestral holdings; whereas she was a human being whose radiant youth and spiritual beauty were an inspiration to all who knew her: we, the members of this society, in loving memory of Helen Green, do hereby change the name of this organization from the Nantucket Protection Society to the Helen Green Society."

The secretary sat down amid applause, tears and murmurs of "Second the motion." Love for Helen Green flowed forward. Hate for her murderer flowed back. Kitty felt it buffeting her, and stubbornly she tried to compose her face to look pure as the driven snow.

The president was on his feet again. "All in favor, say aye. Opposed, no. The motion is passed unanimously. Now I think it will be obvious to every member of the Helen Green Society that a new name for this organization is not enough. The only true memorial we can make to Helen will be to carry on her work. On that score I'm afraid I have some bad news. I have just been informed that the realtor Mrs. Wilhelmina Magee and Mr. James Holworthy of Madaket have filed an appeal with the superior court in Barnstable declaring our new bylaw unconstitutional."

Breaths were sucked in all over the room, and the members of the Helen Green Society looked at one another in dismay.

"Well, we've been expecting something of the sort," continued Mr. Tillinghast. "My only comfort is that Helen herself never knew of this threat to her great work. Without her, of course, we have lost our most eloquent spokesman. But we must carry on. Each of us must feel responsible for fighting this appeal, for carrying the matter all the way to the Supreme Court if necessary. At the end of the evening I shall call a special subcommittee meeting of the governing board to determine ways of raising money for what will undoubtedly be an extremely expensive campaign. Now at this time, we will carry on with our program for the evening. Alden, are you ready? Alden Dove has prepared a slide lecture on the Bay Scallop Fishery of Nantucket. Alden?"

Alden Dove got up and fiddled with a slide projector in the middle aisle of the rows of chairs. Alice Dove stepped out from the front row and pulled down a screen. Then she stood beside the light switch waiting for a signal. Her face was set and grim as usual, but when Alden nodded at her she flashed one brilliant look at Kitty, then snapped off the light.

Blue postcard sky, blue water lapping against pilings. "This is Nantucket Harbor, of course," said Alden Dove. "And this is Coskata Pond. And here's the harbor at Madaket, with Eel Point off to the left. All of these places provide the commercial scallop fisherman of Nantucket with a harvest in the winter months. This is a close-up of the bay scallop as we find it in these waters, *Aquipecten irradians*. It does not reach sexual maturity until its second year. . . ."

Kitty had never been able to keep her eyes open in the dark. To her horror she could feel drowsiness stealing over her. *I will not go to sleep again in a public place,* she told herself firmly. But she couldn't help herself. Darkness meant bedtime. Her head fell forward. She pulled it up again sharply and folded her arms. It fell forward again. She took the Helen Green Society with her into her dream. They were on the beach, dozens of them, walking along the sandy shore, all dressed up in hats and gloves and long loose flapping dark-gray clothes, their faces hostile, glowering. The president was there, marching in the lead, and there was the secretary, her long floppy gray dress slapping against her heavy calves. And there were all the rest of them, hordes of them, an army. They were marching along the beach in one direction, toward somebody lying on the sand. It was Kitty, naturally, lying there, and she was gray too, but the gray was not clothing but naked flesh. She was lying naked on a gray-white beach, her flesh a pearly luminous gray, chill and flaccid like gray-white bacon fat. The people were coming closer, and pointing at her, and making sounds of horror and disgust. And then Kitty lifted her head and looked down at herself and saw to her shame that she was marked with a birth stain, the rich blue-red color of blood, the color of port wine, suffusing one breast, running down into the hollow belly between the crests of her pelvis. She sat up, trying to cover the stain, but the people were retreating, pointing still, making exclamations of revulsion. The light turned on and Kitty woke up, returning promptly to the meeting of the Helen Green Society, jerking her head up from the shoulder of Bob Fern, where it had fallen. Bob made noises in his throat.

"What do you make of that?" whispered Mr. Tillinghast, the president of the Helen Green Society, to the secretary, Mrs. Vickers, and Mrs. Vickers told him what she thought of it in a furious whisper, using language that had never crossed her lips in her entire life before.

22

Could this be the Lamb's Bride, who had departed from this Spirit, and was in the Pollutions of the World through Lust . . . ?

JOHN RICHARDSON,
Quaker evangelist in Nantucket, 1701

"Look at that," said Alice Dove at breakfast the next morning. She was holding the *Inquirer and Mirror* under Homer's nose.

"Look at what? You mean this article right here?" Homer read it, while Alice fed the dogs, thumping their dishes angrily down on the floor.

CONSTITUTIONALITY OF BYLAW QUESTIONED

Mrs. Wilhelmina Magee and Mr. James Holworthy announced yesterday that they have filed an appeal with the Superior Court in Barnstable declaring the new Nantucket Zoning Bylaw unconstitutional.

"We are forming a new group," said Mrs. Magee, interviewed at her home in Monomoy, "which will work in cooperation with our attorney in preparing our case. The first meeting of our new Nantucket Property Owners Rights Association will be held Friday evening, April 3, at 8 P.M., in the home of Mrs. Donald Wilkinson of Siasconset. All interested Nantucket property owners are invited to attend."

"That's tonight," said Homer. "You people are property owners. Why don't you and Alden go, Alice, and come back and tell me all about it?"

Alice glared at Homer. "That woman hates our guts. She'd throw us out."

"A pity," said Homer. "I'll see if I can get somebody else to go. But first I want to talk to Mrs. Magee myself. She lives in Monomoy? Where's that again?"

"This side of town. It's that little resort development of hers. She lives in one of those honeymoon cottages." Alice watched the dogs wolf down their food. "Do you know what she's got there? Plastic starfish."

"No!" said Homer. "To what depths of depravity will some people sink! Do you think she'd believe me if I said I wanted to rent something? Would she know who I am?"

"She'd know," said Alice darkly. "She knows everything that happens on this island."

"Well, then, I'll try something bizarre. I'll call her up and tell her the truth. Sometimes an effective ploy when all else fails."

Mrs. Magee proved agreeable. She said Homer could come on over. He would find her walking her dog. At five minutes to ten Homer parked his car next to a sign that claimed the soil for Herman Melville Estates and Cottages. He got out and found himself face to face with Mrs. Magee's collection of plastic starfish, which were stuck here and there in a pink fishnet draped behind a couple of mannikins in purple pajamas in the window of her dress shop, the Moby Dick Boutique. Below the dress shop the cottages ran prettily down to the harbor. All of them were crowned with miniature roof walks from which honeymooners could observe the luxury craft parked at the marina, that is if the cottages had any ladders to go up scuttle with, but Homer doubted they had any ladders. He winced as he walked downhill

146

past the cottages, trying not to see the blasphemous names affixed to their front doors—*The Ishmael, The Pequod, The White Whale*—and wondered which one Arthur Bird was living in. Perfect place for a fool like Bird.

A woman was walking a dog at the bottom of the slope. Mrs. Magee had said she would be walking her dog. Homer raised his hand in a limp salute and wished her politely in hell. The dog barked and towed his owner up the hill. He was a huge lanky Afghan hound with a fall of blond hair parted in the middle.

"I'll bet I know what your dog's name is," volunteered Homer cheerfully, looking sympathetically at the dog, which was obviously a genetic mistake. "Captain Ahab."

"Why, someone must have told you."

"Just instinct." The dog was looking at Homer furtively with one sad golden eye. They walked back up the hill.

Wilhelmina Magee was an attractive woman with only the tiniest of hairline wrinkles around her delicate features. Her hair was pale spun glass, her eyes were the color of swimming pools, her pants matched her eyes, the shutters of her cottages matched her pants.

"Did you see the film they made of *Moby Dick?*" she said.

"No," said Homer. "Did you read the book?"

"The book? Why, of course."

She lied. Homer studied the rear view of Mrs. Magee carefully as her dog pulled her in front of him along the walk. She lied in her teeth. Because if there was one conclusion a person would jump to at first sight of Wilhelmina Magee, it was, alas, there goes a wretched human soul who has never read Herman Melville. *Because if you had read it, Mrs. Magee, if you had ever read* Moby Dick, *if you had ever followed from day to day the insane pursuit of Ahab after the White Whale, if you had ever beheld the fires of Saint Elmo towering from the yardarms of Ahab's ship, if you had ever heard the crewmen praying for mercy from the blessed saints, if Melville's colossal waves had ever washed over you,* then, Mrs. Magee, *the stickum in your hair would have been dissolved from everlasting to everlasting and your girdle would have lost its grip and the padding would have pulverized in your brassiere and that chilly eye of yours would gleam with holy dread forever after! You're a liar, Mrs. Magee!*

Captain Ahab lifted one hind leg and dribbled on a yew beside the entrance to the Moby Dick Boutique. Mrs. Magee jerked on his leash and tied him to a decorative object resting on the grass, a large anchor painted turquoise blue. She opened the turquoise door. She introduced Homer to Harper J. Cresswell, who was sitting in one of the captain's chairs in a cozy nook next to the window. Harper Cresswell reached out his hand. His jacket of turquoise tweed was so thick and bristly Homer was afraid he'd get a sliver.

Cresswell was drinking Scotch. "Join me?" he said in a rich genial amiable voice, gesturing at a well-stocked cupboard in the wall. Mrs. Magee's ladylike glass of sherry was waiting for her on the coffee table, which was a round piece of plate glass supported by a ship's wheel, the kind with handles all the way around.

Homer thought it over quickly. Much as he liked drink, it was apt to make him sleepy at this time of day, but then on the other hand he didn't want to look too hoity-toity. "Sure," he said.

Fresh from his morning shower, Harper J. Cresswell smelled of shaving lotion and perfumed soap. "Whatsis Min tells me about you?" he said affably, handing Homer his drink. "Goddamned policeman."

"Not anymore," said Homer. "Strictly private now. I'm trying to help out Katharine Clark. She's been indicted for the murder of Helen Green."

"Oh, izzatit? Well, cheers."

They sat down. "What can we do for you, Mr. Kelly?" said Mrs. Magee, crisp and businesslike, folding one turquoise thigh over the other.

"Well, perhaps you could tell me about the day of the eclipse. Were you on the island that day? Did you see it?"

"We were just offshore," said Mrs. Magee. "We were in Mr.

Cresswell's boat, cruising around the island. We saw the eclipse from the deck. We were on the move all during that interval, weren't we, Harper?"

"Well, yes, I guess so," said Mr. Cresswell.

"Were you off Great Point at all?" said Homer.

"We started to go around the island, didn't we, Harper?" said Mrs. Magee sharply. "Going west around Tuckernuck."

"Yeah, but we changed our minds, remember?" said Cresswell. "When Spike began to throw up over the side." Mrs. Magee made a face, and Cresswell turned to Homer. "And just between you and me, friend, I was in no condition to handle shoal waters, so we turned around and headed north. Sure, we were off Great Point part of the time. A good ways out, naturally. We were having a little party, kinda horsing around. I didn't want to take any chances running into Great Point Rip."

"Did you see any activity at the lighthouse while you were cruising? Could you see anything going on there on Great Point?"

"Well, we were pretty busy," said Mrs. Magee firmly. "I mean, we were looking up at the eclipse, weren't we, Harper? Of course we were down in the cabin most of the time, until the sky got really dark the way it did, and then we went up on deck just long enough to see that part of it for a couple of minutes, and then we went down again to have the rest of our lunch."

Cresswell poked Homer, his shining face jovial. "Some of 'em were too sozzled to even get up on deck. Didn't even know what was going on."

"Harper, you're exaggerating." Mrs. Magee frowned. "I assure you, Mr. Kelly, Mr. Cresswell is not in the habit of presiding at drunken brawls in the middle of the Atlantic Ocean." Mrs. Magee had a light quick habit of speech, and her gestures were rapid to match. She snapped open a cigarette case and lit a cigarette in a series of efficient motions.

"Of course he isn't," said Homer soothingly. "Tell me, Mr. Cresswell, that's a forty-five-footer, isn't it, that Big Bertha of yours? Must be a hell of a lot of fun, cruising around in a big sport-fisherman like that. Do you actually do much in the way of fishing?"

"Oh, sure." Cresswell's face sobered somewhat and he talked with a certain authority about his apparatus and the kinds and sizes of the fish he had reeled in off the island of Nantucket. "Of course in Florida I used to catch just about everything. You name it."

"Ever do any diving? Spearfishing? That kind of thing?"

"Oh, heck, no. Me? Can't even swim. But Min, here—to look at her you wouldn't think it, but she dives. She's got a form-fitting rubber outfit that's really something." Cresswell made a shape in the air and guffawed.

"But of course nobody was in the water at that particular party, I'll bet," mused Homer gaily, "unless somebody was having such a good time he jumped in with all his clothes on."

"Oh, good heavens, no," said Mrs. Magee.

"Change the subject," said Homer. "I'd like to talk about the last Nantucket Town Meeting. I understand you are unhappy about the vote on the new bylaw, Mrs. Magee. The paper said this morning that you and Mr. Holworthy are making an appeal to the superior court."

"That is correct." Mrs. Magee reached forward and knocked the ash off her cigarette. "It isn't American. Free enterprise is supposed to be the way of life in this country, and some of us who have faith in the democratic system have sunk our hard-earned money into our belief in this way of life, and now we're supposed to accept the loss of our investment as if it were in the cause of conservation, and it's not." She flicked ash. "It's power. Those people wanted to take power into their own hands."

"Who? What people?"

"Oh, that woman, Helen Green. I mean, I'm sorry she's dead, but . . . And Alice Dove. That whole fucking Nantucket Protection Society." Mrs. Magee had come to life. Her artificial gentility had disappeared. Her eyes were the frozen blue of polar ice. She raced on, talking fast. Homer listened with open mouth. Maybe

150

she had read a chapter or two of *Moby Dick* after all.

She stopped and jammed out her cigarette.

"Attagirl, Min," said Harper J. Cresswell.

Out of doors, Captain Ahab lifted his narrow jaw and howled.

23

"Ahab has that that's bloody on his mind."

Moby Dick

Bob Fern was leaning over Jupiter's fence when Homer drove up to the house after his interview with Mrs. Magee.

"He's looking a little better," said Bob. "Those wounds on his breast are healing up nicely."

"Do you think he'll ever fly again?" said Homer.

"Can't tell until we see if his feathers grow in again after he molts. If all those primaries come back, I don't see why he shouldn't fly. But if they don't, well, that won't be so good." Bob looked up from the scarred white shape of the great bird in the pen and turned to Homer. "I'm afraid I've got a little piece of bad news," he said.

"Just a little piece? Well, come on in and let's have it. Hold on there, you pooches. You're not supposed to come in till your mammy comes home from the bank."

Homer held the door slightly ajar, shoving at muzzles and paws, making room for Bob Fern. Bob squeezed inside the house, took a scrap of paper out of his pocket and put it down on the table next to a bird's nest, a bag of thistle seed, the marble paperweight with Alice's and Alden's initials on it, a jar containing regurgitated mouse bones from an owl's stomach, and Alice's field glasses. "It's a poem," said Bob.

"Oh?" Homer took a look at the scrap of paper. "Oh, that," he said. " 'Joseph's Coat.' We know all about that. It's that ballad of Kitty's. They clipped that from her apartment."

"Not the one I copied, they didn't. A lady brought it in. A Mrs. Wilkinson. Rich old lady, lives in 'Sconset. She brought it to Chief Pike after she read about the case in the paper. Said she thought it might mean something."

"Mrs. Wilkinson? Where have I heard of Mrs. Wilkinson before? Oh, I know. The Property Owners Rights Association. They're going to have their first meeting at her house. Where in God's name did Mrs. Wilkinson get hold of the damned thing? Not that it matters. The district attorney already has Kitty's own copy."

"But the one I saw is Joe Green's."

"What?" Homer stared at Bob Fern. "Kitty never gave one to Joe Green."

"Well, he had it. Anyway, this woman *says* he did, because he came to her house and asked for it back. The day of the eclipse. He told her he had lost a piece of paper on the beach the night before. She found it, all right, but instead of giving it back to him she brought it to us."

"So that's what he lost. He told me he lost a piece of paper. It means he knew—he knew how Kitty still felt about him. Maybe that was why he couldn't sleep. He was walking around with it. He was restless with it." Homer read the poem again. It took him a moment to feel his way through Bob Fern's rounded penmanship to the grim images of Kitty's language.

> Drag the hem of Joseph's coat
> Through the bloody cloven throat.

Dead, the sacrificial goat,
Kneeling in the rain.
Up speaks the goat by some black art,
"Brothers, take my beating heart
To Joseph's house, to him impart
My love's dark talisman,
Its utterance of sorrow,
Its bleeding message plain:
'Put on your coat again,
Your bloody coat again.' "

Homer remembered what Kitty had said about it. *I was feeling maudlin that day. I stood out in the rain in the parking lot behind my apartment house and bawled, with the rain running down my face and my hair all wet. Then I came in and wrote this stupid thing, and then of course I felt better, with all that masochism out of my system. It was supposed to be something like one of those old bloodthirsty ballads. . . .*

Bob Fern was reading the poem over again too, trying to come to terms once more with the obscurities and complexities and depths and heights and passions and intensities of the strange girl with whom he had fallen so hopelessly in love. "You see what it looks like," he said. "It looks like the two of them were in some kind of communication *before* Mrs. Green was killed. Over there in Barnstable they'll think there was some kind of plot between Miss Clark and Mr. Green. What do *you* think it means, Mr. Kelly? All that blood in there!"

"Well, goddamnit, any fool can see that the sacrificial goat is Kitty, goddamnit, and the damn-fool coat is her feeling for him, and the blood is— Do I have to spell it out? Good God. The blood is her suffering, or pain, or something, don't you see? Excuse me, Fern."

"But the trouble is, it looks like the bloody throat could be Helen Green, and the bloody coat is, well, maybe it's Miss Clark, and when it says here, 'Put on your coat again,' it means, Come back to me even though I cover myself with Helen's blood, you see."

"Fern," snarled Homer, "why don't you join Arthur Bird? The two of you should write a book. Make your fortune. *The Poetical Misadventures of R. Fern and A. Bird.* That's a damned lie. Kitty's the bloody throat; she told me so. I should have known you fools on the other side would get the whole thing wrong side up."

"Well, whatever it means," said Bob Fern bravely, "what was Joe Green doing with it the night before?"

"Damned if I know," said Homer gloomily.

"Are you going to show it to Kitty—I mean, Miss Clark?"

"No. And for God's sake call her Kitty. She won't eat you, you know, Bob, even if she *is* a knife murderess."

"She isn't! How can you say that? She's too good! She's too fine!" Bob Fern's breath was coming fast. He was glaring at Homer, his color coming and going. "I *know* she didn't do it!"

Homer smiled and patted Bob's glowing cheek. "Good. That makes two of us."

Bob turned away and stared at the mouse bones in the jar. "There's another funny thing. Helen Green was all over the place that Saturday morning. She was seen at the Maria Mitchell Observatory, and Altar Rock, and the Old Mill."

"She *was?* No kidding! What in Christ's name was she up to?"

"Nobody knows. She apparently just drove up to all those places and walked around for a minute or two and then drove away without talking to anybody. They were all places where people were getting ready to watch the eclipse."

"So they were. I was at Altar Rock myself later on. What the hell do you suppose she was doing?"

"I don't know." Bob turned around again, his expression fierce. "Homer, I don't know how much longer I can stick it out. Chief Pike gave me a talking-to this morning. Said I mustn't let my . . . feelings get in the way of my duty to my badge. But right now I feel like . . . just ripping that badge off and throwing it in Nantucket Sound!"

"Now, Bob, you're letting that bloodcurdling poetry of Kitty's carry you away. Maybe you ought to forget about helping Kitty, and just concentrate on being a model Nantucket police officer."

"No, sir," said Bob Fern, his jaw hardening, his shoulders stiffening. "I've made a vow, a secret vow—secret until now!— to do everything in my power to prove to the world the innocence of Katharine Clark."

"Good boy," said Homer. "That's the ticket." He watched Bob stalk out of the house and depart in his car with stern steadfast backings and staunch forward rushings, resolution and devotion in every jounce and bounce of his old Chevrolet as it disappeared down the rutted drive. "I'll bet he signed it in blood," decided Homer. "I'll bet he signed that vow in blood from his own big goofy thumb."

24

Evil and good, they braided play
Into one cord. . . .

MELVILLE, *Clarel*

Homer climbed into his car and drove to Kitty's, chewing over in his mind the tasty bits of news Fern had offered up on the sacrificial plate of his tin policeman's badge. There was something deliciously tantalizing in the thought of the restless rovings of the two Greens, man and wife, during the twenty-four hours before Helen's death. There was Joe, on the one hand, wandering around the island all night long with Kitty's poem in his hand. And there was Helen, on the other, rushing from place to place the next morning, looking for something. Searching all over, trying to find it. Something or somebody. But what? Or whom? Joe had lost that piece of paper—could Helen have been looking for that? But why would she look for it in those three places? Joe hadn't been anywhere near any of them. Or had he?

Homer found Kitty poking around the sloping ground in front of her house with a muddy book in her hand. Her knees and face were muddy. "Is this blueberry?" she said. "This thing here?

Maybe it's broom crowberry. I wish I weren't so ignorant. I hate to keep bothering Alice."

"Why don't you ask Bob Fern?" said Homer. "He knows all that stuff. Besides, the poor fool is in love with you."

Kitty put out her hand to catch a raindrop. "There, I knew it would begin soon." She strode into the house in front of Homer, her head down. "I wish he wouldn't get himself in trouble on my account. I don't dare look at him. I feel like a basilisk. You know, that dragon that kills with one glance of its horrible gruesome eye."

"A basilisk." Homer laughed. "Well, thank heaven I'm safe. To me you're just a client who happens to have horrible gruesome eyes. Strictly business arrangement. Listen, basilisk, I met Mrs. Magee this morning."

"No! What was she like?"

"Oh, she was all right. You just have to kind of wrench yourself around and see things from her point of view. When she stopped being refined I sort of liked her. Say, what do basilisks eat? Besides the corpses of their victims? Basil, naturally—har har. What have you got in your icebox a fellow could . . ."

"Well, I'll take a look. Sit down." Kitty took some hard-boiled eggs and a loaf of rye bread out of her refrigerator and began shelling the eggs. "I had a letter from my publisher this morning," she said solemnly.

"Oh?"

"My book is doing very well."

"Mmm. I suspect it is. For all the wrong reasons, I suppose."

"They sent me a check. Biggest I ever got." Kitty reached for an envelope on the windowsill. "Here it is. Take it. I don't want it around anymore."

"Oh, go on. Look, girl, we've been through this before. I've been well enough paid already. The money is coming out of my ears, for chrissake."

"It is? Really? Good!" Kitty was surprised to learn that the Commonwealth of Massachusetts was so generously rewarding its charity lawyers. "You're keeping track, aren't you? We'll have a grand accounting and setting to rights when—after it's all over."

"Oh, sure, sure. Now look. I have a job for you. How would you like to go to Mrs. Magee's Property Owners Rights Association meeting tonight?"

"Me? Oh, Homer, last week she wouldn't even show me a cottage. She won't stand for any criminals at her meeting."

"Well, then, I suppose I'll have to go myself." Homer picked up his sandwich, then put it down on his plate, a big smile on his face. "I know. I'll wear my cloak of invisibility. Did I ever tell you about my cloak of invisibility? I mean, we've all got our little mythological devices. You've got a basilisk eye, I've got a cloak of invisibility."

"I hope it's an extremely large cloak. What are you anyway, Homer—seven feet tall?"

"No, no, nothing like that. Look, I'll show you how the thing works." Homer got up and ducked out of the kitchen. Kitty could hear him breathing in the parlor. Then he shambled in again, smiling vaguely in no particular direction, put out his hand at Kitty feebly, withdrew it before she could grasp it, said something that sounded like *Gdeebmnnn,* bumbled behind the backless chair into the corner of the room and let himself down clumsily onto the floor, where he sat hunched behind his enormous knees with his eyes half closed and his mouth drooping open. "Howziss?" he said drowsily.

"Perfect," said Kitty. "I can hardly see you. You're sort of transparent "

Homer's cloak of invisibility worked surprisingly well. When he loomed up in the doorway of Mrs. Wilkinson's big house on the North Bluff at Siasconset, his image registered clearly for only a moment or two on her sharply perceptive retina. Then his terrible posture and wretched articulation and the poverty of the air supply from his lungs and his general air of inconsequence and self-effacement had their effect, and Mrs. Wilkinson soon forgot him in the press of meeting other guests. Homer was able to shuffle into the living room and settle down on a four-legged stool behind a large chair in one corner and withdraw into anonymity, carefully avoiding the look of startled recognition on the face of Mrs. Magee, who was sitting beside the fireplace preparing to conduct the meeting. In a moment the last arrivals had come in, and the business of the evening got under way.

Mrs. Magee carried the ball. She began by reading a list of property owners who had already pledged their support to the cause of overturning the new bylaw. It was a long list. Homer amused himself by comparing Mrs. Magee with her hostess, Mrs. Wilkinson, who sat on the other side of the fireplace in a match-

Old Town pump. Siasconset

ing crewelwork chair—Mrs. Magee the businesswoman, the realtor, her spun-glass hair glinting against the dark wood of the paneled wall, her turquoise knitted outfit form-fitting, fabulous; Mrs. Wilkinson an old war-horse, her Fair Isle sweater dyed to match her heather-mixture skirt. They sat in the two handsome chairs like two queens of Nantucket. Evil queens, decided Homer, giving them their due. Representing no majesty but money, no ancient ancestral claim, no roots in the history of the island, no care or concern for its fragile grace. Here they were in the same place working for the same cause—but of course they were different women altogether. Mrs. Wilkinson could sit quietly in the arrogance of inherited and wedded wealth, gazing with insolent indifference at the motley lot in her living room, while Mrs. Magee had the quick nervous gestures of someone who had clawed her way up, who would never be at rest.

She had finished reading the list. She was introducing the man on her left. "With us this evening," said Mrs. Magee, "is Mr. Hamilton Brine, an attorney who has tried many cases of this nature before the superior court. He will be representing Mr. Holworthy and me in the suit we have filed against the Town of Nantucket, declaring the recent act of the Town Meeting unconstitutional. But before we hear from Mr. Brine, why don't we all introduce ourselves one at a time and state the nature of our objections to the bylaw? Mrs. Wilkinson, would you begin?"

Mrs. Wilkinson stirred in her chair and leaned forward, narrowing her old eyes as she sucked on her cigarette and coughed. "Before he passed away, my husband, Donald, bought sixty acres here in the neighborhood of 'Sconset because they were about to be picked up by a cheap developer. Donald thought a lot of nasty little houses would destroy the picturesque character of the village and lower the property values. So he bought the land himself as an investment, thinking he might divide it up into a few substantial estates someday. Now of course that investment has become worthless." Mrs. Wilkinson leaned forward and stubbed out her cigarette with grim emphasis.

161

Mr. Holworthy was next. He was a freckle-faced sandy-haired fellow of mild address, who had, it turned out, a true reverence for the principles upon which his country had been founded. "It just seems to me that the new bylaw isn't part of our democratic tradition here in the United States of America," he said. "Like it says in the Declaration of Independence, all men are created equal—well, we're not equal if some people can develop their property and some people can't. It's the principle of the thing that bothers me." Homer, crouched obscurely in the corner, reminded himself that in addition to his anxiety about these noble abstractions, Mr. Holworthy might also be slightly concerned about the loss of his million dollars.

Harper J. Cresswell agreed with Mr. Holworthy. He too had lofty ideological differences of opinion with the Nantucket Protection Society. Again Homer had to supply for himself Mr. Cresswell's strong interest, both financial and sexual, in Mrs. Magee and her various enterprises. Likewise with Samuel Flakeley, whose sense of patriotism had apparently been deeply and profoundly shocked by this betrayal of the grand designs of the founding fathers of the nation.

The next speaker was a bony little woman in thick glasses and an unbecoming dress. "My name is Doris Pomeroy," she said. "I've only got a very small piece of land, just outside of town. I've been going out there on Sundays, planting cedars and pine trees. I've been saving up for years to build myself a little place there. And now I can't. I tell you I'm just heartbroken about it. I just hope there's something we can do."

Homer sat up straighter on his four-legged stool. The testimony had taken on a different character.

"I am Erasmus Smith of Nantucket. I was born here, went to school here. I own half an acre next to my own house lot, that's all. But I was planning to send my kid to college on it someday."

"Donald Hemenway, Shimmo. Likewise. I've scrimped and saved to buy that piece of land I own on the south shore. Used to go there as a boy and watch the waves roll in. Always dreamed

162

of living there, building a house there. Had two jobs the last couple of years, trying to pay for it. My wife worked too, baby-sitting. So we could have a place of our own, not live with my folks anymore. *Jesus, what was that?"*

They were all turning around, craning their necks over their shoulders, looking at Homer, who was sprawled on the remains of his four-legged stool. His cloak of invisibility had evaporated like the emperor's new clothes.

25

. . . amid the tornadoed Atlantic of my
being, do I myself still for ever centrally
disport in mute calm . . .

Moby Dick

It was springtime around Kitty's house. The sun knocked on the
windows and had to be let in, with a block of wood or a window
stick propping up the fragile sash. The balmy April air had begun
to unfold the lilac buds beside the door, and the shad-blow along
the driveway was blossoming in palest white. The deciduous trees
had given up some of their gray dignity in a light-green froth, a
veil of infant leaves. The weedy front yard was splashed with
dandelions. Even the briers behind the privy were a bold harsh
green. The privy itself began to be a problem, and after consulting
Alden Dove, Kitty took care of it by dumping a twenty-five-pound
bag of peat moss and ten pounds of lime down the hole.

She was learning the names of more living things. She borrowed books from Alice, from the Atheneum, from the Maria
Mitchell Library; she bought some at the bookstore. She started
with simple ones written for children, picture books meant to be
taken to the beach to identify treasures picked up at the water's

edge on hot summer days—the shells of periwinkles and moon snails, the egg cases of skates.

"Go to the Head of the Harbor," said Alice. "The shore near the Coskata Woods is a good place to explore." Kitty took her books with her and wandered up and down the pebbly beach, bringing home a foul smelly horseshoe crab and the shells of conchs and razor clams and scallops and the long parchment egg case of a whelk and sea clams in a bucket. She took a fancy to the commonplace scallop shells, which had a Renaissance look, as if

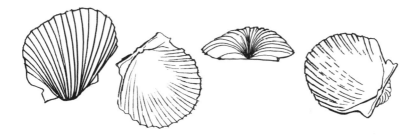

they had come from sculptured niches under the sea for mermaid dignitaries or fishy Medici. She leaned them in a row along the back of the mantelpiece in the parlor, sorted by size and color, gray ones together, and browns and greens and translucent whites. In front of them she arranged the rest of her collection. But one shell was missing, the broken whelk she had been so romantic about. Kitty went to her denim jacket, fished in the pocket, and looked at the whelk in dismay. Nothing was left of it but broken fragments, and the twisted column running down the middle.

If I were superstitious, thought Kitty, *I wouldn't like that.* She wasn't superstitious, exactly, but she was ceaselessly metaphoric, and she was unable to prevent herself from seeing the twisting bony fragment of shell in her hand as a cyclone, a tornado, a funneled storm. She thought of the spiral turnings of the staircase

165

in the lighthouse. She thought of the narrow chamber at the center of convoluted things. If you went around and around often enough, and worked your way closer and closer in, you might find it, the narrow dark chamber, and then you might curl up like an unborn child and go to sleep. Even hurricanes, after all, had quiet places in the middle of them. Her own storm was coming in

September. *Oh, shut up, shut up.* Kitty slapped the remnant of the shell on the mantelpiece, hoping it would crack in two. It didn't.

Then Alice gave her Rachel Carson's *Edge of the Sea*, and Kitty spent the next week with it, spellbound by the brutal complex life of the seashore, endless in its variety. She sat at her kitchen table with Alice Dove, reading the book aloud.

"Listen to this, Alice. I don't understand about the tides:

During much of the year the spring tides drop down into the band of Irish moss but go no lower, returning then toward the land. But in certain months, depending on the changing positions of sun and moon and earth, even the spring tides gain in amplitude, and their surge of water ebbs farther into the sea even as it rises higher against the land. Always, the autumn tides move strongly, and as the hunter's moon waxes and grows round, there come days and nights when the flood tides leap at the smooth rim of granite and send up their lace-edged wavelets to touch the roots of the bayberry; on their ebbs, with sun and moon combining to draw them back to the sea, they fall away from ledges not revealed since the April moon shone upon their dark shapes. Then they expose the sea's enameled floor—the rose of encrusting corallines, the green of sea urchins, the shining amber of the oarweeds.

I don't understand that," said Kitty. "It sounds as though she's talking about the highest and lowest tides happening at once. What does she mean?"

"Give me a pencil and paper," said Alice, "and I'll show you. Do you know how the moon makes the tides?"

"Gravitational attraction, isn't it? The moon pulls on the water."

"Yes. The ocean bulges up in the direction of the moon. So as the earth turns under the moon on its axis every day, the bulge stays in the same place under the moon. The bulge is high tide." Alice drew the moon and the earth with its bulge of water. "The earth is turning counterclockwise in this picture, so if you were on an island at the top there, right under the moon at twelve o'clock, having high tide, then six hours later you would be over here at the side having low tide. And the higher the high tide is, the lower the low tide the same day, because more water is pulled away from the low places. Do you see?"

HIGH TIDE

WATER

LOW TIDE

EARTH

LOW TIDE

"But what does she mean by spring tides?" said Kitty. "Is the tide highest in the spring?"

"No, no, the spring tides have nothing to do with the spring. The spring tides are the highest tides of the month. Don't forget, not only does the earth turn on its axis once every twenty-four hours, the moon is moving too. It orbits the earth once a month. That means that the angle between the moon and the earth and the sun is changing all the time. Here, I'll draw another picture.

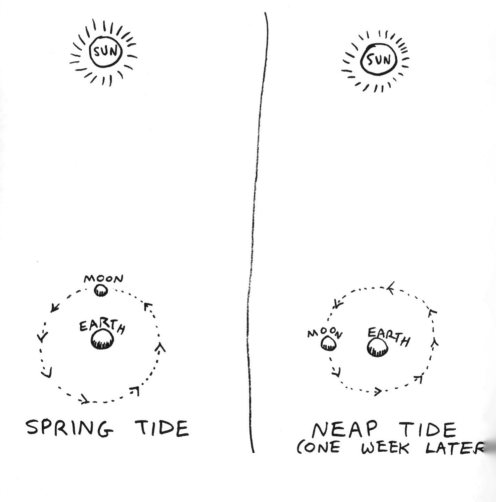

SPRING TIDE

NEAP TIDE
(ONE WEEK LATER

You see, the moon isn't the only thing that causes the tides. So does the sun. It's much bigger than the moon, but it's also much farther away, so it doesn't pull as strongly, but it still counts. So in the picture on the left, which shows the time of new moon, both sun and moon are pulling in the same direction, and you get very high tides. Those are called the spring tides. A week later the moon has moved partway around the earth, it's at the quarter, so that it's pulling in a different direction from the sun. The result is that both sun and moon are flattening out each other's pull, and you get the lowest high tides of the month, the neap tides."

"I see," said Kitty. "The spring tide means the sun and moon and earth are all lined up. Neap tide means the sun and moon are pulling at right angles to each other."

"That's about it." Alice put her pencil down. "Of course there are a lot of other complicated things about the tide—what happens at full moon, and so on, and the effect of shorelines, and the moon's elliptical orbit. What she's talking about there, when she speaks of the very highest tides of all in the spring and the fall, six months apart, is something else that happens only twice a year, when the moon is lined up with the sun, but also it's moving *in the same plane* as the sun's path in the sky, so they're pulling *even more closely* in the same direction. At those two times of year you get the highest spring tides of all. And the water ebbs out farthest of all, exposing parts of the ocean floor that otherwise never see the light. That's what she means there, where she says—let me have the book—the flood tides 'fall away from ledges not revealed since the April moon shone upon their dark shapes.' That's the autumn spring tide she's talking about. It pulled the water farther back than it had been since the spring tide of April, six months before."

"You're smart, Alice," said Kitty.

"No, I'm not. If you make part of your living from the sea the way we do, you have to know about the tides."

Kitty took the book back. "Listen to the rest of this: 'At such a time of great tides I go down to that threshold of the sea world to which land creatures are admitted rarely in the cycle of the year.' Alice, I want to do that. When will that day be?"

"Not till next fall sometime. We'll have a look at Eldridge's tide tables back at my house." Alice stood up and looked absently at the shells and stones on Kitty's mantelpiece. "Of course on Nantucket Island the differences between the various kinds of tides aren't all that great. It takes a combination of tide and storm to make a big difference. But on a long sloping beach you might get the effect she talks about, the uncovering of some of the sea floor once or twice a year. We'll look at the tide book, and then I've got a chart of the length of Nantucket's tidal beaches. Come on."

But at Alice's house they couldn't find the tide tables anywhere. They weren't on the bookshelf where they belonged, beside the refrigerator. "It's your fault, Alden," said Alice. "You never throw anything away. It's buried somewhere under all this stuff."

Alden was resentful. "That's not my stuff. Most of this junk is yours." Angrily he swept a pile of magazines to the other end of the table with a mighty shove.

"What does it look like anyway?" said Kitty.

"Yellow book, paper cover." Alice was turning over stacks of mail, sorting through piles of things on the sofa—a pair of rubber boots, some mismatched gloves, a couple of scarves, some thermal underwear, a blanket, a pile of stiff laundry pinched up at the shoulders where it had been gripped by clothespins on the line behind the house. Under a cushion she found the paperweight with the initials AD, and an empty egg carton. She pricked herself on the cactus that was a china dog's tail and screeched and sucked her finger. Alden slammed out the door to look in the animal shed.

Kitty went outside too and tried the toolshed. There was a shelf inside the door. On the shelf were Alden's egg-delivery accounts, a kerosene lantern, some rolled-up charts and maps.

"Find anything?" said Alden, sticking his head in the door.

There was a yellow object on the floor beneath the shelf, under a gun of some sort, a shotgun. Half a shotgun—the barrel was missing. Kitty reached for the yellow thing. Alden got there first. He grabbed it and pulled it free. "Here it is," he said.

"We found the book, Alice," said Kitty, walking into the kitchen. "It was out in the toolshed. Under a gun."

"A gun? We don't have a gun."

"You know that gunstock I have out there," said Alden. "That shotgun Joe Green gave me. It's just for a camera," he said to Kitty. "I'm going to mount a camera on the gunstock sooner or later, when I get around to it." Alden left to deliver eggs, and Alice and Kitty sat down at the table with Eldridge's *Tide and Pilot Book.*

"We've missed the highest spring tide for this time of year," said Alice. "It was last month, around the time of the eclipse. That makes sense. Both sun and moon were pulling together in exactly the same direction. So six months later means September. Let's look at September. Here it is, the first week in September. That's when you want to go looking at exposed pieces of the sea floor. Next we'll look at my *Selected Resources of the Island of Nantucket* to find the longest tidal beach. Now where did I put that?"

"The first week in September," repeated Kitty, aware of a core of icy chill within her lungs. The first week in September was when her trial was to begin. She clasped her cold hands and watched Alice claw through the piles of papers and books. Well, the first week in September would be all right. Looking at the dark sea bottom newly turned up to the light—it might be as good a way as any to spend the last day before her own inmost lining was to be turned outward like a glove.

26

Stab me not with that keen steel!
Moby Dick

Homer was spending a lot of his time tracking down the owners of the various craft that had been seen outside the harbor in Nantucket Sound on March seventh. Both Bob Fern and Charley Piper had provided him with lists of names to work with, and he had been plugging away at them, but the search was dull and dispiriting, it took him far afield, and it continued to be without result. He had talked to the three healthy young girls who called themselves the Cormorants, who had taken little sailboats out of the harbor on the day of the eclipse. They were scattered all over New England in three different private schools. Homer could think of no reason why any of them would have had it in for Helen Green.

Next he pursued the man who was beating his way back down the coast on rainy weekends in his small ketch, trying to get it home to New Jersey, and at last he caught up with him under the Triborough Bridge by setting out from the Bronx in a rowboat.

The man, whose name was Alfred Klubbock, was hardly able to do more than curse and complain. What had started as a weekend's adventure had ended as a month-long nightmare of taking a train from Philly every Friday night to wherever he had left his fucking boat the week before, and then freezing his ass off in the rain trying to get the fucking thing home again, and losing his way in the fucking fog, and running aground, and discovering he was out of gas, and trying to negotiate the Race into Long Island Sound on the ebb current, which was dead wrong. No, he hadn't seen anything at Great Point; where in the fuck was that? Homer bade bon voyage to Mr. Klubbock and rowed sloppily back to the Bronx, unutterably depressed.

In May Homer couldn't stand it anymore. He cabled his wife and met her for a holiday in Bermuda. After this brief respite, appeased in body and soul, he flew back to Nantucket and picked up where he had left off. First he checked up on Kitty. She seemed all right (although it was hard to tell about Kitty). Then he called an expert in the Coast Guard and arranged to take lessons in scuba diving and spearfishing. "Okay if we start right now?" he said.

"Now? Well, I don't know. It's still kinda early," said the expert.

"Well, how would it be if we had an extra lesson now, and you could just show me all the equipment and so on. I'm really interested in the whole subject. If you were off duty, maybe I could come over right now? I'll pay extra for this special lesson, of course. I didn't mean you should throw it in free of charge."

"Well, all right, okay, I guess that's okay with me."

The day was warm and moist. Below the bluff at Siasconset, Homer could see the ocean tumbling up the beach in a soapy foam, and when he turned off the staccato roar of his engine, which had lost its muffler, he could hear the softer roar of the surf breaking against the shore in long curling combers, flooding up the sloping sand and sliding back down and withdrawing, then rolling in again with an impulse weakened only by the interruption of the Old Man Shoal, a mile or so offshore. There had been wrecks out there in the old days—Homer had read about them —and the watchers who had manned the lifesaving stations had gone to the rescue, or had stood helplessly by while doomed mariners drowned. Now the Loran beacons and the charts of local waters and the vigilant Coast Guard kept navigators in safe channels on the pathless sea. Homer slammed the door of his car and walked up to the cement-block building that housed the men of the Loran station at Low Beach. He rang the bell. Ensign Kenneth Hawkins swung open the door and led Homer into the rumpus room at one end of the building, where he had laid out his diving and fishing apparatus all over a sofa and a Ping-Pong table.

Loran beacon, Low Beach

"Wow," said Homer. "Do you really need all that gear?"

"Oh, sure, if you're going to go into this thing seriously." Ensign Hawkins was a clean-cut muscular fellow with black eyebrows that met in the middle. "How old did you say you were? Hmm, is that all? You don't look in very good shape. Did you do much with athletics in college?"

"College?" said Homer. " 'A whale-ship was my Yale College and my Harvard.' " He was quoting Melville. "No, no, I never went to college." Well, that was a lie, but he certainly hadn't been to the kind of college Ensign Hawkins was talking about. "And anyway, I can hardly swim; I can just barely stay afloat."

"You can't *swim?* Then why . . . ?"

"Well, I mean I haven't got down to all the fine points. I'll just pick 'em up as I go along." This artifice was proving harder to keep up than Homer had thought it would be, but what he wanted from Ensign Hawkins was a nice natural demonstration, not one that was all mucked up with amateur crime detection. "I'm paying you for this demonstration, aren't I? Just show me what all this stuff is."

"Well, okay, sure. You're the boss. We'll begin with the suit. Its principal function is to keep you warm. Here's your gloves. They're partly for warmth and partly to keep your hands protected from sharp objects or stinging organisms of any kind. This here is your diving knife, in case you get tangled up in something under water. These of course are your swim fins so you can really go places without working hard at it. The main rule under water is to just *relaaaaax* and take it easy, so you don't use up too much oxygen."

"*Relaaaaax,*" echoed Homer, nodding his head.

"That's right. And that brings us to the breathing equipment. Here's your snorkel. That's for using right at the surface, so you can float with your face under water. But here's the real McCoy. This is your scuba-diving gear. With these things you can go anywhere under water, because you don't have to keep coming up for air. But before you use scuba equipment you really have to know what you're doing, or you can get into real trouble, man."

"Trouble," agreed Homer.

"You said it. You have to wear this depth gauge so you know where you're at, and this watch so you know how long you've been down. And then of course you have to know how to come up from way down deep so you don't get the bends."

The bends. Homer found himself remembering the anguished face in the newspaper clipping in the library of the Whaling Museum, and he winced. Maybe it was the bends that had killed that poor kid who had been diving down to the wreck of the *Andrea Doria*. "What about this stuff over here?" he said, turning to the Ping-Pong table, where Ensign Hawkins had laid out a neat row of weapons with pistol handles and long shafts ending in sharp steel tips.

"Those are your spear guns. Different types for different situations, different sizes of fish."

"What are these rubber things for on this one? Oh, wait a minute, I know. They're slingshots. Right?"

"That is correct. Under water the density is a whole lot greater than in air, so you need extra force to get anything going fast enough to hit a fish with enough impact to kill it. That's what all these devices do. They've all got a spring or a rubber sling or a CO_2 cartridge or something like that to dart the spear into the fish."

"I notice the points are different. Some of them have toggles, like the harpoons in the Whaling Museum. Some of 'em don't. What's the difference?"

"Well, it's just the opposite of what you might think. The big fish take a straight tip. The toggle thing with the swinging barb is for the smaller fish. It punches a big hole in the fish, so with the kind of force a big fish can exert on it, it would pull right out. So you use this straight tip here on a big fish."

"How big is big?"

"Oh, you get a really big fish of one hundred pounds or more, then you need this straight tip. But you don't get them around here much. I'm going to take this gun to California with me on my next leave, go after tuna."

"So for a hundred-and-twenty-pounder you'd probably use a straight tip?"

"What kind of fish do you mean?"

"Angelfish," mumbled Homer, after a moment's thought.

"Angelfish? Go on. They don't come any bigger than my hand."

"Well, anyway, for this big fish you'd use a straight tip? Could you pull it out from far away?"

"Pull it out? No, of course not. You're trying to land the fish, aren't you? What good would it do just to kill it and leave it there?"

"Well, heh heh, in case you weren't hungry or something."

"Well, I certainly don't think it would be very sportsmanlike to go around killing fish just for the hell of it, and then leave the carcasses around to rot. What kind of freak are you anyway?"

"Just ignorant," said Homer humbly, "and I want to know more. Tell me which of these spear points you would use if you didn't want to make a big gaping hole in the fish, this big hundred-and-twenty-pound fish, and you just wanted to kill it and then pull your spear point back again?"

"Jesus. Well, I guess if you were dumb enough to want to do that, you'd maybe use this one here, this little one. It's for small game, close-up, but it would probably kill a big fish. You'd never bag it, though." He was looking at Homer thoughtfully.

"Say," said Homer, "it just occurs to me—what if you were using a spear gun in the air instead of in the water? Suppose you were aiming at a hundred-and-twenty-pound fish that was up there out of the water, say about ten or twenty yards away—what kind of spear gun would you use then? The thing would be a lot more powerful and deadly in the air, wouldn't it?"

"This hundred-and-twenty-pound fish is out of the water?"

"You know," said Homer insanely, "like a porpoise! Jumping up out of the water!"

177

"Porpoises are protected by the state," said Ensign Hawkins. His manner was becoming hostile.

"Well, then, suppose I used it against some land animal, like a deer or something. What would I use to kill it and then be able to pull the spearhead out again?"

"Are you sure you're not talking about a *human being?*" guessed Ensign Hawkins shrewdly, his breath beginning to come fast. "I think you are planning the murder of a human being, and I'm not going to be a party to it. If you think I'm going to answer any more questions, you've got another think coming, brother."

Homer sighed. "Look, you jerk, I'm trying to figure out how a murder was done, not how to do one." Then he explained what he was up to. Ensign Hawkins was extremely doubtful at first, but when he was finally won over, his eyes lit up.

"Well," he said, "why didn't you say so right away? Yes, of course I remember. That woman that was killed at the lighthouse during the eclipse. You mean you think somebody might have done it from the water with a spear gun?"

"That's one possibility I'm exploring."

"Well, say, now! I tell you what I would have used, if it was me." Ensign Hawkins's one long eyebrow was rising with excitement. "This spear gun here—this one with the spring action and the plain tip. Only I'd practice for a while on a target that had about the same holding capacity as the human body and the same density and everything, and I'd figure out the distance, and how hard to cock it and so on, and I'd really practice—because if you were only accustomed to underwater shooting you might get your aim all wrong. Say, these things would be really deadly, I'm telling you. They're bad enough under water."

Homer picked up the spear gun Ensign Hawkins was talking about and hefted it in his hand. It was light and strong, with a sharply honed steel tip.

"The big problem would be getting it to go straight in air," said Hawkins. "You know what else I'd do? I'd get a big huge roast beef and use it for a target, because it would have more or less the same density as the body, wouldn't you think? Or do you think a woman's body might be more, like, soft and spongy?"

Ensign Hawkins patted his rib cage inquisitively, and Homer could feel the fatty muscle overlying his own stomach flinch. He wrote out a check for a full course of scuba-diving lessons and said good-bye.

But Ensign Hawkins hated to see him go. He accompanied Homer outside, happily describing various gruesome accidents of spearfishing history, until he saw Homer's car. "My God, man," he said, "how long have you been driving around with that soft tire? Want me to pump it up for you? It's a long way back to town."

Homer was desperate to get away. "No, no," he said, "I'll stop at a place I saw on the road, a couple of gas pumps, not far from here. They'll have an air hose there."

"Oh, you mean Boozer Brown's place. He's illegal. Not even supposed to be there. Pretty crummy place, if you ask me. Crummy guy too, you know what I mean? I wouldn't go there if I was you. And you ought to do something about that little muffler problem you've got there."

"I know, I know," said Homer. He made his engine roar loud enough to drown out Ensign Hawkins, who was still shouting at him cheerfully, and drove noisily away.

The car did feel funny. Now that Homer knew about his soft tire, the car felt funnier and funnier. By the time he had driven back to the place on Milestone Road where the wrecked cars and the gas pumps were, he was limping along slowly, hoping he didn't have a flat. He turned in and parked beside the air pump, squeezing into a narrow space between the pump and one of the wrecked cars, a station wagon with a splintered windshield and a bashed-in door. Clumsily he connected the hose to the tire and watched the pressure gauge.

"Wanshum gash?" A big slob of a man in filthy pants and a torn greasy T-shirt had come up behind him and was looking on genially. It was Boozer Brown, obviously. No wonder he had not appealed to the fastidious ensign. Homer was delighted to observe a smooth curved shape in Boozer's pocket. He must be carrying a hip flask like a gangster in an old movie.

"Sure, I need some gas," said Homer, feeling he ought to pay the man back for the use of his hose, since the place certainly didn't seem to be a regular gas station at all. There was a sort of shack behind the gas pumps, but it was more like a house than a gas station, and not much like a house at that. Homer backed his car around to the gas pumps and leaned out the window making conversation, while Boozer filled him up. "Nasty little keepsakes you've got there," said Homer, nodding at the wrecked cars.

"Oh, yeah, I'm in lotsha trouble becuzha them. That woman Min Magee, she wantsh me tarred and feathered. She shezh I'm deshtroying the najural bewdy of the island. Wanzh me to put up a fensh. Cosh me a thouzhand bucksh. Old battleaxsh, why doezhn't she juzh look the other way? Shmy playzhe, I oughta be able to do what I want."

Homer studied the nearest car, the station wagon with the shattered windshield and the twisted door. "Well, I think maybe it's a good idea to have these things around where people can see them," he said. "Cautionary sculpture. A lesson to us all."

"Thash what I shaid. A lesshun. Shpeshly for the kidzh. Show 'em shpeed killzh. Coursh, that one wazhn't shpeed, exzhackly. That one wazh shomebody'zh dirty lil practical joke."

"Practical joke?" said Homer, looking at the wreck. "Some sense of humor. Was anybody hurt?"

"No. Wazh a miracle." Boozer leaned in the front window, and Homer, gasping for air, leaned back as far as he could. "Belonged to that novelisht, whashizname, Jozheph Green. Only he wazhn't driving. Car hit a telephone pole on the shide away from the driver, sho nobody wazh hurt."

Homer gaped at Boozer's bleary eyes and inhaled his suffocating breath. "It was Joe Green's car? What—do you mean somebody did something to his car? For a joke?"

"I'll show you. Come on in. Took it inshide for a keepshake. Here, come right on in."

Homer walked through the open garage door that was the entrance to Boozer's house and looked around in pleased surprise. The inside was half garage, half bachelor's quarters, with a sink, a grubby refrigerator, a shower stall, a toilet, a sofa, a desk, a stove and a Coke machine arranged around a grease pit.

"Here it izh on the wall. Shee thizh thing? Itzha tie rod. Keepsha front wheelzh connected. You know. Well, I shuppozhe itsh pozhible the adjushment link could work looshe by itshelf, but take a look at that bolt there. Shee how clean the fredzh are?"

"Freds?"

"Zhredzh. Threadzh. You know."

"Oh, the threads!"

"Shomebody loozhened the cashle nut, sho the bolt would fall out. It mushta been loozhened all at onshe. Thash why itsh sho shiny. If it had worked looshe by itshelf, it'd be moshly rushty."

Homer felt a surge of something like joy. "Who was driving?" he said, trying not to sound too eager, too interested.

"Fella named Tillinghasht, neighbor of Green'zh. Green muzhta had a grudge againsht Tillinghasht, that'zh my opinion. Green loozhened the cashle nut and loaned Tillinghasht hizh car, and pretty shoon there wazh Tillinghasht driving along the Polpish Road with the shteering all gone to hell."

"When did it happen? Do you remember when the accident happened?"

"Sure I do. It wazha night the Boshton Bruinzh beat the Red Wingzh for the Shtanley Cup. I wazh watching on TV. I wazh mad azh hell. All the other guyzh with wreckerzh were buzhy, they shaid. They couldn't go pick up the car. Well, you know azh well azh I do why they were buzhy—they were watching the playoffsh too—sho I had to go. Mished the besh game of the sheazhon."

Homer drove home rejoicing, after promising to come back and have a new muffler installed and his transmission and differential checked and his oil filter changed and his chassis lubricated and his radiator drained and flushed. The man was a genius, an automotive genius. His illegal garage was sacred as a church.

27

*"But I am not a brave man; never said I
was a brave man; I am a coward; and I sing
to keep up my spirits. And I tell you what
it is, Mr. Starbuck, there's no way to stop
my singing in this world but to cut my
throat."*

Moby Dick

It was almost hot. Wet and hot. A mist steamed up from the
ground, mingling with the fog that hung in the middle air, and
the fog in its turn blended with the heavy low-hanging clouds that
obscured the sky. There had been foghorns baying in the night.
Kitty put on a shirt and a pair of jeans over her bathing suit,
picked up her bucket and trowel and her notebook, and drove to
a beach called Dionis on the north shore of the island. One of her
tourist pamphlets had described it as a popular bathing beach. On
a day like this she could have it to herself.

The low bluff was like a rough forehead sprouting hair. The
bluffs to left and right were lost in mist. Kitty put her things down
on the sand and looked at the low waves seething softly at the
bottom of the beach. Beyond them there was no line to tell where
the water ended and the gray sky began. The world was all one
substance, fog, bog, shaggy and ragged and moist, dripping,
drenched, flooded, engulfed. The island today was like a sponge,

laden with water, floating in the salt sea under this ocean of thick fog.

She took off her shirt and jeans and waded out into the water and dove in. After the first shock of cold she felt at home, and she swam with strong strokes parallel to the shore, then turned and swam back. After a while she began to feel cold again. She headed toward the beach and rose dripping into the heavy air. With her hair streaming and her nose running and her eyes weeping, she walked back to her discarded clothes. It occurred to her to think of herself, too, as a kind of sponge, a swampy tissue flowing with rivers and inland seas. She began to list and catalogue them, the seas and rivers, and soon she was excited, delighted with the knowledge that she was beginning to organize and arrange a poem in her head—a long one; it was going to be quite long— for the first time since the day of the disaster. She pulled her clothes on over her waterlogged bathing suit and sat down on her wet towel, scribbling in the damp notebook in which she had been drawing pictures of sea lettuce and sea squirts and the arrangements of needle clusters in various kinds of pine trees. It was a list, of course, just a list to begin with.

Many rivers flow inside a man.
He is a pouring and an emptying,
A dark rushing of underground streams,
A hollow vessel brimming at the lip,
A cave of ancient jars of precious ointment,
A fountain,
A cask with a dripping bung.
His flesh is a bog,
His liver and lungs are spongy with water.
The red organs flash back a glistening film
At the surgeon's lamp. . . .

Kitty laughed, exhilarated. There was no end to them, the liquids in the body. There were digestive secretions and blood and urine and sweat and sexual fluids and menstrual blood and mother's milk. And the warm moisture of the breath from the lungs. And tears. She didn't know yet where she was heading. There would have to be some point to it, some watery meaning. And the whole thing would have to be nailed together tight as a ship's hull, because a single lapse of power was a puncture through which the whole thing would leak out, and then the poem would founder like a wooden ship on perilous seas. Kitty brushed splashes of rain off the page and scribbled some more. Those biles and humors she had been wanting to do something with—here at last was the place for them.

> And do not forget the various biles,
> Yellow and black,
> Akin to the bilious and melancholic
> Humors of the soul,
> Nor the phlegms and sputums of disease,
> The stinking effluvia of wounds and sores,
> The vomit of final convulsion,
> The black seepages of death.

Oh, horrible, horrible, glorious. Grinning, Kitty mopped at the wet page, slapped the notebook shut and stood up, shivering from the clamminess of the wet bathing suit against her skin. She gathered up her belongings dreamily, walked back to her car and drove home slowly through patches of mist lying over the road.

There was a note impaled on the thumb-latch of her front door, and a dandelion drooping from the rusted knocker. Kitty left the dandelion where it was and brought the note inside to read.

Joy! Joy! Somebody was trying to kill her before! Call me!

Homer

"Somebody was trying to kill her before?" said Kitty, when Homer answered the phone.

"You bet your boots somebody was trying to kill her before." Homer was shouting into the telephone. Kitty had to hold the receiver away from her ear. "Thanks to an automobile mechanic named Boozer Brown I can now inform you, Katharine Clark, that somebody tried to kill Helen Green three weeks before you set foot on Nantucket Island. Listen to this: Joe Green has a new car. Why does he have a new car? Because his old car was wrecked —I just happened to stumble on it this morning. And this man Brown tells me that somebody had untwisted a nut from a bolt in the front wheel linkage, so the next time the car was driven the thing came apart and the car ran into a telephone pole. Green's car! Joe Green's! How do you like that?"

"Was Helen in it? Was she the one who had the accident?"

"No, but she was supposed to be. Here's what happened. Joe left in the morning for the mainland to give a speech somewhere. Helen stayed home to attend an important meeting of the Nantucket Protection Society, because they were making plans for that big town meeting when they wanted to put the new bylaw through. Only then at the last minute she stayed home sick, and her neighbor Tillinghast borrowed the car, because his own car was on the fritz. He set off for the meeting in it, and so he had the accident on the way to town. He came out alive by a stroke of luck. I'm so happy, I'm dancing around the house, upsetting all of Alice's porcelain figurines and Chinese vases—aren't I, Alice? Well, birds' eggs and bottles of rat poison, then. Oh, no, that's not right either. Don't glare at me, Alice. I shouldn't have said rat poison, because rats after all are a part of the great chain of being, marvelous in their own ratty way, aren't they, Alice, dear? Reverence for life, and all that. Forgive me."

Kitty stared doubtfully at the shells on her mantelpiece. "Do you think anybody will believe that, Homer?"

"Who do you mean? The judge? The jury? Well, it's true they might not believe Boozer Brown, but I'll go right to the top, I'll get the world's greatest experts on auto mechanics, people who have taken advanced degrees in spark plugs and carburetors. I'll get some guys like that to testify that Joe Green's front-wheel linkage bolt didn't work loose all by itself. I've just called Boozer, and he's promised to wrap the thing up in an old sock and stick the sock in a can of axle grease and keep the can of axle grease in his Coke machine along with his bottles of booze."

"I don't know, Homer," said Kitty gloomily. "It sounds too good to be true. One small bolt compared with all they've got against me."

"Oh, have no fear. I'm going to fasten my whole argument together with that bolt. And look here, if somebody failed to kill her once, they may have tried and failed another time. There's that loose stair carpet after all, and her fall down the stairs. I'll bet there were more things like that. I'm going to look into it."

"Homer . . ." There was a pause, and then Kitty spoke up shakily. "Do you know how a starfish eats a clam?"

"No. How?"

"It forces the clam apart with its arms and then eats it with its expelled stomach."

"No!" There was another pause. Kitty could feel Homer wondering about her at the other end of the line. "Say, look, Kitty Clark, are you all right? Maybe you'd better stop reading about clams and starfish and so on. Nature in the raw is pretty strong medicine for tender sensitive natures like yours. Those books ought to be kept in locked cases in the library along with the pornography, in my opinion. Do you want Alice and me to come over? No? You're sure? Well, all right. So long."

Kitty hung up. It had suddenly become electrifyingly clear to her while Homer was talking that *somebody* had killed Helen Green, *somebody real,* and that whoever had done it had acted with malice and deadly intent. And not only that, but this person was now destroying a girl named Kitty Clark as well, by letting her take the blame. And still more, this malevolence and violence were a part of the natural order of things. And that was the whole trouble. Homer had understood about the starfish and the clam. He had said they should lock up those books with their horrible stories. Well, maybe they should.

Kitty sat down at her kitchen table and looked at the scribbled words in her notebook. But the euphoria of her morning's work was gone. All she could think about was the savagery of nature. It was all very well for nature lovers like the Doves to have a reverence for life, but they should understand that their reverence was not shared by the life forms they revered. The life forms themselves were concerned with one thing only—murder. Every one of those fragile delicate creatures at the edge of the tide and down under the water, each individual being that was itself so wonderfully made and marvelously complex, was existing and surviving from one day to another only by a horrifying grasping at the death of other fragile complicated creatures—and the sum of all this grasping was a billion simultaneous tragedies, taking place at that very instant in the oceans of the earth. Kitty shuddered and found herself wondering how *they* felt about it, all the multitudinous mollusks which were at that moment having their shells drilled into by moonsnails, all those forms of sentient life that were now being ground up or torn asunder or clawed and punctured in their soft mortal parts. Were they afraid? Were they screaming with terror and pain in some part of themselves? Or was there instead some sort of vast and cosmic resignation that assuaged the horror of this immense incalculable slaughter?

That was what she should say to herself, Kitty told herself bitterly. She should simply resign herself, vastly and cosmically, to whatever was going to happen to her. She should simply remind herself that she was expiring in order to satisfy some necessary appetite in the world. She was part of Mother Nature's great untidy plan.

But it wasn't going to work. She was not resigned. She couldn't help asking what, exactly, was the nature of the necessary appetite in her own case?

28

To grope down into the bottom of the sea
after them; to have one's hands among the
unspeakable foundations, ribs, and very
pelvis of the world; this is a fearful thing.
What am I that I should essay to hook the
nose of this Leviathan!

Moby Dick

Dearest Mary,

Behold, my love! Your mild soft-spoken gentle shy retiring husband is now a new Ahab! his eyes hot coals! his ivory leg apace upon
the deck! in his breast one fierce desire, to drive this ship across the
world to the den of the sea where lurks the white whale in all his
murderous immensity! To find (in short) who it was that killed that
woman Helen Green. I smite my chest, and it rings most vast, most
hollow! I shall drive 'round the whole terraqueous globe before I'm
done! to find that murdering bastard for whom poor Kitty Clark
is to become a pendant pearl at the yardarm end, like Billy Budd.
The trouble is, she's a lamb for the slaughter, she's just the sort to
step up to the hangman's noose like Billy and cry, "God bless
Captain Vere!"

Well, anyway, I'm off to a fair start. I'm as sure as I can be in
my own mind that someone was patiently trying to kill Mrs. Green
for at least a month before the day of the eclipse, with a series of

189

carefully planned accidents. I don't know if I can make this tenuous stuff convincing to anybody else. Kitty doesn't take much stock in it herself. Here's the list—

1. Somebody tinkered with Helen's car in such a way that it caused a nasty accident. Her husband managed to be away that night, which looks a little queer.
2. She fell downstairs one day because someone had loosened the stair carpet.
3. A railing collapsed under her. She was invited to lunch at the neighbors' house, and they were out on the porch looking at birds through a small telescope mounted on the railing, Helen and Mrs. Tillinghast, when the railing gave way, and Helen almost fell twenty feet to a stone terrace, but Mrs. T'hast grabbed her and pulled her back.

I just ran that last one down this morning. Mr. Tillinghast was pretty upset about it, apparently, because his wife had been complaining about the rickety porch for some time and he hadn't done anything about it, and she was mad as hell, as who wouldn't be, but I wonder whether somebody didn't make it still ricketier for this particular occasion when Helen was going to be there.

You see, what I'm supposing is that somebody was trying to get rid of Helen Green in a *passive* way, by merely arranging pitfalls for her to fall into amiably all by herself. No crude stranglings or vulgar confrontations with pistols or shotguns. But then when all of these passive perfectly respectable things failed, it was unfortunately necessary to be more direct.

The point is, of course, all these earlier attempts on the life of Helen Green happened while my client was peacefully teaching classes in versification at Boston University.

Ah, well, damn. It's just so many feathers in the scale compared with the lead weight of those pictures of Kitty standing there with her bloodstained knife. I'm afraid I haven't got enough yet. Not enough. And here it is June.

190

Which means, thank God, there are only ten more days until you come. One for each finger of my two hands. I think I'll chop off one digit as each day goes by, rejoicing in the increase of bloody stumps.

Your loving husband,
Homer

29

*Will I, nill I, the ineffable thing has tied
me to him; tows me with a cable I have no
knife to cut.*

Moby Dick

All of a sudden it was summertime. The tourists who had begun
to trickle to the island on Memorial Day were increasing in
number every week. From a midwinter low of forty-two hundred
souls there would be a high of twenty thousand after the Fourth
of July, with more thousands pouring off the boat every Saturday
and Sunday for a quick look around. The island's resident citizens
detested the off-islanders, but offered them a wary hospitality just
the same, because most of Nantucket's revenue was derived from
the tourist trade. The vacationers were a kind of repulsive but
plentiful natural product like the quahogs in the harbor, to be
harvested for gain at so much apiece.

They flowed off the boat every day, the tourists, and billowed
up Main Street. Eddies of them swirled into the Whaling Museum and the gift shops and the restaurants and Mitchell's Book
Corner; swells and surges of them rolled along the narrow streets
in the direction of the Maria Mitchell birthplace and the Jethro

Coffin house and the Old Mill and the seventeenth-century jail; pools and puddles of them collected in the Hadwen house while the lady guide repeated herself tirelessly on the subject of the Hepplewhite table and the Sheraton sofa and the ivory button on the newel post that meant the house was all paid for. Jets and spurts of tourists streamed out the straight country roads, doggedly pedaling bicycles to Siasconset to see roses, pink and red and white, scrambling over the cottage rooftops and fences. They went swimming and splashing and wading in the quiet water of the northern beaches along the southernmost edge of the cold tidal basin that extended northward to the Gulf of Maine and Georges Bank, or they ran shouting into the pounding surf on the south side, which was the northernmost edge of the warm mid-Atlantic Bight. They visited the shops before they went home again, and bought souvenirs shaped like whales, or real whales' teeth, or T-shirts printed with whales, or lightship baskets. The police arrested outraged youths with tents and knapsacks and sleeping bags camping on the beach. The season was at its height.

Kitty kept running into Joe Green. There he would be at the end of a bookstack in the Atheneum or driving past her as she walked up the road to the Doves' house or turning a corner and coming upon her as she hurried up Main Street. In these encounters he was forever recoiling, turning, fleeing, averting his face. Kitty didn't come to town more often than she could help, partly to avoid the look of recognition in the eyes of strangers on the street, partly in fear of these disastrous convergences.

But on so small an island it was impossible not to meet. And even when she was alone at home Kitty was aware that Joe was not far from where she stood. She was rather like an iron ball, a magnetic pole on one end of an axis that was balanced on some sort of fulcrum, and at the other end of the axis there was another iron sphere, Joe. She could never rid herself of the knowledge that he was there on the island somewhere, and that his end of the axis was moving about, bobbing here and there, lifting and pausing and descending in massive counterpoise to her own. The solid axis

between them was made of accusation and guilt, of suspicion and vexation and repugnance, but it had fixed them together in a bond of wretchedness and despair.

Kitty was sick of it. She went back with relief to her study of spartina and arenaria and hudsonia and the small scuttling animal life of the beach. In the cheerful sunlight of a June morning the fiddler crabs were more amusing than they were carnivorous.

"Cosmic resignation, clam!" shouted Kitty, as a herring gull dropped one in front of her on the crumbling asphalt at the end of Hummock Pond Road.

And one Sunday morning she asked Bob Fern to take her out into the harbor in his scalloping boat and to put her ashore at the northern end of Coatue, the fragile scalloped strip of land that protected the harbor from the sea.

From the other side Coatue had looked barren and bleak, but now she could see that it was like the rest of the island in the strong twisted individuality of its vegetation, its windblown cedars and low-growing bearberry, its rugosa roses flowering pink and red and white. Kitty strolled along the curving shore, heading southwest from Wyer's Point to Bass Point, from Bass Point to Five-Fingered Point, and then at the tip of Five-Fingered Point she turned and looked back. What she wanted to find was prickly pear cactus, which was supposed to grow out here somewhere, bristling in the face of New England's harsh coastal storms. But instead she was attracted by the commonplace eelgrass that had drifted up from under water and lay in dried black drifts, carried up by the incoming tide. The water had gone back down, but the eelgrass still lay there, marking the rim of high tide. Then Kitty thought about what Alice had said about the tides, and she looked higher up the beach. Yes, there was another line of eelgrass there. Was that where the water had come up in the highest spring tide of all? Back in March or April? Kitty walked along the upper line of eelgrass, and followed it farther and farther from the shore up toward the low crest of the narrow peninsula. The tide must have come very high here indeed. The eelgrass had washed right over the crest and down the other side. All of the low vegetation was dead here. There was nothing left of the bearberry but brittle gray dead twigs. It must have been killed by the salt water running over between the harbor to the sea. Kitty looked at the quiet harbor and shook her head. It was a wonder this narrow crust of land sufficed to hold the water in at all.

She headed southwest again and walked the length of Coatue, found a prickly pear cactus and started back, hungry for the lunch she had hidden in a paper bag under a thorny rosebush above Wyer's Point. By the time she had walked the mile and a half of the return journey and looked under thirty rosebushes before she found the right one, she was tired. She sat down and ate her way through the sandwiches and the cookies and the orange, and then, feeling lively again, she jumped up, twisted the paper bag into a narrow wad that would fit in her pocket, and set off around the curve of the harbor in the direction of the Coskata Woods. She had to wade across the shallow inlet to Coskata Pond, her tennis shoes slung around her neck with their strings tied together. Then she swung along easily, enjoying the baking warmth of the sun on her bare shoulders. Alice was going to drive over to Wauwinet and pick her up at three. Plenty of time yet. Kitty watched the darting shadows of the terns. They were cheeping lightly over her. Then she winced, as one of the shadows sharpened and darted at the shadow of her head. The bird had plunged at her. Then there was another sharp cheep and another darting shadow. She looked up. The terns were circling over her, uttering light wind-borne cries, dropping at her one by one like small strafing planes. What if their sharp long beaks were to pierce her scalp and hurt her? Then Kitty remembered about the terns. It was June; they were nesting on the beach. She must be walking among their eggs, which looked just like the pebbles on the stony shingle. She started to walk faster, watching her footing, careful to step only on large stones or on the sand. But the terns were still dropping at her. She clasped her fingers over her head, and then she could feel the breath of their wings on her fingers. She began to be frightened. She started to run in earnest.

Suddenly she saw a house on the beach, with a big four-wheel-drive vehicle parked beside it. The windows were shuttered but the door was open. Kitty ran toward it, the terns in pursuit. Or perhaps it was other terns now, new waves rising above her in alarm as she invaded new territories. She ran toward the rough board steps of the house, and as she ran she had an odd sense that the house was shrinking away from her, withdrawing. The door was shutting! Stubbornly Kitty ran up the steps and stood on the sun-bleached boards of the little stoop, tapping hesitantly on the door. The warm boards creaked under her feet. There was no answer.

"Hello?" called Kitty. There was still no sound, and yet she was certain that someone was standing on the other side, breathing silently, waiting for her to go away. She rattled the latch. "Please let me in!"

The door was jiggling a little at last. She could hear the tiny noise of the hook being removed from the screw eye, and rattling down, and now the door was opening slowly. Well, it was about time. Then Kitty felt the color rush from her face and flood back in, in pulsing waves of beating blood. Her heart began thumping in her breast. It was Joe.

"Get out," he said. "Get out, get out."

Kitty stumbled backward and half fell down the steps. She ran, head down, blindly, her feet white arrows flying out in front of her, the terns diving at her over and over again. At last it occurred to her to run into the water. Surely they wouldn't have built their nests in the water! And there, splashing in the warm shallow water, Kitty cursed herself for a fool. If she hadn't been so stupid she would have figured it out before, and then she would never have knocked on that accursed door. What evil genius was it, what damnable poltergeist, that tormented her this way, thrusting her, shoving her, pushing her again and again into these grotesque intrusions? How he despised her! Well, she despised herself.

Kitty thought for a while that nothing could be worse than that encounter. But there was another one to come. It was her own fault, she realized afterward. Curiosity had killed the cat again. One rainy day she had decided to brave the tourists and visit the Whaling Museum. She manufactured a disguise, a genuine cloak of invisibility like Homer's—a pair of dark glasses, a kerchief tied over her head and a tremendously long oilskin coat that had belonged to Mr. Biddle. The oilskin drooped and dragged. It came down to her ankles. It felt wonderful. Confidently Kitty set forth, feeling altogether comfortable, a shapeless shambles, a deranged maiden aunt.

The Whaling Museum enthralled her. In the library she hung over the glass cases, reading the seamen's logs. Downstairs she admired the scrimshaw, and the ruddy faces of Folgers and Boatwrights and Ropers and Colemans and Coffins and Husseys in gold frames on the wall. In the great room where whale oil had been pressed for the making of candles she gaped at the jaw of a sperm whale as tall as a house, and looked up at the towering press, and inspected the lump of ambergris, and examined the harpoons and cutting-in spades on the wall, and then suddenly she was attracted by the harsh grating sound of a familiar voice. It was Mr. Biddle. He was a museum guide. He was giving a lecture, standing at the stern of a whaleboat. Visitors had gathered around him, listening. Charmed, Kitty started toward him. Mr. Biddle

was talking in a high thready voice, his head nodding and trembling. Someone asked him a question, but he heard not. Perhaps he was a young boy again, thought Kitty, and his hearing was tuned to the shouts and sharp commands of his shipmates, to the hissing rope and the clash of the oars in the oarlocks. As his cracked voice droned on and on, Kitty ran her hand along the smooth gunwale of the boat and imagined it red with spouted blood, the five oarsmen spattered, tossing, clinging, as the vast hulk of the sperm whale rolled in its last convulsions. A small boy squeezed in beside her and patted the gunwale too with his hand. Kitty smiled at him and moved over. Then she smiled at his mother and moved over still further.

But the mother blinked at Kitty and yanked her little boy away and hurried around to the other side of the boat, keeping a blank face aimed at Kitty like a pale defensive shield. Chagrined, Kitty turned away, and bolted for the front door. There she collided full-tilt with someone on his way in.

She fell, and lay for an instant on the floor, her sunglasses wrenched to one side. The man was bending over her, throwing out an involuntary hand to help her. The light from the doorway blurred around the edges of his hair. He said her name, *Kitty*.

Violently Kitty jumped to her feet and thrust past him, stumbling away, her long coat flopping and slapping, her arms and legs mere chunks of logs, stumps of wood. The trouble with an island was you couldn't get away. It was too . . . damned . . . small.

30

But give me my tot, *Matt, before I roll*
over;
Jock, let's have your flipper, it's good for
to feel. . . .

MELVILLE, *Tom Deadlight*

Somebody was driving up the lane to Kitty's house. Was it another bloodsucking tourist? No, it was Homer's purple Chrysler
with the crushed front fender. He would probably be hungry.
Kitty looked in her refrigerator, went to the front door, and
staggered back, gasping, whooping with laughter.

Homer was wearing a colossal wetsuit, complete with goggles
and flippers. He lifted his huge frog feet, stumbled over the sill
and fell into the rickety stair railing. The newel post collapsed.
Kitty had a laughing fit. She couldn't stop. "A toad! A monster
toad! Don't touch me, toad! I'll turn into one enormous wart!"

Homer picked himself up and began fumbling with shattered
pieces of banister, grumbling. "We come into this world, I tell
myself, to create, not to destroy, and the next thing I know I'm
lying on another pile of splinters. Ouch. There's one in my
thumb."

"Poor Homer. Let me see." Kitty squinted at his thumb, took

hold of the free end of the splinter and pulled it out. "Homer, don't tell me you drove over here with those flippers on your feet?"

"Of course not. I put them on just now entirely for your benefit. What's more, I almost drowned on your behalf. Somehow I got my breathing apparatus on upside down. They didn't understand how that could happen, they said it was impossible, but I did."

"Who said it was impossible?"

"The other members of the Nantucket Scuba-Diving Club. You know I'm taking these lessons from Ensign Hawkins and he invited me along to dive with the club. Say, Kitty, how about a little drink for a friend who has suffered untold hardship in the cause of righteousness?"

"A toddy for the monster toad! Come on in the kitchen, toad," said Kitty. "I'll see what I can do. Pick up your feet!"

Homer lifted his flippers high and flopped after Kitty. "She was there, all right, our Min. Wilhelmina Magee, I mean. Funny, she looked like a realtor even under water. I had a feeling she was laying out house lots down there. 'This lovely property is known as Davy Jones' Locker. Second clam from the corner to the octopus on the rock. Fifty thousand clams.' Ha ha—joke."

"Homer, you don't really think Mrs. Magee killed Helen Green? I mean, even if she is a scuba diver, I can't see her jumping off that big boat and swimming around Great Point and back again."

"No, no, not Min Magee. The one I was interested in was a guy by the name of Spike Grap. Spike was on Cresswell's boat. He was supposed to be zonked out the whole time, dead drunk. Speaking of which, where's my—oh, thanks. Big strong fella, charter member of the Scuba-Diving Club. Dead-eye fisherman with that spear gun of his. It's not exactly the kind of device that could have been used on Helen Green, but he was complaining that somebody stole the one he had before. He had to buy a whole new outfit, suit and all. What I was hoping to do today was see him in action. But no sooner had he walked out into the water than I began splashing and howling and gagging and making a fool of myself with my breathing apparatus on wrong and had to be rescued by a couple of guys who were laughing so hard they almost drowned me a second time."

"Honestly, Homer, I do think you're great. To keep trying this way, I mean"—Kitty's straight face dissolved—"even when you have absolutely no talent whatever—" She was off again, leaning back, gasping.

"That's what I get," growled Homer, "sacrificing my life, almost. That's what I get when I crawl up to your door seeking the warm hand of sympathy and the balm of human kindness. Laughter. It hurts, that's what it does."

Kitty struggled with herself and at last subsided. She sat down primly and tried to focus her attention upon the subject at hand. "Tell me some more about Spike Grap," she said. "He sounds interesting to me."

"Well, about all I know about him so far is that he has a financial interest in Mrs. Magee's business. She has a new corporation now, Magee Enterprises. That woman never stops. She's a walking incarnate gathering together into one person of all the pressures that could destroy this island someday. She reminds me of something Melville said about the devil, that the marplot of Eden is sure to slip in his little card. That's Mrs. Magee all over, slipping in her little card." Homer shook his head. "Well, anyway, back to Spike Grap. My diving friend in the Coast Guard, Ensign Hawkins—he thinks Spike is the culprit. 'There's your man,' he says to me in funereal tones."

"Well, why not?" said Kitty. "He knew all about those spearfishing guns, didn't he? Maybe the spear he claims was stolen from him was the murder weapon and he hid it or buried it or destroyed it somehow."

"Oh, sure, he's an appealing suspect in a lot of ways. Hawkins was all for buttonholing Spike there and then, with the Nantucket Scuba-Diving Club all standing at attention, saluting, goggles on, fins together. He thinks Spike is sick because he's so fanatic about diving; it's a monomania. He doesn't even have a girl friend; he's probably in love with a fish. Obviously a homicidal maniac, Hawkins says."

"Well, couldn't he be right?"

"Oh, no, I don't think so. I talked to Spike. He's a monomaniac, all right. All he talks about is fishing. Bluefish, rock bass, blackfish, flounder, codfish. Oh, of course I'll keep after him. I'll see if I can get anybody who was on Cresswell's boat that day to admit Spike wasn't out cold there on the bunk in plain sight whenever anybody went to the john, snoring on his stomach in his red-white-and-blue-striped blazer. I suppose they could all be lying. And then there's the problem of how to make the dratted spear go straight in air. I haven't figured that one out yet. Hello, what's that?"

Kitty looked out the window and wrinkled her nose. "It's just rubberneckers. They usually turn around and drive right out again. Oh, no, they're stopping. Hide, quick! In a minute they'll be peeking in the window."

"*What?*" Homer took one look out the window at the eager family pouring out of the car—mama, papa, sister, brother, Auntie Mae and Uncle Frank—and leaped to his feet. "*Oh, no, they won't,*" he thundered, hurling himself out the door in his monster toad suit, pulling his mask down over his face, taking tremendous leaps in his frog feet, hollering, snatching up an eight-foot fence rail. In a moment he came lumbering back, his chest heaving.

"They'll sue you," laughed Kitty.

"Let 'em." Homer sat down, then reared up once again at the unmistakable sound of another approaching car.

"Stop!" shouted Kitty. "Homer, wait! I think it's— Homer! Stop! It's Sergeant Fern!"

But Homer was already lunging at the car with his fence rail. And Bob Fern was leaping out of the driver's seat with gun in hand, his jaw clenched, his strong heart thudding in his breast, prepared to rescue Kitty at any cost from the monstrous frog that had her in its power.

"*Stop, stop,*" screamed Kitty.

Homer and Bob Fern stared at each other, then Homer turned away, breathing hard, and hurled the fence rail at the ground.

Sergeant Fern's chest was also rising and falling. However, he put his gun away with dignity, while Kitty, sobbing with laughter, leaned limply against the wall.

"I'll go away if I'm not wanted," said Bob Fern.

Homer turned around and embraced him and clapped him on the back, and apologized and patted his cheek and invited him to come in the house. Kitty apologized too, and explained that Homer was just sticking up for her rights: he had thought Bob was a Peeping Tom like the others.

"What others?" asked Bob Fern.

"No, no, Bob, there's a good boy," said Homer soothingly. "Come on in and tell us what you've got on your mind."

Bob was wearing his Sunday suit again. "I couldn't find you at the Doves' house just now, Mr. Kelly, so I thought I'd see if you were over here."

"Quick thinking, Bob," said Homer. "Come on in. And call me Homer."

"You see, I've just turned in my badge."

"Oh, say, Bob, I'm sorry."

"Well, I did it fast before the chief could fire me. He caught me going through the file. And anyhow," said Bob, bravely cheerful, "I decided I couldn't serve both God and Mammon at the same time."

"That's our Bob!" said Homer. "Although, come to think of it, Mammon helps to pay for the groceries. What will you do now? Here, sit down."

Homer offered Bob the backless chair, but Bob wouldn't sit while a lady was standing. He leaned awkwardly against the mantelpiece instead, and Kitty politely sat down on the chair, suddenly deciding it was what a lady should do at a time like that.

"I live pretty cheap anyway," said Bob. "I've got my scalloping money put away. Something will turn up." He was keeping his eyes firmly fixed on Homer, but the brave show was for Kitty.

She felt it and tried to say something kind. "Bob, I want to thank you for helping us. I'm terribly sorry it's made all this trouble for you." Oh, if only she hadn't laughed.

Bob looked at her courageously. "Nothing is any trouble." Kitty modestly dropped her basilisk eyes, but Bob was carried away. "It just means I'll have more time to work for you," he said, and with an enthusiastic sweep of his arm he knocked some of Kitty's shells off the mantel. They fell with a dismal clatter to the floor. "Oh, gosh, I'm sorry," said Bob, getting down on his knees to pick everything up. "Gee, I'm afraid some of these scallop shells are broken. Forgive me, Kitty. I'll get you some more. I'll go out this afternoon and get you some more, Kitty."

"Oh, no, no, Bob, don't be silly," said Kitty. She bent down and picked up the twisted core of the broken whelk. It was cold to the touch. She held it in her hands and let it suck the warmth out of her fingers and absorb into itself her good humor, the good spirits of the morning.

31

*The subterranean miner that works in us
all, how can one tell whither leads his shaft
by the ever shifting, muffled sound of his
pick?*

Moby Dick

They all went to Homer's house for lunch. "I'll cook," said
Homer, as Alice Dove looked up severely at the three of them
from inside the chicken-wire enclosure of Jupiter's pen.

Alice had just come home from her morning in the Pacific
National Bank, and she was still wearing her respectable bank
teller's dress. "Oh, no, you won't, Homer Kelly," she said. "The
last time you used my pots and pans you burnt a hole in one."

"Don't worry, Alice," said Kitty. "I brought some bread and
cheese from my house. We're all set. Homer just wanted to come
home and take his rubber suit off."

"And I've got some plums and peaches here," said Bob Fern,
beaming at Alice, brandishing a paper bag. "Say, Alice, Jupiter
looks pretty good today."

Alice's face softened. "Oh, do you think so? I wish you'd take
a look at that wing of his and see if you think his new primaries
are coming in."

Obligingly Bob unfastened the roll of chicken wire Alice used for a gate and knelt down on the hard trampled ground beside the big white bird, holding him easily with one arm, spreading out his wounded wing with the other. The gap in Jupiter's feathers was downy at the edges. "Well, something's coming in. Let's hope some of those feathers are going to be big strong ones." Bob let go of Jupiter and stood up to watch him waddle after the kernels of cracked corn Alice had thrown down.

"I'd love to see him fly," said Kitty.

"Maybe he'll dismember his dismemberer," said Homer darkly, "the way Ahab wanted to do."

They went inside. But at the door Alice stopped. "There they are again," she said. She was looking down her driveway. Bob and Kitty and Homer looked too. They saw a man with a tripod over his shoulder walking along the road, trailed by another man carrying a long ruled stick and a shovel.

"Surveyors," said Homer. "What are they doing? Surveying your place?"

"No, no, Helen's land," mumbled Alice. "The land she gave to the Boatwright Trust."

"Oh, is that around here somewhere?" said Kitty.

"All around. Ours just sticks into it a little bit." Alice stumped into the house, her face set. Kitty opened up her loaf of bread on the table and began slicing her Swiss cheese with one of Alice's kitchen knives. Bob Fern took his peaches to the sink and began peeling them. He was smiling like a boy at a birthday party.

Homer was changing his clothes behind the open door of his bedroom, shouting at Alice at the same time. "This Boatwright Trust of Helen Green's—it's some sort of conservation outfit, isn't it, Alice? To preserve the land intact forever, isn't that right?"

"I guess so," grumbled Alice. She picked up a couple of cats from the table and dumped them on the floor. "What I want to know is, what do they keep surveying it for? That's all I want to know."

Homer burst out of his bedroom wearing a pair of brown pants, buttoning a shirt over his sweaty chest. "Want me to find out for you?" he said. "Wait a minute. I'll be right back." He threw open the screen door and pounded across the front yard in his bare feet.

At the top of the first rise beyond Alice's house he caught sight of the surveyors and shouted, *"Hey."* They looked back and waited for him to catch up. "Excuse me," said Homer, puffing to a stop. "I just wondered what you fellows are doing."

"Just checking the lines on this map here so we can put in stone bounds," said the man with the transit. "Dig a few holes. Gonna make some percolation tests."

He had a large roll of paper under his arm. "Mind if I take a look?" said Homer. "My friend Mrs. Dove, who lives right here, she's sort of worried about what you guys are doing."

"Well, I guess it's okay." The man put his transit down on the ground and unrolled the map. "It's this big chunk in here," he said, pointing at the middle of the sheet. "All this part marked 'Boatwright Trust.'"

"My God," said Homer, "that's a big piece of the island. Who's in charge of it anyhow, this Boatwright Trust?"

"Damned if I know. Do you know, Bertie?"

Bertie shrugged his shoulders.

"Well, who hired you guys?" said Homer.

"Oh, we work for an engineering firm in Woods Hole. Becket and Anderson. Come on, Bertie." The transit man rolled up his map again and picked up his tripod.

"Off-islanders, eh?" said Homer. "Well, who hired Becket and Anderson to make the survey and dig the holes?"

"Don't ask me." The man turned around and started up the road again, his transit over his shoulder. Bertie followed with his rod and shovel.

"What about you, Bertie?" shouted Homer. Bertie's back hunched up again to display his ignorance. "Sinister, that's what it is," bawled Homer. "You're the faceless minions of a nameless blind gigantic secret power, that's what you are. You ought to be ashamed of yourselves."

The two surveyors glanced at each other and grinned. Abutters —Christ, they always got so excited.

"It's huge. Holy cow," said Homer, walking into Alice's kitchen again. "Alice, what in God's name is that trust?"

"Don't know." Alice was pouring coffee. "Nobody seems to know," she said, flashing him a lugubrious glance.

"Well, there must be some trustees or something. There must be somebody in charge." Homer looked at the map on the wall. "Show me the boundary lines, Alice."

Alice put down the coffeepot and pointed. "It's this big piece here, called Saul's Hills—that's the old name for it. The Hidden Forest is part of it. It's the *heart* of the island," said Alice, turning away.

"It's about four square miles," said Bob Fern, pacing them off on the map with his fingers. "That's a big part of Nantucket Island, all right. The whole island's only about fifty square miles, all in all."

"Funny they hired an engineering firm from the mainland," said Homer. "I'll tell you what I'll do, Alice. I'll see if I can track down the trustees of this Boatwright Trust. Don't worry. The whole thing's probably run by a couple of white-tailed deer and a flock of partridges. But I'll look into it anyway and find out."

Alice said nothing. She was grubbing away at the breakfast dishes in the sink. Kitty nudged Alice aside and began washing the dishes herself. Bob Fern snatched up a dish towel and took the dishes reverently from Kitty. Alice was making funny noises. She went into her bedroom and shut the door.

"She's crying," whispered Kitty, looking at Homer.

"Well, it means a lot to her," said Homer softly. "She's got strong feelings, after all. She's a woman of passion."

32

". . . Aye, aye! thy silence, then, that voices
thee . . ."

Moby Dick

It took Homer an hour to get through to Mr. James Anderson of
Becket and Anderson, Civil Engineers, Woods Hole, because
Becket was on vacation and Anderson was out to lunch, and then
the line was busy, and then the secretary said Mr. Anderson was
in conference, and Homer could hear him saying, "What does he
want?" in the background and then making demurring noises,
and the secretary made demurring noises at Homer in her turn.
"Put him on," thundered Homer, and the girl, who was new on
the job and easily cowed, did so.

Mr. Anderson was merely fulfilling the requests of the firm
that had engaged him as a civil engineer. "Doris, may I have
the file for the Boatwright Trust? May I ask what business it
is of yours, Mr. . . . ? Oh, I see. Well, all I can suggest is
that you contact Chalmers and Partridge. That's East Forty-
sixth Street in New York. A legal firm. You're welcome. Not
at all. Good-bye."

Homer took the phone away from his ear and looked at it. "I didn't even say thank you, you big jerk."

He sought after Chalmers and Partridge then, and was connected at last with another secretary, who announced that all members of the staff of Chalmers and Partridge were on vacation for the month of July, and if he would care to leave a message he could expect a reply at some indefinite date in the future.

Well, would she look something up for him?

No, she was merely an answering service. She would suggest that he call back the first of August. Enraged, Homer threw the telephone at the floor. Then he picked it up again and called Mr. Tillinghast, the new president of the Nantucket Protection Society, or rather the Helen Green Society. Surely Tillinghast would know about the Boatwright Trust if anybody would.

"Why, yes," said Mr. Tillinghast. "I have the brochure around here somewhere, and I must say, as I remember, it looked just fine."

Ten minutes later Homer was standing in Mr. Tillinghast's front hall, examining the Boatwright Trust brochure, a folded pamphlet of heavy pale-green paper. On the outside there was a drawing of a spray of blueberry and the words "A priceless heritage, Nantucket's unspoiled moors." The pamphlet unfolded to a photograph of a child on a horizon of blowing grass against a background of dark sky and cirrus clouds. The photograph had been taken through a red filter. The clouds were spectacular. There was a map on the next fold, with words below. Homer's eye skimmed over them.

. . . nature, unpolluted and unspoiled . . . irreplaceable beauty . . . preservation of these historic hills . . . headwaters of the island's pure fresh-water streams . . . wildlife . . . birdsong . . .

It was all just exactly what you would expect. Yet something about the wording irritated him. Something wasn't quite right. "Do you have anything else?" he said.

"Well, I've got a copy of the engineering diagrams made up by John Hepburn. Here they are, these charts here."

"You mean the surveying has already been done?"

"Well, of course. It had to be, before the legal instrument could be drawn up."

"Then why is another outfit, from Woods Hole, in there surveying the land again? Look, all I want to know is, who's in charge? I should think there would be some trustees."

"Oh, yes, there will be. My understanding was that a local board of trustees would be appointed once the legal transaction had been formally completed. Why don't you look at the deed? It must be on file at the Registry of Deeds in the Town Building."

"Good," said Homer. "I'll do that right now. One more thing, Mr. Tillinghast. What would Helen Green's land have been worth, I mean in dollars, if she had sold it for development instead of giving it to this conservation trust? Vulgar question, I know."

"Oh, I think I heard a figure going around—five million dollars, I think it was, but that was just a romantic notion. After all, some of the land is under water. I should think . . ." Mr. Tillinghast looked at the map in the pamphlet and mumbled to himself, then raised his eyebrows. "Well, you know, maybe that's not far off, the way real estate values are today. It could have been worth that much. It was an extraordinarily generous gift."

"Five million dollars?" Five million dollars. Five million . . . Homer was still muttering it to himself as he groped through the file in the office of the registrar of deeds. *Five million dollars.* He found the file for the Boatwright Trust. It contained a single sheet of paper. Homer carried the sheet to the woman at the desk. "What does this mean? There's nothing there."

The registrar's assistant glanced at the sheet of paper. "Oh, that deed must be in Boston. It says, 'Department of Corporations and Taxation.' You'll have to go there. This just gives you the name of the trustee."

"That's what this Hermann Dankbinkel fellow is? The trustee?

214

Do you know him? There's no address. Does he live in Nantucket?"

"I don't know him," said the woman, "but he may be in the phone book." She riffled through the Nantucket directory, but there was no Dankbinkel.

"Tell me," said Homer, "is it customary to have a deed filed elsewhere than in the local Registry of Deeds? Why would anybody do that?"

"I have no idea. It's not exactly customary. But it *is* done. It's perfectly legal."

"Well, thanks." Homer copied down the scant information he had uncovered and drove home again, muttering to himself, wondering how anybody could be so unselfish as to give up with a stroke of the pen an inheritance worth five million dollars. It was odd that the deed wasn't registered in Nantucket. Peculiar. Suppose, just suppose, that this Dankbinkel, whoever he was, turned out to be some kind of swindler or chiseler who had found a way of diddling Helen Green out of her land by some tricky legal wording in the trust agreement, and then he had killed her before she found out. The murderer was not Katharine Clark, but Hermann Dankbinkel! Or maybe Dankbinkel was in league with one of the eager builders and realtors on the island. *Five million dollars.* Christ almighty.

Homer sat down with a can of beer in his hand and called up his friend Jerry Neville in Boston. Jerry specialized in writing leases for supermarkets, but he was also the expert on estate planning and realty trusts for his legal firm. "Why would the deed to a Nantucket conservation trust be registered in the State House in Boston rather than right here on the island?" Homer wanted to know.

"Beats me," said Jerry. "I'll send somebody over to the State House to have a look at the deed and call you back."

Jerry called Homer that evening after supper. "It smells," he said. "At least I think it smells, but then maybe I've got extrasensitive nostrils. This Dankbinkel is a Swiss. He's the sole trustee. He's an executive of the Schweizerische Kredit Anstalt in Zurich. That's a Swiss bank. The deed can be terminated at any time by its shareholders, but they're not listed. Are there any shareholders on the island?"

"Not so far as I know," said Homer. "But I'll look into it some more. What if I call up Dankbinkel in Zurich?"

"Not a prayer. Those Swiss bankers are sworn to secrecy to protect the privacy of their clients. I've tangled with some of them before. That's what seems so peculiar to me. Why would a nice wholesome conservation outfit like this one need that kind of anonymity and privacy? I suspect that something not quite nice is going on."

Homer hung up. Alice Dove was looking at him silently. He told her what he had turned up, or failed to turn up, and what Jerry had said. Alice said nothing. She looked grimly down at her folded hands.

"You know, Alice, even that pretty little green pamphlet didn't look right," said Homer. "There was something missing in it, and I've finally figured out what it was. There was nothing in there anywhere about time. You'd think there would have been all sorts of phrases like 'in perpetuity' or 'world without end' or 'forevermore' or 'till the last syllable of recorded time.' Why not? And now the deed itself says that the shareholders can terminate the trust whenever they so desire. Why? Do you know of any shareholders, Alice? Do a lot of people on the island own shares?"

"No," said Alice curtly. "Nobody I know of. Not a soul."

"Funny. I'm awfully afraid somebody was out for plunder. Somebody was making a fool of poor old Helen Green."

216

33

*"Whosoever of ye raises me a white-
headed whale with a wrinkled brow and a
crooked jaw; whosoever of ye raises me that
white-headed whale, with three holes
punctured in his starboard fluke—look ye,
whosoever of ye raises me that same white
whale, he shall have this gold ounce, my
boys!"*

Moby Dick

Mary Kelly came at last. Homer met her plane in Boston, took
her home to Concord, and then brought her to Nantucket and
settled her in a small house he had rented in town on Vestal
Street. He took her around to meet Kitty Clark and Alice and
Alden Dove.

Kitty took to her at once. Mary Kelly had an amplitude and an
untidy luxuriance of parts that was both august and pleasing, and
a calm that seemed embedded in the marrow of her large bones.
To Kitty she seemed a vessel or a bowl in which one could be
cradled and contained, a receptacle for the truth. In Homer's
presence Kitty had tried to keep up a show of courage and confidence, but in the company of his wife no unnatural posture
seemed necessary.

The two women spent a good part of the month of August
together. Kitty took an interest in Mary's feminists, and Mary in
turn joined some of Kitty's expeditions around the island. One hot

muggy afternoon Homer rented the Scout from Mr. Woodrow and took them clamming in the Great Point Lagoon. Enthusiastically he splashed around in the shallows with his clam rake and bucket, while Kitty and Mary drifted idly in the middle of the lagoon in a dinghy they had brought along in the back of the truck.

"I have these dreams," said Kitty.

"What dreams?" said Mary.

"I dream that I have my clothes off, and then people say such terrible things to me. Oh, I don't blame them. People shouldn't go around with all their clothes off. I keep wanting to explain that they should just let me go home and get dressed."

Mary reflected, looking down at the wobbling patterns of light on the ribbed sand under the water. "Maybe it's like that passage in Paul in the Bible. 'Thou shalt be as one stripped for action.'"

Kitty brightened. "Yes, I like that. Stripped for action. I'll tell them that, next time I have the dream." She inhaled a deep shaky breath. As the time before the trial grew short, she was aware

great Point

more often of a rising sensation in the chest, a fluttering in the lungs. "What should I wear to the trial?" she said, trying to sound jaunty. "What would be the fashionable thing for an indicted murderer to wear in court?"

Homer was wading beside them, handing a bucket of clams to his wife. "Red satin," said Mary firmly, clasping the bucket between her knees.

"Good!" said Homer. He picked up the painter and began towing the dinghy to shore.

"I know what I'd like," said Kitty. "One of those big dusters people wore in horseless carriages. And a huge hat and goggles. And I'd get an umbrella, a gigantic black umbrella, and hold it way down over my head so the prosecutor would have to peer up under it to ask me questions."

"Then you could spit in his eye," said Homer.

They drove home along the sandy track. Kitty leaned forward from the back seat, made bold by the presence of Mary Kelly. "Look, Homer, it's high time I paid you something. That money is piling up in my bank account. It's the wages of sin. And surely the state of Massachusetts isn't paying you enough to keep you going for months and months like this. I'm feeling worse and worse about being a charity case. I shouldn't be cheating the state of Massachusetts when I've got four thousand dollars in the bank."

"Look, girl, I'm already embarrassed by those bundles of hundred-dollar bills you keep sending me in the mail. The last one was ridiculous. I don't know why you're so— What did you say? The state of Massachusetts? I'm not a public defender for the state of Massachusetts."

There was some kind of gap in understanding. Homer glanced back at Kitty. Mary Kelly looked from one to the other. "You mean you *haven't* been sending Homer those bunches of hundred-dollar bills?"

"Me? No!" Kitty put her hand to her head. "But aren't you— I thought you were the lawyer officially assigned to me because

I didn't have one. You mean it wasn't the police who called you to come to see me in that jail cell?"

"Jesus Christ." Homer stopped the truck, and for a moment they sat looking out at the low wind-swept forest of junipers that rimmed Coskata Pond. "It was a note in the mailbox. You mean you didn't ask one of the police officers to get hold of me?"

Kitty couldn't speak. She shook her head.

"Well, who in God's name did?"

They sat staring at each other.

"Homer," said Mary, "are you sure it wasn't somebody in the Nantucket Police Department? The local judge?"

"But why would they pick on me? I'm not on the list of Nantucket attorneys. There's a bunch of regular court lawyers who do this sort of thing as a matter of course. Why me?"

"What did the note in the mailbox say?" said Mary.

"Hardly anything," said Homer. "It was typewritten. 'Katharine Clark has been arrested and needs your assistance.' Something like that. And it must have said where she was, in the jail. I assumed she had asked for me and some policeman had put the note in the Doves' mailbox after he couldn't reach me on the phone. Mmm. I wonder if it could have been Fern. No, I don't see how he could have kept on shelling out so much money all this time. What about Arthur Bird? He could afford it."

The truck was hot. Kitty opened the back door and let the onshore breeze blow in. "Impossible," she said.

"Well, good. I'd hate to be beholden to Arthur Bird. But it had to be somebody who knew about the trouble you were in. What about Dick and Letty Roper? No, that's out of the question unless they're a lot less simple than they seem. How about Joe Green?" Homer gave Kitty a sidelong glance. "Let's just think about Joe Green for a minute."

"He hates me," said Kitty.

"Well, maybe." Homer started the engine.

Kitty slammed her door. "No maybe about it," she said.

Mary laughed. "Maybe somebody hired Homer because they

were sure he would louse the whole thing up."

Homer groaned. "Oh, God," he said. "You may be right."

Back in town, Mary and Kitty left Homer washing sand out of the clams while they went off to Main Street to buy salad greens from Mr. Bartlett's truck. Homer abandoned the clams half washed and called up Bob Fern. Maybe Bob would know where the money was coming from.

Bob didn't know. Bob was flabbergasted. "I just assumed she asked Chief Pike to call you in," he said.

"You assumed, I assumed, she assumed, we all assumed," growled Homer. He called Richard Roper and Arthur Bird and Joe Green, hoping to surprise one of them into an admission of having been Kitty's benefactor (or Kitty's enemy, depending on what view you took of the competence of that bonehead Homer Kelly). They all denied it.

It was damned peculiar. Homer ate his gritty chowder and

thought it over, while Kitty and Mary giggled about Mrs. Pankhurst's daughter Christabel, who had gone to prison too, and had had feeding tubes stuck in her too, and had been marvelous, altogether marvelous. Then Homer took Kitty home. When he got back to Vestal Street someone was reeling up to his door.

"Good God," said Homer. "Mr. Brown. I didn't recognize you at first. Come right in. Meet my wife. Mary, I told you about Mr. Brown. He has in his custody a certain very precious bolt or a castle nut or something like that. Have we got a little something for the gentleman? I think there's some beer in the back of the icebox. Well, how's the astute automotive engineer this evening?"

"Oh, fine, I'm jush fine. But I thought I better tell you. The adjushm'n' link bolt'sh mishin'."

"What? The adjustment link bolt? You don't mean—you mean, the one you showed me? With the nice clean threads? It's missing?"

"Shomebody shwiped it. Well, they shwiped the whole cashe a beer. It wazh in a can of axshle greashe, you know, in a cashe a beer in my Coke machine. Shomebody shwiped the whole cashe a beer."

"Oh, goddamn." Homer stared at Boozer Brown in dismay. "But the car—the car's all right, isn't it? I mean, you've still got the car?"

"Car? Wha' car?"

"What car? Joe Green's car. The wrecked car. The one the bolt came out of. You've still got the car?"

"Oh, oh, tha' car. Sure, tha' car. No, car'zh gone too. Mizh Magee got a court order. Made me get rid of it. Zheezh, I didn't know you wanted the car. I juzh paid shigstyfi' dollarzh, they hauled it away. Prob'ly all shqueezhed by now, there on the mainland, in one of those big machinezh. I'm shorry." Boozer wagged his head, his bleary eyes alight with friendliness.

"Oh, Boozer, my God."

"'T'shall right. I'll teshtify." Boozer held up his greasy right hand and rolled up his eyes. "Sh'welp me, God. Don' worry, Mizzer Kelly. Oh, thanksh, Mizh Kelly, don' min' 'f I do." Boozer swilled down his glass of beer, accepted another, told a couple of dirty stories and departed. Homer shut the door behind him and looked at his wife for sympathy.

Mary laughed. "He'll look great on the witness stand," she said.

"Jesus X. Christ," said Homer.

It was a hot night. Moths were blundering against the window screen. Homer sat beside the window watching his wife rearrange her notes at the dining room table. He thought long and hard about Mrs. Magee, who had been responsible for the disappearance of the car that had been doctored to cause an accident in which Helen Green might have been killed. Had she also stolen the bolt in the can of axle grease? How would she have known about the bolt? Of course Boozer was a loose talker. Maybe the whole island knew about the linkage bolt in the can of axle grease in the case of beer in Boozer's Coke machine. And then again maybe it was just some thirsty kid who had stolen the case of beer. Homer watched the moths walking feebly up and down the window screen. One of them had pretty turquoise wings, and suddenly he had a vision of Mrs. Magee in a turquoise-colored golfing outfit swinging a golf club gracefully, watching the ball lift over the low undulations of Saul's Hills, which were now all velvet patches of green with little flags sticking up out of them. Helen Green's land! Homer still hadn't found out who in the hell it was who had been trying to swindle Helen Green out of her conservation land. Tomorrow he would call up that legal firm, Chalmers and Partridge. They would be back from vacation by this time. And it was Chalmers and Partridge who had hired the surveyors who were now planting red-topped stakes all over that land, according to Alice Dove. Maybe Chalmers and Partridge could explain what the stakes were for, identify the shareholders in the

Boatwright Trust, or tell him how in the hell he could get through to the mysterious trustee in whose care Helen Green had left five million dollars' worth of magnificent Nantucket land—the Swiss banker himself, Hermann Dankbinkel.

34

. . . innocence and guilt . . . in effect
changed places.

Billy Budd

It took Homer three days to get through to Jarvis Partridge of
Chalmers and Partridge. Mr. Partridge was upright and discreet.
He refused to discuss the business matters of any client of his with
another party. Was Mr. Kelly a shareholder in the Boatwright
Trust? No? Well, then it would be highly improper for Mr.
Partridge to reveal the private business matters of the trust to an
outsider. Homer hung up in a rage, resolved to go after Dankbinkel in earnest. After all, he told himself, Dankbinkel had an office
there in Zurich with a telephone in it. And here he was, Homer
Kelly, sitting in a chair in a house in Nantucket with a telephone
in his hand. They were both human beings, after all, born of
woman, fellow mortal souls. He would try presenting the matter
to Hermann Dankbinkel himself, as man to man.

Alas, it was already night in Switzerland. Early the next morning, he placed his call. He spoke to Dankbinkel's assistant in the
Zurich office of the Schweizerische Kredit Anstalt. Joyfully

Homer offered up to her his high school German.

(Here follows an English translation of the transatlantic conversation between Homer Kelly of Nantucket and Frau Magdalena Kranzli of Zurich.)

"Good afternoon, dear madam! Or perhaps miss? How goes it? I am Mr. Homer Kelly, of the United States. May I spoke with Mr. Dankbinkel?"

"I am sorry, but Mr. Dankbinkel is not here. Can I help you?"

"I love, please, to know the names of the peoples who have the parts in the Boatwright Trust, in Nantucket, Massachusetts, in the United States."

"Parts? Parts? Oh, I see. You mean shares. You want to know the names of the shareholders. Is that right?"

"Oh, yes, yes, miss or madam, I want this names. Mr. Dankbinkel, he is a trustee."

"But, Mr. Kelly, I cannot give you information on the telephone. I am sorry. I must ask Mr. Dankbinkel first."

"Where is Mr. Dankbinkel? When comes he at home?"

"I don't know. Mr. Dankbinkel will call you when he comes in. Good day."

"No, no! Halt, please, miss! It is a matter of live or die! I must have this names! Now! These minutes!"

"No, no, I cannot."

"What is it with you, miss? Don't you have a head on top of your neck? Don't you stand on your own two foot?"

"How dare you speak to me like that? You are rude and insulting!"

"Oh, no, no, my good loveliness young lady! How beautiful you are! I love you! I blossom you a kiss! Only give me please the name of the shareholders of the Boatwright Trust! Now, most beautifuls young lady! These minutes!"

"I will not speak with you any longer. Good day!"

"Halt! No, no!"

The phone went dead. Homer stared at the receiver, his chest heaving, shouted *"Schweinehund! Dummkopf!"* into it, and kicked the telephone table across the room. Then he picked up the phone, which had lost a few chips here and there, and called his friend Jerry on the mainland.

"Well, you might try Interpol," suggested Jerry. "Aren't you an old friend of the district attorney of Middlesex County? Maybe he knows somebody over there who knows somebody."

It was true that the district attorney was an old friend and colleague of Homer Kelly's. A man of modest talents, he had once been Homer's superior in the East Cambridge Courthouse, and Homer had worked long and loyally for him. Now Homer called up his old friend and told him about his problem with Dankbinkel.

"Well, I might be able to work something out," said the D.A. "You know, Homer, I think the Swiss police chief who buddied with me in Paris at the convention last fall was from Zurich. Or maybe it was Geneva. He showed me around gay Paree while everybody else was taking a tour of the French countryside. Saved my life. You know how I feel about the country. I'll see what I can do. You've really got something on this Donkbingle? I mean, no kidding, this is something really rotten? Okay, I'll just get in touch with the *Polizeikommissar* in Zurich and ask him to serve a paper on Donkbingle. He'll do it. That is, if he's the one I remember. The Geneva fella wouldn't do you any good, right? Well, I'm pretty sure this chap was from Zurich."

(Here follows an English translation of the transatlantic conversation between Homer Kelly of Nantucket and Herr Hermann Dankbinkel of Zurich.)

"Hello?"

"Mr. Dankbinkel?"

"This is Hermann Dankbinkel. Is this Inspector Kelly?"

"Mr. Dankbinkel! Mr. Dankbinkel! Thank God! Good morning, Mr. Dankbinkel!"

"Good morning. Police Commissioner Haessler has requested me to tell you something about the Boatwright Trust, Inspector."

227

"Yes, yes, that is truly, yes, indeed!"

"Good. I have here the names of the shareholders. Do you have a pencil?"

"Yes, yes! I have the pen of my aunt!"

"I beg your pardon?"

"No, no, never mind. I have a pencil!"

"Good. Hmm. There is only one shareholder listed here. Her name is Green. Helen Boatwright Green."

"Helen Green? She was the only shareholder? But she is dead! Helen Green is die dead!"

"Oh? When did she die? This document is only good for a year. I have another document. The Boatwright Trust was to have been taken over by another trust."

"Halt! I cannot understand you! Another document? What is this other document?"

"Mr. Kelly? Vy do vee not spake in English?"

"Ja, ja—I mean, yes, indeed, by all means. Go to it. Go right ahead. I'm all ears."

"I haff not zuh English perfected. I spake vrongly, no doubet."

"No, no, beautifully! You speak beautifully, Herr Dankbinkel! But please tell me about that other document! The Boatwright Trust was to last for one year only? And then it was to be superseded by another trust?"

"Yes. Zuh uzzer trust vas to haff taken over zuh assets of zuh Boatwright Trust on a certain date. I haff a letter of intent to zat effect. It vas to be a landed property trust—how do you call it? —a real estate trust. I vass no longer to be zuh trustee. I vas to be replaced by a Mr. James Harmon. Zuh trust is named for him. Zuh Harmony Real Estate Trust."

"You mean, James Harmon of Harmony Hotels? Aaahhh." Understanding flooded in upon Homer. Helen Green had indeed been duped, she had been gulled, she had been swindled. It was just as he had thought. The slender hand of Wilhelmina Magee had slipped in her little card. Somehow or other Mrs. Magee had jumped into the action through a loophole, or a defect in the wording, or through some even more sinister opportunity, some threat of reprisal, perhaps even murder. She had inserted herself between the beneficence and generosity of Helen Green's intent and its object, she had perverted it to her own ends. "This is not merely a substitution of one free gift for another, is it, Herr Dankbinkel? It is not a gift to Mr. Harmon? Surely there is money involved, a sum of money?"

"Oh, yes, of course, a great deal of money. Fife and a half million dollars, Mr. Kelly, vas to be paid by zuh Harmon Corporation to zuh vooman who signed zuh letter of intent, on completion of zuh exchange of assets from zuh one trust to zuh uzzer. But zuh exchange never took place."

The woman. Wilhelmina Magee! "Who signed it, Herr Dankbinkel? Can you tell me if the name Wilhelmina Magee is on that letter of intent?"

"Vilhelmina who?"

"Magee, Wilhelmina Magee. M-a-g-e-e."

"Vilhelmina Magee." There was a pause. "No, zere is no such name here anyvere," said Herr Dankbinkel.

"Well, then, who signed the letter?"

"Vy, of course it vas zuh shareholder, Helen Green. She vas zuh only vun who *could* sign it."

"Helen Green?"

"Inspector Kelly? Are you still zere?"

"Yes, yes, I'm still here."

"Tell me, did zhu reeng bevore?"

"Before? Yes, of course. I've been calling since yesterday."

"No, no, I mean a vile ago. Lahst spreeng? Lahst veenter? You spoke to my assistant, Frau Kranzli?"

"No, not I. Did someone call last winter?"

"Ja. You see, Frau Kranzli did not know she was supposed to be —how you say it *auf englisch?*—*umsichtig.* Discreet! She was —how you say it?—*eingeschüchtert,* frightened, by being called oop on zuh transatlantic telephone. It vas likevise a call from Nantucket. And she vas answering hiss qvestions ven I came into zuh room, and zen of course I cut him off short and hung oop qvickly, and reproved my assistant. She cried tears down her face. I don't remember zuh man's name. *Frau Kranzli, erinnern Sie sich auf den Namen des Mannes der letzten Februar telephoniert hat? Nein?* No, Inspector Kelly, she does not remember eezer."

"It was a man who called? From Nantucket?"

"Yes. He belonged to some Conwerzational Committee, for making conwerzation."

"Conwerzation?" Homer rolled his eyes to the ceiling and tried to think of something else to say to Herr Dankbinkel, whose voice was beginning to crackle and snap, to wane and wax and wane. The connection was failing. "What did they conwerse about?" he said idiotically. "The Dialogues of Plato? Truth? Goodness? Beauty?"

"Vot? Vot?" The telephone squealed and buzzed. Herr Dankbinkel's voice was growing fainter and fainter. "Conwerse about? Conwerse about? Vy, zuh trees, of course, zuh green trees and zuh flowers, zuh booshes, zuh green grass . . . "

And then Herr Dankbinkel's voice faded away altogether, and as it faded it seemed to Homer that Herr Dankbinkel was drifting back into his childhood. A miniature Herr Dankbinkel in a tiny sailor suit was skipping through a childlike little park in a little toy city in Switzerland, with giant plastic flowers blossoming under trees as round as green balloons. Then Homer understood. He dropped the receiver and threw up his hands and shouted at Herr Dankbinkel across the entire expanse of the Atlantic Ocean and all of southern France and up and up into the foothills of the Alps. "Conser*wation*, Herr Dankbinkel! You got the *ess* and the *wee* in the wrong places! You meant a Conser*wation* Committee, Herr Dankbinkel! God bless you!"

35

To you, Arch Principals, I rear
My quarrel, for this quarrel is with gods.
MELVILLE, *Timoleon*

So it was Helen Green herself, the bitch, the dirty little hypocrite. It wasn't Min Magee or Samuel Flakeley or James Holworthy or any of those other fine upstanding realtors and commercial developers who was about to lay violent hands on Nantucket's sacred soil and dump hotels and parking lots all over it. It was Helen Green herself. That Boatwright Trust of hers was a fraud, a swindle, a dummy organization for a deal with Harmony Hotels. Helen Green, damn her, the leader of the forces of virtue, who was self-righteously demanding that everyone else give up the profit on his acreage for the sake of a bunch of varying hares and a few bucketfuls of blueberries—it was Helen Green who was betraying them all while she was pretending to set them such a noble example. Well, her noble example was a filthy lie.

Homer stretched and scratched his chest and yawned and got up and sought out his wife. "She was double-crossing them," he said.

"Who was?"

"Helen Green."

"Oh, no!"

"She was going to get five and a half million dollars from Harmony Hotels for her chunk of land. And there's another thing. Somebody else got wind of this deal last February. Somebody in the Nantucket Protection Society. Somebody discovered that Helen was going to sell her land to James Harmon of Harmony Hotels. And it was last February that the first of Helen's accidents began. I'll try to track down the transatlantic phone call from Nantucket to Zurich last February, but it was probably made from a public phone. You see what this means, don't you? It means Helen Green was killed by somebody *on her own side.* I mean the side we used to think she was on. Somebody who was in favor of birds and bees and trees and so forth was trying to kill her, beginning last February. It wasn't one of those real estate types after all. They've all got hearts of gold."

"Homer, you haven't got much time. This is Saturday. Doesn't the trial begin on Monday? Can you get it postponed?"

"Yes, it begins Monday. No, I can't get it postponed."

"Well, let me help." Mary got up out of her chair at the dining room table, took a picture off its nail on the wall and turned it over. "There, I've turned Mrs. Pankhurst back to front. I'm all yours. Let me do something."

"Good. Make me a list of six reasons why I can't introduce all this new stuff into Kitty's case. You know, all the ways it might be called irrelevant and immaterial. See what you can think up. Then I'll call Jake O'Donnell in Cambridge and ask him how I should argue back."

"Who's Jake O'Donnell?"

"You know. Trial lawyer, hopeless cases. Snatches them out of the fire."

"Hopeless! But Kitty's case isn't hopeless! Homer!"

"It is if we can't get all this stuff about Helen into it. Right now

I want to call up Bob Fern and see what he makes of what Dankbinkel told me."

Bob was shocked. "Why, I'm absolutely disgusted," he said. "To think Mrs. Green would do a thing like that! What did she think would happen when the bulldozers went in there and they started to build the hotel? Everybody would know she'd been a traitor to her cause."

"Well, she would have cried all the way to the bank, as they say," said Homer. "But I think the reason for the dummy conservation organization and all this secrecy was that she was planning to be an innocent victim. After all, everyone assumed that she had given up all claim to that land. Nobody knew she was still the sole shareholder in the conservation trust. So when the time came for the hotel chain to buy the land from some transatlantic bank, she would pretend she had been betrayed, and she would sue the Swiss bank and the hotel people, only of course she would sue very gently and ineffectually, and the upshot would be that the hotel company would be in legal possession. And then she could quietly deposit her five and a half million in the Swiss bank and nobody would be the wiser. She would just be one more poor victimized idealist."

"Oh, I see now," said Bob. "But what does all this mean for Kitty?"

"Well, I think it helps. I've got a motive now for all those earlier attempts on Helen's life. Somebody knew what she was trying to do, and was doing his damnedest to stop her. And of course all of it has nothing to do with Kitty—that's what's so good about it. It was all very much a Nantucket Island matter. So if I can just focus enough attention on Helen's perfidious arrangements, maybe I can take the heat off Kitty. I wish to hell I had more time. Here I've been concentrating on Min Magee and all her friends and relations and I should have been nosing around the members of the Nantucket Protection Society. The only ones I know even by name are Alden and Alice and Mr. Tillinghast.

Who else is there? Just a lot of respectable folks. Is Joe Green a member?"

"Yes, he is. So am I. Don't forget me," said Bob Fern.

"I won't, I promise. Now, in order to have killed Helen Green during the total eclipse of the sun on March seventh of this year, this respectable person in the Nantucket Protection Society would have to have been floating around Great Point somehow. Maybe it was somebody in that goddamned red cabin cruiser I haven't been able to track down. You see, Fern, I should have been finding out which of those people have motorboats or sailboats or rowboats or whatever. There's Alden, of course, he was out scalloping that morning, but he was hard at work in the harbor hauling up bag after bag, and he never went outside the harbor mouth, where Charley Piper was keeping track."

"*I* did," said Bob. "You should be investigating me." He laughed in a shaky voice. "How do you know it wasn't me?"

"I don't," said Homer. "Look, have you got a list of the membership of that society? You do? Could you bring it over? I want you to tell me about all those people."

Bob was melancholy when he walked into Homer's front hall. "It's a pity you haven't got that piece of Mr. Green's car anymore. You really need it to make this whole thing hang together."

"A pity? That's an understatement. Damn Boozer anyway."

"I saw Mr. Doolittle walk into the Jared Coffin House this morning," said Bob. "You know, the district attorney from New Bedford."

"Tom Doolittle?" Homer whistled. "They're sending in their big gun. Look, Fern, you can help me. I've got to get some confirmation of this deal between Helen Green and the Harmon Corporation, so I've got to go after James Harmon, and here it is Saturday afternoon, and I've got a thousand other things to do. I'm going to give you the whole job. We'll go over the Nantucket Protection Society membership list another time." Homer scribbled a number on a card and gave it to Bob Fern. "Call up my friend Jerry Neville. He'll tell you how to go about it. Call me in when you think you need me."

Joe Green was next. Homer stood on the granite doorstep of Helen Boatwright Green's house once again and rang the bell. Joe opened the door slowly and stood looking at him, and once again Homer had the sensation that the man was brimming with unspoken speech. But the question about Helen's financial arrangements with James Harmon of Harmony Hotels produced only apparent surprise. Joe threw back his head. He opened his mouth, then shut it again. "I knew nothing about that," he said at last. "Helen kept her business affairs pretty much to herself."

"You had separate checking and savings accounts?"

"Yes. In the Pacific National Bank. Dick Roper sent me an accounting a while ago and asked me to examine the contents of Helen's safe deposit box. I found the key in her pocketbook and took a look in the box. There was some family silver in it, and some stock certificates. That was all. And a copy of her will."

"Her will. You are the principal beneficiary, I understand?"

"Yes, I am."

"Does it seem out of character to you, Mr. Green, that your wife might have taken part in this underhanded agreement with the president of a chain of hotels?" Insulting question to ask of a grief-stricken husband.

Again the hazel eyes became keen, and the lids drew back to show the entire circumference of the iris, and the mild face braced itself. But Joe said nothing, and then, with what seemed a massive effort, he mumbled something inaudible, withdrew clumsily and closed the door in Homer's face.

On his way back to Vestal Street Homer pondered the thwarted power that was now so fiercely driven back upon itself, and wondered if it had ever been unleashed, whether it was a force with which Joe might somehow have destroyed his wife. Homer had jokingly compared him with Bluebeard, because he had not wanted Helen to enter his house on the beach, and

Bluebeard after all had murdered his wife. Bluebeard had murdered dozens of wives. And Joe had refused entrance to Kitty too, that day when she was running away from the terns. Kitty had told Homer about that encounter. Maybe Joe's shack was like Bluebeard's chamber. Maybe it was full of murdered women. Maybe Homer should get a search warrant and take a look at that place. Was Joe telling the truth or was he lying when he said he knew nothing about Helen's business affairs? Ignorant he might have been, but who was it, after all, who was going to end up with the five and a half million if the hotel deal went through? Helen wasn't going to get it. Joe was. And if the hotel people didn't think it was going to go through, why were they out there every day putting up lines of stakes for a roadbed and marking out a huge rectangle that looked very much like the outline of a giant foundation? Why were there twenty or thirty of them out there all the time now, the way Alden said?

At home Mary was ready for him. She had made up a nasty list of judicial objections to the miscellaneous extraneous evidence Homer wanted to introduce into the murder trial of Katharine Clark. Homer took a look at it and groaned.

"Mary, holy cow, you should go over to the Jared Coffin House and work for the prosecution. Good God, look at that one. What am I going to say to that one? Well, hell, what did I do with my index cards? I can't do anything without those index cards. And how about some supper? My God, I'm a starving man."

Heroically Mary Kelly suppressed a retort that was the fruit of her six months' examination of the slow upward movement of womankind. She became her husband's devoted assistant and self-effacing slave. She found him his index cards. She made him some supper. She typed up his notes. She sat solemnly at her typewriter looking at the back of the picture of Emmeline Pankhurst, and then she frowned at the keyboard and typed up some more queries. She slipped them silently under Homer's nose.

"Oh, damn, damn," said Homer, looking them over. "All right, you're right. I'll ask Jake." He picked up the telephone and dialed

Jake O'Donnell on the mainland. Mary abandoned him and drove out the Polpis Road to see Kitty.

Kitty was glad to see her. Kitty was restless. Mary told her what Homer had learned from Dankbinkel. Kitty didn't seem to be paying much attention.

"Tomorrow's my last day," she said.

"What are you going to do with it?" said Mary.

"Well, if it doesn't rain I'm going out with Alice Dove. Tomorrow's the day of the highest and lowest tides in six months, since last spring. We're going to do what Rachel Carson talked about. We're going to see if we can find a piece of the floor of the harbor that ordinarily never sees the light of day, and look for various kinds of underwater life. The Head of the Harbor has the longest tidal beach on the island. We're going to go out there at low tide. Alice said we should hope for a northeast wind, and that's what the weather report is for tomorrow. I hope it doesn't rain."

"Why do you want a northeast wind?"

"Because it would make the low tide even lower. How is it out there now? Which way is the wind blowing?"

They stood outside Kitty's door, looking up. The wind was northerly. Mary felt it on her face, on her lips. It tasted a little salt. It tasted free. How would it taste to Kitty the day after tomorrow? When the Commonwealth would pick her up, then let her go, when each day after that it would pick her up and let her go, until perhaps one day it would pick her up in its iron grasp and not let her go again.

"I'm going to Quaker Meeting tomorrow," said Mary. "Want to come with me?"

"You're going to pray for me, is that it?"

"No, I just want to see what it might have been like to be a Quaker on Nantucket Island. Why don't I stop by for you?"

"No," said Kitty, "we haven't got time. Alice and I are going out early. The first low tide is around nine in the morning. But look for Mr. Biddle at Friends Meeting. He's my landlord. He'll be there."

"Well, then, how about having supper with us tomorrow night?"

"Well, I don't know. Look, tell Homer how grateful I am, how much—"

"Oh, for heaven's sake." Mary wondered if Kitty's dignity would be offended if she were to embrace her, decided it would, started for her car, then changed her mind and went back and hugged her hard. Kitty seemed pleased.

Back at the house on Vestal Street Mary found Homer still talking to Jake O'Donnell. He was arguing and making notes, cursing and laughing. He didn't hang up until Bob Fern came in at midnight. Bob was all excited.

"I talked to Mr. Harmon," said Bob. "James Harmon of Harmony Hotels. I got him on the line with your friend Jerry Neville. It was a three-way call, but mostly I just listened."

"Did he admit it?" said Homer. "Did he admit the deal with Helen Green?"

"Oh, sure, but the way he told it, it wasn't a deal, it was a regular—you know—business arrangement."

"Well, did the business arrangement go through? She signed the letter of intent, apparently, but did she sell it in actual fact?"

"No! Wait till you hear! She was *going* to sign the actual bill of sale, and they had a date all set up, and she was going to meet his representatives at a place on Martha's Vineyard on the afternoon of March *seventh!* The day of the eclipse! Only she was killed first! She must have been killed so she wouldn't be there, so she couldn't sign it!"

"March seventh? By God, that's great! Good for you, Bob. Well, what did they think when she didn't show up? I notice they're still out there surveying as if they were getting ready to build."

"They're gambling on the supposition that they'll win a case in probate court, that her signature on the letter of intent is sufficient, that it is no different from an item in her will. They're just waiting now for this trial of Kitty Clark's to be over, he said.

238

Obviously they just want to be sure that nothing too unpleasant will come up."

"What did Harmon say about the phony conservation trust?"

"Oh, he didn't seem to have the slightest qualms of conscience about that. I gather Mrs. Green had arranged all that with somebody else, and as far as Mr. Harmon was concerned, it was just a temporary holding arrangement. That was the way Mrs. Green had explained it to him. It wasn't his fault, he said, if she had described it falsely in public. He had agreed to keep his negotiations with her a secret, and to say nothing about her involvement in the land development, but he seemed to think that was normal business practice."

"Did any money change hands?"

"Not yet. He said he was ready to pay the specified amount into her estate, five and a half million dollars, whenever the court agreed that the land was his."

"Had he talked to Joe about it? Joe's the beneficiary."

"No. I asked him that. He said no. Helen had not wanted him to discuss the matter with any outsiders except for Dankbinkel and she had specifically mentioned her husband as someone who should not be involved."

"Good, good! Bob, you're magnificent. I'll just call back Jake O'Donnell and tell him all this."

Mary went to bed exhausted. Homer never went to bed at all. When the Old South church bell began ringing the next morning, he was just finishing his preparations. He was fresh as a daisy. He had reshuffled and rearranged all his cards and reassembled them under a new set of headings. He had a clever index to the whole thing and a handy set of little tabs he had constructed with scissors and tape. He demonstrated it proudly to his wife, ate a large breakfast and asked for Kitty.

"Kitty?" said Mary. "She must be out at the Head of the Harbor by now, looking at the sea floor."

"Well, I guess I'd better drive out there in the truck and get her. We've got a lot to talk over before tomorrow."

"Oh, no," said Mary. "Poor Kitty! Look, it's her last free day."

"Well, for Christ's sake, I've got to get her ready for the witness stand. Tell you what. I'll just go out there and tell her to be back here by the middle of the afternoon. I'll go right now, while I still know where she's at, and then I'll come home and go with you to Quaker Meeting. Do me good. After all, like Melville's Ishmael, I cherish the greatest respect for religion, no matter how comical."

36

Such deeps were bared as when the sea
Convulsed, vacates its shoreward bed,
And Nature's last reserves show nakedly. . . .

Timoleon

Kitty woke up and looked anxiously out the window. It was a gray morning, but it wasn't raining, not yet anyway. She got up and put on her jeans and a shirt and made breakfast, thinking about the shape of time. Last spring it had seemed formless and abundant, but lately it had become a compressing hollow space, large and open at one end, small and constricted at the other like a funnel. And she was about to drip out the small end, thought Kitty, into some kind of jar. She smiled grimly, thinking of herself as a nice little crystal teardrop, dripping out of the funnel. The day ahead of her had a narrow and contracted shape. Her chest felt tight. She couldn't breathe. She unbolted her door and threw it open.

It wasn't going to rain. The clouds were thick but they were high. The wind was blowing from the northeast, just the way Alice had hoped it would. And there was the pickup truck coming up the lane. Kitty was surprised to see two people in it.

241

"I thought I'd come along," said Alden, hopping out. "Take a holiday." His hands and face were streaked with grease.

"Well, of course," said Kitty. "Why not?" But Alice apparently disapproved of this arrangement. Her mouth was pursed up tight. Kitty climbed in beside her, and Alden got back in and started the engine, backing and turning and heading out to the Polpis Road. He laughed at the chill atmosphere of Alice's disapproval. "Alice is mad because I left things every which away."

"I told him," said Alice, "we had to be out there at low tide, and I couldn't wait, and he suddenly decided he had to come along. He was fixing the car; he was all greasy. The animals haven't even been tended to. He just dropped everything."

"You're not going to find anything in particular, you know, you girls," said Alden, obviously renewing another argument he had been having with his wife. "Just because the tide may be lower than usual, it's hardly worth it. After all, I dredge along the bottom of that harbor all the time, don't forget, and if there were anything special, don't you think I'd find it?"

"How can *you* tell?" said Alice sharply. "By the time you get anything small and fragile up onto that culling board of yours, it would be all smashed. You can't even touch some of those things, or they just disappear."

Alden was furious. He swore under his breath. Alice said nothing. She sat fiercely upright beside Kitty with her hands clasped tightly in her lap. But then she unclasped them, and made an effort, and smiled at Kitty as if to dispel the atmosphere of wrath. She began talking about the jars and buckets she had brought along to put things in, and how Henry Thoreau had collected things in his hat. Kitty knew perfectly well that Alice was really talking to Alden, reminding him that it was Kitty's last day, that they mustn't spoil it.

They drove along the shore of the harbor. At the outlet to Coskata Pond Alden stopped the truck and they all got out. Alden climbed up into the back of the pickup to get the buckets and jars, and Alice whispered to Kitty that she must forgive them for being upset. "Those surveyors are all over the place now, there are more of them every day, and we're both absolutely beside ourselves with worry."

"Tide's low, all right," said Alden, walking up with the buckets. "I don't know when I've seen it this low."

They sat down on the pebbly shingle and took off their shoes. Kitty looked over her shoulder at the small house that belonged to Joe Green, but it was boarded up. Nobody home. She got up and examined the sloping beach. "If the tide is this low now, I wonder how high it went during the night," she said. "All the way up to here, I guess. That's pretty high. I wonder if it washed over Coatue again."

"Washed over?" said Alden, looking at her.

"There between Five-Fingered Point and Bass Point. When I was there in June I saw eelgrass all across that narrow place, as though the water had washed right over from the harbor into the ocean sometime or other. I wouldn't have noticed it if I hadn't been reading about the Haulover, that place on the other side where the tide broke down a big stretch of beach and connected the harbor with the sea, so they could haul their boats right across, way back in the eighteen nineties."

"Can't break through there anymore," said Alden. "The bluff's way too high now."

"But there isn't any bluff over *there*," said Kitty. "Not on Coatue. That little strip of land is narrow, and it's not much above sea level at all. So sometime last spring the harbor had another outlet to Nantucket Sound right there. I felt pretty pleased with myself to notice that. Maybe it will wash over there again this afternoon. Why don't we come back at high tide and see? When will that be? Three o'clock!"

Alice said nothing. And Alden was gone, running ahead of them toward the distant rim of water, swinging his bucket. The water in the harbor was flat and still under the gray sky, a mirror with a planar surface. The wet sand too reflected the sky, but only in parallel ribbons and stripes because it was ribbed like the roof of a dog's mouth.

They came to the end of the open beach and began splashing in the shallows. Alden was wading ahead of them, running back and forth. Alice found a sea worm and scooped it into a jar. Kitty hurt her foot on a broken bottle. She found an old scalloping dredge covered with barnacles. She found a string, a narrow rope, and pulled on it. The rope dragged, then stopped, refusing to give at either end. Somebody's lost mooring, probably. Kitty followed the rope and came upon a long dark object, its shape shifting and changing as the clear waves lapped over it. She picked up the rope again and pulled. The dark shape gave. It loosened itself from the sucking sand and became a heavy weight in air, streaming with trickling sandy water.

It was some kind of gun, some sort of fishing apparatus with a corroded gun barrel. It was a device for killing fish under water, with a spring mechanism to make it fire. Homer had talked about these things. He had been looking for one. Kitty hooked her bucket over her arm, held the spear gun in one hand and pulled the other end of the rope, which was stuck on an encrusted piece of driftwood. She bent down and loosened it. Ow! it was sharp. The sharpness was a rusted metal tip like an arrowhead. "Hey," said Kitty, "look what I found." She lifted the weapon high in her two hands.

Alden and Alice looked up. Then Alden began running toward Kitty. "Wait, Alden," called Alice.

"*Hallooooo!*" There was another shout. It was Homer, standing up in the front of his Scout, waving at them from the shore. He had parked beside the pickup. He was getting out.

They turned and headed for the shore. "Why don't you throw that old thing back?" said Alice. She was at Kitty's shoulder, her hand on the spear gun.

"No, no; I want to show it to Homer," said Kitty.

"Let me carry it," said Alden, slopping up beside her, breathing heavily in her face.

"No, really, I'm all right."

Homer met them halfway. "Say, what have you got there?" he said to Kitty.

Kitty gave him the spear gun. He was delighted with it. "Will you look at that!" he said. "The thing has been tampered with. Wouldn't you say the gun barrel had been added to it, Alden? You know, now that I look at it, I can see it's exactly how you would solve the problem of getting a thing like this to fire straight in air. I think you've made a find, Kitty Clark. This is our lucky day. Where'd you get this thing?"

"Out there in the shallow water," said Kitty, pointing. "We came out today to see what it was like at the time of highest and lowest spring tides, the highest and lowest in six months. The last time it was like this was during the eclipse, remember? At high tide today the water will be really high again. I want to come back to see if it will wash over Coatue, the way it did before."

"It did? You know, it's a miracle the harbor is here at all." Homer drew the wet rope through his fingers and looked at the rusted spear tip. "What do you think, Alden? I swear, I think this must be the thing that killed Helen Green. Somebody must have dumped it out there in the harbor at high tide. Of course we still have no way of knowing whose it was, but maybe it will help to dangle it in front of the jury anyway."

Alden pushed his sunglasses up on his greasy black forehead and stared at the spear gun, then shook his head dumbly.

"Do you suppose it was Spike Grap's?" said Kitty. "The one he said he lost?"

"It could be," said Homer. "Of course his apparatus wasn't doctored up with a gun barrel like this, but whoever stole it could have fixed it up for himself. Of course if we could just find somebody who had a tidy little shotgun from which the barrel had been removed, that would be a tidy little discovery, but I suppose that's asking too much. And we haven't got time to go looking for one now."

Kitty opened her mouth to speak, then stopped and glanced at Alden. Alden met her eye, then looked away. Kitty looked back at Homer, and bit her lip. Alden had a gun without a barrel. She had seen it in the toolshed. Alice knew about it too. And they knew that she knew. And they knew that she knew that they knew. And then a grim memory struck Kitty. Alden had got the gun from Joe. He had said the gunstock in the toolshed came from Joe.

"Well, I'll be on my way," said Homer, climbing back into his truck. "And I'll just take this delightful thing with me, and keep it safe and sound. Listen, Kitty Clark, I came out here to tell you we've got to sit down this afternoon and talk about what's going to happen when they get you up there on the witness stand. How about two o'clock at my place? Matter of fact, right now I'm about to go to church. Congratulate me on my piety."

And then he was off, careering along the open beach in his Scout. Kitty watched him go, encouraged as usual by his colossal self-confidence and by the sheer mass and size of him sticking up out of the front seat. Then she turned around, and found Alice and Alden gone.

That was funny. Where were they? She was all alone with a flock of sanderlings, dipping and soaring over the changing tide, and there were terns skimming along the surface, plunging after little fish. The terns must be the same ones who had dived at her before, but now they were no threat. Their eggs had hatched, or perhaps they had been crushed. The terns had forgotten. They seemed to bear her no ill will.

"Kitty!" Someone was calling her. Someone was walking into the open door of Joe's small house, far away. It would be Alden, of course. Where was Alice? The call came again. *"Kitty!"*

Once bitten, twice shy, thought Kitty, remembering the last time she had tried to enter that house. But Alden was calling her. Amiably she walked along the beach until she came to the sandy wooden steps that led to Joe's front door. There she hesitated a moment, remembering the violence of his rejection on that miserable day in June. *Get out,* Joe had said. *Get out, get out.*

Well, this time she was being invited in. Kitty peered blindly through the open doorway at the darkness, and then slowly, defiantly, she stepped into Bluebeard's chamber.

37

"Go to prayers, d——n you! To prayers,
you rascals—to prayers!"

White Jacket

Homer sat slumped on a narrow bench, staring sleepily at the high seats of the elders at the front of the small gray room where Nantucket's Quakers had sat of old. He was drowsier than he would have thought possible. Beside him Mary was deep in reverie, her head down, her hands crossed in her lap. Was she asleep? Around them in the Meeting sat a score or so of Friends, keeping a profound stillness. Homer wanted desperately to shift his position, but the last time he had tried it, the bench had shrieked in protest. Resignedly he tried to forget his discomfort and his sleepiness and center down like the others, if not on prayerful thoughts, at least upon a vision of the ancient breed of island Quakers who had sat here in the past. They had all been the spiritual descendants of that saintly old lady Mary Starbuck and her husband, Edward, and they had sent their God-fearing young sons out upon the deep in search of whales, and then later on they had excommunicated scores of rebellious boys who took ship on gun-bearing

vessels during the Revolution, and then still later on they had fought among themselves, Hicksites and Wilburites and Gurney-ites, and because of the schisms they had lost ground, and then they had all but disappeared. Now they had revived again, but these gentle people no longer engaged Leviathan. *Oh, God,* thought Homer, *I'm so damned uncomfortable. If I could only think of something spiritual to say I'd get up and stretch.* There! What was that? At last somebody was getting up, scraping back a bench, clearing her throat. Gratefully Homer uncrossed and recrossed his legs and glanced at his wife. Mary stirred, smiled at him, folded her arms across her chest and lowered her head once again to listen.

The speaker was Letty Roper. She had been doing some serious thinking, she said. She was troubled, she said, by the idea of vengeance. Tomorrow a trial was to begin, a trial for murder, and what was a trial, she said, but an act of vengeance? She was deeply troubled by the thought of vengeance. " 'Vengeance is mine, saith the Lord,' " said Letty, and sat down.

Slowly the silence gathered again and filled the room. It was not a mere absence of sound but a positive substance, a collective absorption, a general sober pondering of Letty's concern. The thick quiet went on and on. Homer wondered at it. Would no one else be moved to speak? Quaker Meeting had never been in-tended, he knew, to be a debating society.

Someone was rising, there in the back. There was a creaking of a chair and a dropping of an object and a blowing of a nose and a long explosive clearing of a throat to prepare the members of the Meeting for a quavering sermon from an old man in the last row. It was Obed Biddle. Homer had often encountered Mr. Biddle in the Whaling Museum, and he recognized his voice at once.

Mr. Biddle's inmost thoughts were the Lord's. " 'Moses stretched out his hand over the sea,' " said Mr. Biddle, " 'and the Lord caused the sea to go back by a strong east wind all that night, and made the sea dry land, and the waters were divided. . . .' "

Homer couldn't resist the temptation to turn his head around and look, and he was delighted with what he saw. The old man was taking the part of Moses. One lank arm was outstretched, exposing a dirty shirt cuff, his head was swaying forward, his glittering old eyes were fastened upon the waters of the Red Sea and upon the children of the Israelites standing upon the shore. Mr. Biddle was speaking about the vengeance of the Lord. He was answering Letty Roper's troubled scruples the best way he knew how.

". . . And the people of Israel went into the midst of the sea on dry ground, the waters being a wall to them on their right hand and on their left. The Egyptians pursued, and went in after them into the midst of the sea, all Pharaoh's horses, his chariots, and his horsemen. And in the morning watch, the Lord in the pillar of fire and of cloud looked down upon the host of the Egyptians, and discomfited the host of the Egyptians, clogging their chariot wheels so that they drove heavily, and the Egyptians said, Let us flee from before Israel, for the Lord fights for them against the Egyptians. Then the Lord said to Moses, Stretch out your hand over the sea, that the water may come back upon the Egyptians, upon their chariots, and upon their horsemen! So Moses stretched forth his hand over the sea, and the sea returned to its wonted flow when the morning appeared; and the Egyptians fled into it, and the Lord routed the Egyptians in the midst of the sea. The waters returned and covered the chariots and the horsemen and all the host of Pharaoh that had followed them into the sea; not so much as one of them remained! But the people of Israel walked on dry ground through the sea, the waters being a wall to them on their right hand and on their left. Thus the Lord saved Israel that day from the hand of the Egyptians, and Israel saw the Egyptians dead upon the seashore!"

Mr. Biddle's voice had risen until it was a harsh cry. He sat down at last with a clattering thump of his cane, and the members of the Meeting breathed gratefully and welcomed the silence

251

once again. Homer closed his eyes and allowed himself to be diverted by the oceanographic problem. The whole thing must have been a perfectly natural phenomenon. The east wind and the low tide must have combined to carry the water a long way out from the shore of the Red Sea, and then the people of Israel had been able to scuttle across a shoal that was normally under water, and of course there had been water both to the right of them and to the left. But then later on when the tide was coming back in again, the Egyptians had been tempted to follow, but by now it was too late. Before they knew it they were in the midst of the sea, with their chariot wheels dragging in the mushy sand and the water rising around them. The running tide was coming in fast, engulfing them, drowning them. The same thing could happen right here on Nantucket, if you had a bunch of scampering Israelites and a whole mess of chariots churning across the Old Man Shoal or Great Point Rip.

Homer opened his eyes for a moment, drowsily, then closed them again upon an apocalyptic vision. The pillar of fire and the pillar of smoke that had summoned the children of Israel rose up and up in his mind, twisting together in a mighty pattern of light and dark, rising to the throne of Almighty God, who appeared not as a man but as the sun itself at the staggering instant of total eclipse, mysteriously withdrawing himself behind the black moon ("Look not upon the face of thy God"). And suddenly this vision brought with it a streaming host of concomitant revelations. Perhaps the event described in Exodus had taken place at the time of the spring tide, there at the Red Sea. So it would have been a new moon or a full moon, and it might even have been the highest spring tide of the year, since it had sucked the water out so far and then drawn it back in again so high. It must have been pretty much like the time of the eclipse here on Nantucket. There was an east wind then too, and of course during the eclipse the gravitational attraction of the moon was *precisely* in the same direction as the attraction of the sun. . . .

It was five minutes before the hour in the Quaker Meeting

House. The Meeting now seemed destined to end in silence, and the members of the congregation were composing their thoughts for a final moment of contemplative prayer. But they were reckoning too soon. A madman in the front row was leaping to his feet, moved by as powerful a spirit as had ever possessed him. To his wife's horror and to the dumbfounding of the sober members of the Meeting, Homer Kelly threw both arms in the air and addressed the deity in a thundering roar. *"My God, my God, I see it now. It was the moon. The moon did it, after all. Just the way Kitty said."*

Homer jerked his dazed wife to her feet, dragged her out of the room, and the Meeting broke up in confusion.

38

". . . Stand up amid the general hurricane,
thy one tost sapling cannot, Starbuck!"
Moby Dick

Joe's house was empty. What kind of game was this? Kitty walked slowly to the middle of the room. "Alden?" she said uncertainly. But it was not Alden's presence she felt in the soft incoherent darkness around her. With a rush of dread Kitty became aware of the vengeance of Joseph Green. The place was his, it belonged to him, and he hated and detested her. Then there was a slight noise behind her, and Kitty screamed as the door slammed shut with a great shuddering crash of wood against wood. She ran back to it and rattled the latch, but the door held, and outside there were scraping sounds, and then a succession of jarring thumps as heavy pieces of lumber were shot across the door. They were great two-by-fours—Kitty had seen them on many a Nantucket house that faced the wind. She hammered with her fists on the door, and then shouted for help, her voice hoarse and cold with fear. "Alice? Alden?"

Silence.

Kitty turned her head, listening, looking this way and that for a cranny of light. But the darkness was absolute. Joe had bolted and barred the door. Was there another door at the back? Kitty thought there was, she thought she had seen it when she came in. Slowly she blundered across the room and felt for it and found it. But if the second door had been open before, it was closed now, and latched and bolted and barred like the other. She turned away from it and faced into the black volume of the room.

She had been blinded with one stroke. There had been the bright light and gray air of a clouded morning, and now suddenly she was imprisoned in the dark. But more terrible than the darkness was the menacing presence just outside, the sense of being closed in by walls of loathing as well as by walls of wood.

What did he want with her? What had he done with Alden and Alice? And what would he do with her now? In the midst of her fear Kitty remembered that she had been afraid in the dark like this before. It was the same dread that had engulfed her during the eclipse of the sun. The power of the moon had overcome the world. It had struck her down as it had struck down Helen Green.

Get a light. Stop gibbering. There must be some kind of light in this room. There would be no electricity, but there would surely be a kerosene lantern or a flashlight or something. Kitty shuffled along the wall, padding on her bare feet, feeling her way. She bumped into the back of a wicker chair, edged past it and nudged the edge of a table. Patting her hand over the table, she felt a row of books and a knobbed object that puzzled her until she ran the palm of her hand over the sloping keyboard—a typewriter. Groping further, she found what she was seeking, an erect glassy surface, a lamp chimney! Good. Now all she needed was a match. Kitty patted and patted the table, and fumbled along the wall past the front door and the window and the corner of the room and another window. Then her hand brushed against cobblestones. A fireplace! There would be a mantel, and on the mantel there might be a match. Quickly Kitty's eager fingers ran along the rough cement of the mantel shelf, colliding with a big clumsy object, which fell to the floor with a fluttering thump. There! Now her fingers were closing over a small box. Good, good, it was kitchen matches. With trembling fingers Kitty struck one against the side of the box. The light flared up, and swiftly she held out the match and stared into all four corners of the room. Thank God, she was alone. She began to breathe more easily. Her thumping heart subsided. She struck another match, walked back to the table, and lit the wick of the kerosene lamp. Then she picked up the lamp and carried it around the room with her, looking for an exit. One by one she struggled with the doors and unlocked the windows and heaved them open and thumped at the plywood shutters that covered them on the outside. Nothing gave way. She was locked and barricaded in. Well, then, she would look for something to beat her way out with.

What was that?

Kitty stood still in the middle of the room, the lantern in her hand, listening. Had there been a small sound?

It had stopped. Perhaps she had been mistaken.

She put the lantern on the mantelpiece then, and bent down to pick up the scattered object that had fallen to the floor. Sheets of paper were everywhere. They had tumbled out of a box and slipped under wicker chairs, under the bookcase, into the dead ashes of the fireplace. Patiently Kitty sought them all out, getting down on her hands and knees. She put them in a heap on the table and began straightening the pile. Then she stopped, transfixed by a word that jumped out at her from the topmost sheet of paper. It was her own name, *Kitty*.

She read the entire page. Then, without being able to stop herself, she read the next. It was not in consecutive order, but like the first it was spotted with her name. And what the pages said —it was all true. Those things had really happened. She remembered them clearly, only here they were seen from the other side, from Joe's side. What did it mean that he had written about her? And what, dear God, was he doing to her now?

There! The sound had come again. But it was a different sound this time, a kind of soft rustling, a windy rumbling from under the floor. Kitty turned around, then screamed again.

The house was on fire. Flames were licking up between two of the floorboards, bright tongues of flame. Instinctively Kitty seized a book from the table and slapped at the blazing crack, then thumped at another crack, and another. But it was useless. It was not the floorboards but the supporting timbers under the floor that were on fire, fanned by the wind blowing under the house.

She had to get out. Kitty snatched up one of the andirons from the fireplace and smashed it at the blank wooden surface of the window beside the door. But the solid shutter had been screwed in place, and the screws held. She smashed at another, then dropped the andiron in a fit of coughing. Smoke filled the room. The chimney wall behind Kitty suddenly thundered into a sheet of fire. Reason left her. Shrieking and coughing, she ran from window to window to window, then around again, pounding on them in turn with her fists. Then around again. From window! to window! to window! Then at last she flung herself against the front door, her hair aflame.

The door burst open. Pitching forward, Kitty staggered down the steps and fell. Then she rolled over and over, grinding her hair into the sand, struggling to breathe. At last she lay face down, gasping and shaking, as the cottage began to roar behind her and a streak of flame burst through the chimney and the roof gave way.

She sat up for a moment, shuddering, her eyes weeping, and then she pulled herself to her feet and walked quickly down to the water, wading into it, feeling its cool lapping touch on her bare feet. Then she looked up sharply. Where were Alden and Alice? Had Joe tried to kill them too? The truck was still parked where Alden had left it, but it was empty. Kitty shook herself, and began hurrying along the shore, heading south. She came upon her shoes, and sat down and put them on. Then she looked back at the truck again and saw to her surprise that it was no longer empty. Thank God, there was Alden! He was starting the engine, he was coming her way. Kitty jumped up, shaking with relief, and started running toward him. Alden drove faster, accelerating, charging along the beach in the truck, rushing toward her. Kitty stopped and waited for him. But instead of slowing down to pick her up, Alden revved his engine and plunged at her.

Startled, Kitty stepped back into the water, then flung herself out of his way, drenching herself all over, catching a glimpse of his intent face, his eyes shadowed under the visor of his hat. Now he was turning the truck sharply up toward higher ground, and bounding around in a narrow curve, his tires softly conforming to the shape of the pebbled beach. Now he was plunging at her again. Swiftly Kitty made up her mind. If it were like the terns, if it were like the time the terns had dived at her here in this place last June, then she could simply swim away from danger where the truck could not follow. But it wasn't like that, because Alden could swim after her easily and catch her and hold her under water until she drowned. No, no, she must try something else. Craftily Kitty ran north along the edge of the water, splashing half-in, half-out of the incoming tide. The truck lurched after her, a little higher up the beach, wallowing in the wet sand, sticking, lunging, rearing back and forth to free itself, pulling free with a grinding, rending roar and bucking forward once again. Splash in, splash out, draw him farther to his peril! Kitty was gasping but she couldn't stop to draw breath because the great whining high front of the truck was close behind her. Then suddenly it fell back, and glancing over her shoulder Kitty saw that it was caught once again, caught and held this time, and she darted ahead. Behind her the four wheels of the truck were burying themselves in clay that lay beneath the sand, clay that had fallen from the eroding cliff above the beach, that had lain at the bottom of a lake in glacial times, and now the wheels of the truck were churning and foundering in the clay and miring themselves further and further down.

Kitty was off and away, she was racing for the line of trees at the top of the bluff. Behind her she could hear the engine die, and looking over her shoulder again she saw Alden leap from the cab and stumble in the sand. His head was up, his gaze was upon her fleeing back. But she was up at the top of the bluff now, and deep in the juniper thicket, she was tearing at it, heedless of the clawing branches, making a wedge of her body, her elbows up before her face, thrusting, thrusting, her clothes catching and tearing on the furred bristling stems of the rugosa rose, on the intricate thorns of the cat brier, her arms pricked and lashed by the dense needled branches of the twisted junipers. With all her enfeebled power Kitty butted and shouldered her way through the dwarfed entangled oaks—and the trees fought back at her with the same harsh knotted strength that had netted them together before the wind. They clawed and clutched at her, and soon her arms and legs were slashed and bleeding, but she was hardly conscious of any pain. She was only aware of the sound of branches breaking behind her, of the ripping shove and thrust of the heavy body of Alden, who had more mass and weight and could force his way through faster. Again in this tangled maze he had the advantage. In her panic and confusion Kitty remembered bitterly the pretty lesson she had composed for herself, the vow she had made to thicken and intensify the days and weeks, to make them dense like the trees of the island—and now it was that very density that had caught her, and hedged itself about her. Her only hope was to hide, to find some nest into which she could burrow down, where she could lie very still while Alden went crashing over her, where she could curl herself very small in some dark spiraled chamber that was gathered in upon itself, huddled away from the light. . . .

Alden stopped suddenly beside a dwarf oak that was taller than the rest, and looked up at it, his chest heaving. Then he wiped his arm across his bleeding face and leaped into the sinuous branches. From there he could get a wide view of the treetops, and immediately he was rewarded. There was movement in the tops of the low junipers. Something was disturbing them. She was there ahead of him, circling around to the left. If he went around a little further to the west, then cut across, he would be upon her. . . .

Kitty had found a place at last, a low tent within a wild grapevine that was scrambling up into a red oak tree, and the floor of the tent was softly carpeted with poison ivy and fading ferns. She crawled into it and dropped down, shaking from the outpouring of her adrenal glands. Blood was brimming from a hundred small wounds and scratches, and she felt lightheaded, as though she had been picked up and whirled around by a twisting storm until she had spun her way at last into its dark silent heart. The interlaced twigs of oaks and junipers were tightly woven over her, and there was a cloud of mosquitoes gathering around her head; but looking off to one side she could see the same flock of gray sanderlings she had noticed before, wheeling and dipping over the water as if they were all one creature, as if they had been trained by a dancing master, as if they were moving to a music they alone could hear, as if the tide were swelling and receding in three-quarter time. They had a tricky way of turning so that they all darted into shadow at once and disappeared, and then reappeared together as the gray light struck them all one way. *Come, follow, follow, follow, follow, follow, follow me! Whither shall I follow, follow, follow? Whither shall I follow, follow thee? Dip and soar! Oh, why are you flying without your clothes? And the sanderlings threw up their wings in horror and danced away, while Kitty's fingers moved in the fine gray sand, and the purple blood fell in round droplets that rested on the sand in perfect spherical beads—beautiful!— their rich red color on the fine gray sand.*

39

" . . . What d'ye say?"
"I say, pull like god-dam."

Moby Dick

Homer's euphoria had disappeared, replaced by an uneasy sense of foreboding. He had dropped off Mary at the house on Vestal Street and then he had gone around to Bob Fern's place on the west side of town and picked up Bob, and now the two of them were on their way to Alden's place to wait for Kitty and Alice and Alden, and then of course there were all those things Homer had to go over with Kitty. But first he wanted to sit down with Bob and Alden, all three of them together, and go over the whole thing again. Together they ought to be able to come up with the name of somebody in the Nantucket Protection Society who might have called Dankbinkel last winter, somebody who would then have had a reason for killing Helen Green. Somebody who might also have taken a boat across Coatue from the harbor to Nantucket Sound, across that place between Bass Point and Five-Fingered Point that Kitty had discovered, where the water had washed right over.

"Homer, tell me how that went again," said Bob Fern, "that part about the Red Sea and the eclipse of the sun. You said the moon did it, just the way Kitty said. I don't think I've got it straight in my own mind."

"The moon did it because it eclipsed the sun, don't you see? Not only did it make the island dark enough for murder but it created the highest tides of the season, and lifted the water right up over Coatue."

"Yes, I understand that. But what about the crossing of the Red Sea? What does that have to do with it?"

"Because it's just the same, don't you see? It says in Exodus that there was a strong east wind all night, just the way there was here, and it did the same thing it did here—it increased the normal effect of the tide. And here on Nantucket the moon and the sun and the storm together raised up the water till it came close to the very foot of the lighthouse, and together they lifted the harbor up and over the barrier to Nantucket Sound. So somebody went straight across Coatue from the harbor and headed up the Sound for Great Point and shot Helen Green at the instant of total darkness. But then the damn fool made a fatal mistake. He slipped back across Coatue into the harbor and dropped the spear gun over the side where he thought the water was deep enough, forgetting how far out the tide would go that very day. The thing must have lain there exposed to view that selfsame day! Only nobody saw it. And nobody would have discovered it at all, if it hadn't been for Kitty's determination to go out there again precisely six months later at the next time of highest and lowest tides. And then of course it happened for Kitty the way it happened for the Israelites. God made the sea dry land, and she walked across it in the midst of the sea. And bless her heart, she found that thing I left locked up on the back seat of the Scout. Blast those guinea hens. Do you see Alden's truck anyplace?"

"No, just Alice's car. I guess they're not back yet." Homer and Bob Fern got out and stood beside Alden's toolshed looking around. The two brown goats came running up to the edge of the fenced-in pasture and stared at them, bleating.

"Look at that," said Bob. "Look at that poor nanny's milk bag. I'll bet nobody milked her this morning. And say, Homer, Jupiter's gone."

"Well, good for him," said Homer. "He must have flapped up over the fence. I wonder if Alice knew. She didn't mention it this morning. Listen to the dogs! What are they making such a racket for?"

"Maybe they're after Jupiter," said Bob. He ran behind the house and found two of the dogs barking at one of Alice's cats, which was hissing at them from the top of the laundry pole, its claws dug in, its fur on end. Bob shooed away the dogs and rescued the cat, and Homer rushed off to the chicken shed, where a third dog was yipping in a high treble above a tremendous angry squawking of furious hens. The air inside the shed was full of feathers. Frightened chicks were tumbling around in the incubator, and the hens were hurling themselves at poor Fly, who was yelping in a corner.

Somebody had left the door open. "Here, boy," said Homer. "Good dog." He batted his way through flapping wings and took hold of Fly's collar and dragged him out, glancing up to make sure there was no great white swan perched in the rafters. Then he slammed the door between himself and Fly and went back to take another look. *What was that?* There was a shotgun in the rafters. Homer reached up and snatched it down. It was a shotgun from which the barrel had been removed.

Bob Fern had been mildly surprised at being dragged away from his lunch by a man babbling incoherently about the moon and the crossing of the Red Sea. Now he was further stunned when Homer burst out of the chicken shed shouting at the top of his lungs, cursing himself for a blind fool, hurling himself into his car. Backing up, he almost ran into Bob, who was trying to dodge around the car and get in the other side. "My God," cried Homer, "I left them all out there together. It was Alden, Bob, it was Alden—it was as plain as the nose on my face all the time

—and I went off and left him there with Kitty. Christ in blazes, we can't go out there in this thing. I've got to go back to town for the Scout. God damn it, Fern, she found the spear gun. He didn't like it when she found the spear gun. I saw his face! I should have recognized his face!"

"Alden's face?" said Bob politely. "You recognized Alden Dove?" Bob's head crashed against the windshield as Homer jammed on the brakes at the intersection of the driveway with the Polpis Road, and Bob clenched his teeth and groaned.

"The *Andrea Doria!*" shouted Homer. "Good God, Bob, Alden was a diver, he went down to that sunken liner, the *Andrea Doria*. And his partner had an accident, he died in the attempt. It was in the paper, Alden's photograph, with black grease on his face, and it wasn't until I saw him just now, and there was grease on his face again, and it was all contorted with some kind of trouble, and there was something else—I know, he had his glasses pushed up on his forehead just like the diver's mask." Homer was gesturing wildly with one hand to show Bob, and the car was veering all over the Polpis Road. "The two faces were one and the same. The diver was Alden! Alden Dove!"

"Try Joe Green's place," said Bob Fern quickly. "He's got a jeep. You wouldn't have to go all the way back to town. Here, here, slow down, this is his driveway."

"Good for you, Bob. Good for you. God damn his soul in hell if the jeep's not there."

The jeep was there. And so was Joe Green himself, running to open the door as Homer's car roared up and shrieked to a stop. Homer shouted at him, and Joe rushed out of the house and threw himself into the jeep. Homer and Bob Fern jumped from the car into the jeep as Joe backed it up, and Homer nearly fell out again as it gathered speed down the driveway. Joe burst out onto the Polpis Road without slowing down. He said nothing. His eyes were alight, his galvanized hands gripped the wheel.

"I'll feel like a fool if we meet them on the road," shouted Homer, straining forward in the bucket seat. But there was no

The Polpis Road

great lumbering vehicle coming their way on the Polpis Road. There was nobody on the road at all until they stopped at the air pump at Wauwinet to lock the front wheel hubs and get the jeep into four-wheel drive. The Nantucket Fire Department was there before them, a bunch of men in rubber coats and boots, letting the air out of the tires of one of their pumping trucks.

"Fire somewhere?" yelled Homer, tumbling out of the jeep.

"Column of smoke," said the fire chief. "Big pillar of smoke off there at the Head of the Harbor."

Bob Fern and Homer were wrenching at the tires with a screwdriver and a tire iron, while Joe Green kept the engine throbbing and pulsing, one hand on the knob that controlled the four-wheel drive. He whammed it into place as they jumped back in the jeep, and they were off again, bounding along the sandy track in the wake of the fire engine, which had a good head start.

They could see the smoke now, off to the left. "It's my shack," said Joe. He was driving now like a crazy man. The jeep was jolting from crest to crest of the washboard track, and the three men inside it rose and fell on the hard seats, bucking up and slamming down. At the place where the road forked Joe whirled the steering wheel and they bore down on the fire truck. Men were dropping off the running boards, snatching at the hoses, coupling them together, shouting at each other, running around the smoldering shack.

"My God, what's the use," moaned Homer, climbing down, sick at heart.

The roof had fallen in. If Kitty had been in there she would have been crushed to death. Homer and Bob Fern stumbled around the house to the beach, but Joe began attacking the smoking timbers with his bare hands, lifting them, wrenching them out of the hold of the nails, heaving them aside. The fire chief rushed at him, shouting, "Get away from there, you fool. It's no use."

Bob Fern found the pickup truck in the rising water of the tidal stream that flowed from Coskata Pond. The tide was swirling around the hubs of the tires. Bob waded out to it with Homer. "My God, what's it doing here?" cried Homer. "Something's wrong. He would never have left it here."

Bob was splashing back to the shore, he was standing and turning, examining the stretch of beach that ran around to Coatue, looking out over the water, twisting swiftly around to stare at the bluff, where Joe was climbing up, clawing at roots and clumps of beach grass.

It was Joe, therefore, who found the broken place in the massed barrier of tangled juniper, and the fragments of torn cloth clinging to twigs and thorns. The trail was little more than a succession of snapped stems and broken branches, but he thrust himself along it, shouting, *"Kitty, Kitty."*

Dimly Kitty heard her name. Someone was calling, "Kitty, Kitty!" Surely the man who was standing over her was not calling her name, because the call was far away, and he was nearby. She could feel his presence, hear his breathing, but she didn't want to open her eyes and look at him. She just wanted to burrow her head still farther down into the ground and listen to the distant music of her name, which was coming closer and closer, accompanied by percussive noises, brittle and sharp, snapping and crashing like drums and castanets, like marble lids falling back and shivering into chips and shards.

Kitty woke up suddenly, rolled her head back, and saw Alden and Joe. And Joe was looking at Alden, his torn face full of joy. Joe's bleeding hands gripped the trunks of two trees like the hands of Samson in the temple of Dagon. Alden was bleeding too. There were red gashes all over his arms and face. The two men seized one another like dogs and fell cruelly into the underbrush, and Joe's arm was around the other's neck, lifting and pounding the gray face into the ground. Then the man underneath rolled away and staggered to his feet and crashed off through the thorny trees, lurching and falling, and they could hear the breaking of branches as he stumbled through them, growing fainter and fainter until there was no sound but that of their own voices, murmuring one another's names over and over.

Bob Fern saw them coming out of the woods, and he started toward them, but he couldn't bear to look at their faces. She was all right, thank God. The hell with the rest of it, as long as she was safe. Then Bob saw something else, and he shouted at Homer. Alden Dove was there, in plain sight, a hundred yards away, leaping up into the back of his truck, snatching something out of it, jumping down and running up the shore of the tidal stream in the direction of Coskata Pond. Bob and Homer took off after him, but Alden was too quick for them. When they came pounding up to the shore of the pond he was nowhere to be seen, and when they ran around the pond to the Atlantic shore on the other side they saw nothing but the sanderlings skimming and darting over a seamless lapping of small waves where a man weighted down with steel tire chains had gently lowered himself below the surface of the water. The slight disturbance was of no interest to the sanderlings after all, and they soared away to continue their dancing flight in another place.

40

*"Oh, oh! Yet blindfold, yet will I talk to
thee. . . ."*

Moby Dick

Letter from Joseph Green to Katharine Clark, written June 24,
delivered September 3:

Kitty, you have just been at my door and I have turned you away.
Oh, Kitty, there were a couple of boats out in the harbor. They
were full of people with telescopes and field glasses. They were
following your every move. They could do you more harm than the
terns. The terns won't hurt you, Kitty. Oh, Kitty, Kitty, the only
way I can love you is to hate you. I recite that lesson over and over
to myself, so that I won't by force of desire snatch at you in the
street or fall on my knees in front of you in a public place. I have
trained myself to turn away from water when I am thirsty and from
food when I am hungry so that I may get used to a world turned
upside down. Every bone in my body wants to hurl itself into your
defense, to throw itself in the way of the machine that is grinding
and tearing at you, and yet the only way I can help you is to remove
myself, to stay far away, to keep up the pretense that I want

vengeance for the death of my wife. Otherwise—and this is what I must beat and beat and beat into my head—if I were to approach you, if I were to show any trace of tenderness toward you, it would only give credence to their conclusion that you had a reason for coming to that place to kill Helen. Therefore I am compelled to show myself the coward, over and over and over again, and draw back as if to protect myself from some vile association, as if to show that I had no part in any kind of plot between you and me. All I can do, and it is little enough, is to put someone else in my place to help you, and to try to depend on him. But sometimes he infuriates me, Kitty, he is so slow, so clumsy! But I suppose I don't know what else I would do if I were in his shoes.

Kitty, Kitty, when I saw you standing over Helen's body I understood in that instant in one shock of revelation as if a thunderbolt had halted every life process and charged it with one purpose and drenched it with one thought that from then on I would have to strangle every natural impulse to go to you, to hold you, to comfort you; that to truly love you I must make you hate me.

Oh, Kitty, the worst thing is to see your sober face.

Kitty looked up. "I never hated you. If I looked sober I was just struggling to keep my dignity. Loving you was just a big gloomy fact. It was a kind of stupid lodger I couldn't get rid of."

They were walking along the shore of the harbor at Quaise. Joe gripped Kitty's hand painfully. He took another letter from a thick packet of them in his pocket and gave it to her. It was dated July 1.

Kitty, today when I saw you going into the Whaling Museum in that ridiculous long coat I ached for you so badly I followed you in, and I think I would have made a fool of myself in front of all those people and ruined everything if you had not run away. I no longer trust myself.

Perhaps it is idiotic to try to tell you about Helen. Probably you don't give a damn what happened between me and Helen. But I have to tell you just the same that it didn't take me long to come to my senses and see her in comparison with the true soul I had lost, to discover that the stupefying golden vision that had come floating to me across the moors was nothing more than that, only a vision. Being a golden vision was Helen's stock in trade, it was her profession. Oh, of course it is true that the island and her ancestral heritage were important to her, but only as a background for what had become more and more a public performance. At home when I refused to be an audience of one I discovered that there was nothing left of her but petulance. It was a wretched awakening. I told her we should never have been married, that I had made a mistake. But she kept saying that I was being ridiculous, that I should wait, that she knew I'd change my mind. We were blundering along somehow, going from bad to worse. And all the time I wanted to turn time backward, to go back to you. But I knew you were not someone to whom I could go with glib apologies and sad stories. So I wrote a book for you instead. It was your book, not Helen's. It was a kind of long crazy letter addressed to you.

"I never read your book," murmured Kitty, looking up.

"Well, why should you? I should have guessed. I suppose I assumed out of vanity you would read anything I wrote."

"I thought it was what everyone said—I thought it was about Helen. I was afraid it would make me unhappy."

"Read on," said Joe grimly.

And then when Bird gave me your poem "Joseph's Coat" I was beside myself. . . .

"Bird?" said Kitty, looking up in horror. "He didn't! When? When did he give it to you?"

"The day before the eclipse, in all that rain and wind. He popped out of a bush beside the door with his big black umbrella, and slipped me an envelope and said, 'I think you might be interested in this,' or something of the sort. I almost threw it back in his face, but then I didn't. I could forgive him almost anything because he was a student of yours, and sometimes he told me things about you, and then I would try to jump over his perversions of them and see you clear."

Kitty was mystified. "But where did he get it? If he had it the day before the eclipse, before I came to the island at all, then it wasn't the one the police found afterwards in my apartment. And there weren't any other copies of it. Unless—aha. Now I know. He took it out of my wastebasket. I had my students in for dinner. *That's* where he got it. I threw the first attempts away. They were even worse than the one the police found on my desk."

"Worse? Oh, Kitty, you don't know what it meant to me. I thought it was your answer to the book I had written to you, don't you see? I was a fool."

In one way your poem made me miserable because I could see so horribly clearly what I had done to you, but at the same time it overwhelmed me with joy to know that in spite of that you still seemed to love me. That night I couldn't sleep, I was so glad because of it. I walked around with it all night. And then at the lighthouse I was still so full of the thought of you that when I saw you running across the sand I felt I had evoked you. I didn't know what was going to happen, but I didn't care. And then afterwards, after we found you with Helen's body and I knew that to go near you was to condemn you, I remembered "Joseph's Coat." Kitty, I had lost it! The night before, walking on the beach, I had lost it! And I knew that if they found it you would be in even more danger than before. And now, oh, Kitty, I know they have it, because they've asked me what I think you meant. What have I done to you? From the very beginning I've blundered cruelly in and out of your life.

"*You* have blundered into *my* life? Oh, Joe." Kitty threw her head back and laughed. "And you were wrong about that awful ballad. They had it already. They had taken it from my desk."

Joe turned to her and kissed the scratches on her sunburned cheek. "Do you know what I missed most? It was the way you laugh. I kept remembering the time my sink backed up, and you fixed it, and you kept making jokes about it, remember? 'Forward, turn forward, O slime in thy flight! Let Joe have a drain again, just for tonight!' I thought of you with that rubber plunger in your hand more than anything else."

"Now there's a compliment for a sensitive and beautiful woman."

"Oh, Kitty." Joe kissed her with a thirst he seemed unable to slake, and Kitty closed her eyes. When she opened them again she saw Jupiter. There was no mistaking him. He was beating his way strongly against the longshore wind, his body tipped slightly to balance his left wing. Now he was changing the direction of his flight, banking so that the sunlight lay in downy patterns on his breast, heading inland, steadying his wings in a long descent until he was an arc of purest white against the dark jack pines.

Kitty and Joe pursued him. "He's coming down in the pond beyond the house," said Kitty.

Sure enough. When they skirted the shore and peered through the cattails and marsh grass and pickerelweed, they could see him skimming on the glassy surface of the pond, rising to flap his wings heavily and descend again near the opposite shore. And then they saw the reason why he was there. A woman in a man's old jacket and a pair of rubber boots was wading out into the shallows, holding out her hand to him. It was Alice Dove.

41

. . . Thou hast been a Man . . . that the Lord has been near, and favoured with many Openings, and if thou hadst been faithful to the Gift of God thou mightest have been serviceable, but thou has been unfaithful, and a Cloud has come over thee, and thou art laid aside as useless.

JOHN RICHARDSON,
Quaker evangelist in Nantucket, 1701

A couple of days later Kitty went to Vestal Street and Homer read aloud to her the deposition Alice had written for Police Chief Pike.

I swear that what I have written in my own hand is the truth.
Alice M. Dove.

Mr. Pike tells me Homer guessed about Alden and the *Andrea Doria.* It's true, Alden was one of the divers on that salvaging expedition that ended so badly. He had been a frogman in the Navy, and he was an expert spear fisherman too, there at Pearl Harbor where he was stationed. So afterwards he joined that expedition that was going after the money and jewels in the *Andrea Doria.* But the diving was too dangerous and they couldn't see anything, and they had to keep fighting off sharks. And then the accident happened. It was Alden's fault. On the very last dive he thought he had blasted his way into the ship's vault at last. He had a locked box in his hand, and he was convinced it had all the money in it, all the passengers' money, all the millions of dollars they had put in the safe. And then the other diver yanked at him, and jerked Alden's arm. All he meant was, that it was time to go back to the surface, but he made Alden drop the box, and it sank down and disappeared. Alden was so enraged he grabbed the other man and tore out his breathing apparatus, and the poor man drowned.

After that Alden never dived again. He only spent a year in prison because his crime was judged to be manslaughter, not murder. When he got out he changed his name (it wasn't Alden Dove before), and he came to Nantucket to live. For a while he worked on somebody else's scalloping boat, until he could make a down payment on his own, and then he met me in the bank when he was arranging the loan. Somehow we hit it off right away, and decided to get married, and then we bought our place at Polpis. It's meant everything to the two of us, that place of ours, heart and soul.

I've always felt lucky to be married to Alden, timid spinster that I was, and we've been pretty happy together on the whole. Before we were married he said he had to get something off his chest, and he told me about the *Andrea Doria* expedition and what happened then. He had always had a violent temper, he said, and it was a curse, and he was trying to get over it. After we were married I felt sorry at first that we didn't seem able to have any children, but when I saw what Alden was like on his bad days I decided it was just as well. He was afraid of his temper himself, and whenever he had one of these attacks he was always miserable about it afterwards. He only laid a hand on me once, when I crossed him about something, but I gave back as good as I got, and I swear he never touched me after that. But he took out his feelings on things, time and time again. You'd think one kick at something would be enough, but that just seemed to feed his anger. He wouldn't be content until he'd broken it. He was good as gold in between, and we both thought he was getting over it, he was doing so well. But then this matter of Helen Green's land came along.

As soon as she announced that plan of hers, to set up a conservation trust all around us, Alden began to worry. He wanted to be sure it was going to be just what she said it was. Well, the more he looked into it, the more suspicious he got, and he went to Boston to look at the deed, and then he called up that Swiss bank and found out that Helen was doing something wrong, but he wasn't sure what. So he told me to look in Helen's safe deposit box and see if I could learn anything. Of course that was pretty tricky. I had to steal her keys when we were at a meeting together and copy them—it was something like making casts of birdtracks—and I copied all of them. And then one day I snatched a chance to look in her box, although I almost got caught at it. What I learned was pretty bad, the arrangement she was making with Harmony Hotels.

Well, I went home and told Alden. I was crying, I was so mad. His face turned white, and he didn't say a word. He just went out and walked all over Helen's land for hours. When he came back he had made up his mind. And it was soon after that that her accidents began. Alden didn't tell me, but when that railing collapsed under Helen I remembered that he had gone off the night before with the wrecking bar in his hand, and I guessed he had pried the nails loose from the porch. I was horrified. But the very next day I saw what Helen did to Jupiter, and I made up my mind I wouldn't try to get in Alden's way, because she was doing such terrible things. Oh, of course when she ran over Jupiter's mate it was an accident, I could see that. She was driving too fast. But then she got out of the car and picked up an oar from a dory that was lying there beside the marsh, and then she started hitting the bird with it, because the poor thing wasn't dead yet. And then when Jupiter rushed at her she hit him with it too. She broke the oar, she hit him so hard. Joe knows. He came running down the hill from the house. But by that time Helen had the shotgun out of the car and she was spraying buckshot at Jupiter with it. She would have killed him if Joe and I hadn't stopped her. Joe gave the gun to Alden later on, because Helen was using it on the dogs that came around the house.

So Alden kept trying one thing after another. But nothing seemed to work. The time that was left before the paper was to be signed was getting short, and Helen was still alive. And then Alden found out to his dismay that he had only one chance left, because Joe told him Helen had gone to Martha's Vineyard, and she was coming back only just in time to see the eclipse at Great Point. So Alden knew he would have to kill her on that very day. And of course the first thing he thought of was those two minutes of darkness. So he worked it all out in his mind, how to go about it. And afterwards he told me what he had done. The first thing was to help himself to Spike Grap's scuba-diving equipment and spear gun when he was at Spike's house delivering eggs. Then he transferred the barrel of Helen's shotgun to the spear gun, and practiced with it over at Mr. Biddle's place, because the house was empty, and nobody was there. Then he fixed up some things to make his boat look different. He cut some big boards to the right measure and painted them with fast-drying paint—it was that barn red we used on the chicken shed—and then he made some false cardboard numbers to paste over the Coast Guard numbers on the bow. And then he saved up scallops. That was really clever of Alden. For several days he hid half his catch under water at a sheltered place in Haulover Pond, so the scallops just kept on accumulating.

And then there was the big storm the night before the eclipse; he hadn't expected that. So when he went out into the harbor the next morning, pretending he was just going scalloping as usual, he discovered that the water was right up over Coatue, and he got the idea of going across to Nantucket

Sound right there. He wouldn't have to be seen going out through the jetties at all. He could just lift off his engine and pole his way across Coatue. So that's what he did. And then he took off the winch and the culling board and set up his big box—he just put the painted boards together with a few screws so that his boat looked like a cabin cruiser. Then he put on the scuba equipment and greased his face black so if anybody saw him sticking his head out of the water they wouldn't know who he was. And then he just headed for Great Point, put down his anchor and swam under water across the Rip and down the Atlantic side until he was near the lighthouse.

And then two things almost ruined his plan. First, there were so many people there, when he hadn't expected to see anybody but Helen and Joe. Second, it had never occurred to him they would have a key to the lighthouse and would disappear inside, but they did. But it didn't matter after all, because Helen came out again, not once but twice. So he had two shots at her. He missed the first time, and he was disgusted because he thought it was his last chance. But then she appeared for the second time, and Alden could see her silhouetted clearly against the light around the horizon. He shot at her again. This time he didn't miss. And then he just swam back to his boat and headed for Coatue and poled across that narrow place again. This time he had to wait for a couple of small planes to stop circling around overhead, and then he had to wait some more for Bob Fern's boat to go back to Straight Wharf, because it was right there at the Head of the Harbor. But after he got across Coatue, he just took the box off the boat and put his winch back on, and dropped the weapon over the side (of course that was a mistake, and it haunted him afterward; he was afraid somebody would dredge it up, and he kept trying to dredge it up himself, but he never did)—and then he went right to Haulover Pond and picked up his bags of scallops. And then he went back to the wharf and showed his catch to Charley Piper, and

Charley was impressed. So of course it was like an alibi: he'd been in the harbor all that time, working hard to get such a big catch at the end of the season.

So that's all. Of course it was a help that Homer was there in our house, because we knew what he was up to—like the time Boozer Brown hid that piece of Joe Green's car: Alden just went over there and took that case of beer.

There's one more thing I want to say, I've been so miserable about it. I worked against Alden without realizing it. Taking Kitty out there to the very spot in the harbor where he'd thrown the spear gun over the side! I never guessed he would have dropped it where it would show up at low tide. If she hadn't found the spear gun he would never have tried to kill her, and then maybe she would have come through that trial all right. Of course when Alden asked me for the key to Joe's shack I had no idea what he was about to do, so I gave him all the keys I'd copied from Helen's key ring, and one of them fitted. But when I saw what he was doing to Kitty, trapping her in there, starting a fire with kerosene, I couldn't stand it, hearing her scream. I unlocked the door to let her out and then I ran away and started walking home, crying my eyes out, keeping away from the beach and from the road. And then at home I discovered Jupiter was gone. So I put some cracked corn in my pocket and went looking for him, walking all over the island from one pond to another. I used to do the same thing when I was a girl. I slept two nights in Ram Pasture beside Hummock Pond. And at last there he was, coming down right near that place at Quaise where Helen Green had almost killed him. So we had come full circle.

And another thing. Before he left the house on the day of the eclipse, Alden told me to remove all those documents from Helen Green's safe deposit box. Well, I knew just how to do it. The bank was open that day because of the influx of visitors to the island, so I was right there doing my job. And then when everybody went outdoors to see the eclipse I ducked back inside the bank with my copy of Helen's key. There was nothing to it. It was just as though everybody had been struck blind or put to sleep for two minutes. I could have done anything.

I took the papers home and Alden burned them. So Helen never signed them. What will happen to that land of hers now? If this awful mess has been for nothing it will break my heart. Well, it's broken anyhow.

That's all I have to say.

Alice Dove

P.S. I forgot to mention what happened to the box Alden made for his boat. He set it up in Jupiter's pen and Jupiter's been living in it ever since.

P.P.S. And one more thing. That paperweight we've got with our initials on it, AD   it's not really our initials, of course. That chunk of Italian marble was the only thing Alden was able to bring up from that sunken luxury liner. It's a souvenir of the *Andrea Doria.*

42

"There she blows! there! there! there!
she blows! she blows!"
"Where-away?"

Moby Dick

Bob Fern came over to the house on Vestal Street at dawn to help
Mary and Homer get their stuff to the boat. He had insisted they
get up early because he had a couple of things he wanted to show
them, he said.

The first was a rumpled tabloid called *The Naked Truth.*
Homer and Mary goggled at the front-page picture of a grinning
Arthur Bird with—good God, could it be Helen Green? It was
Helen Green. Sometime or other the damn fool had succeeded
in having his picture taken with Helen Green. The headlines that
went with the picture were staggering.

"I WAS AN INSTRUMENT OF DESTINY!"

FINAL SECRETS OF MURDERED WOMAN REVEALED

Intimate Family Friend Was Confidant of Helen Green
ARTHUR BIRD BEGINS FIVE-PART SERIES IN THIS ISSUE:

It was I who told Helen Green about the other woman in her husband's life. Two weeks before her death Helen came to me. She had discovered the truth about his *literary infidelity*. She knew that his novel had been written about *another woman*. Therefore *it was I* who told her all I knew about Joe Green's BLAZING ROMANCE. *It was I* who knew Kitty Clark had been his wife in all but name, that she still wanted Joe, that she was coming to claim her own on the very day of the eclipse, the day that was *destined to be* Helen Green's last day on earth.

(STORY page 6)

"It was *you*, you goddamned interfering snoop, you creep, you bastard, it was *you* who did your damnedest to drag everybody down into the dirt you wallow in. Destiny, bullshit! Destiny's stool pigeon!" Homer dropped the paper on the floor and jumped on it.

"Me too," said Mary. She jumped up and down beside Homer.

"Move over," said Bob. The whole house shook. Bob sat down on a box labeled PANKHURST. "It explains one thing anyhow," he said. "Why Helen was running around the island that morning, going to the observatory and Altar Rock and so on. She was looking for Kitty."

"That's right, so it does," said Homer. "She was going to tell her to get lost. And that's why she was in such a hurry to meet Kitty at the lighthouse. She wasn't going to invite her up. She was just going to say, 'It's my bloody husband and my bloody lighthouse and my bloody island and my bloody sun, moon and stars, so, sister, you can just bloody well get the hell out.' And another thing—Joe told me somebody had broken into his shack and thrown the first draft of his novel around. It must have been Helen. She had a copy of his key, we know that. So it *was* Bluebeard's chamber. And Bluebeard's wife went into the forbidden room and discovered the corpse of his dead love right there in the shape of that first draft of Joe's novel, the one that had Kitty's name all through it. Aha!"

Mary leaned over and picked up *The Naked Truth*. "Does anybody want this anymore?"

281

"Hell, no," said Homer.

"Well, then, help me tear it up. I'm going to flush it down the john."

Bob Fern wanted to show them something else. So after they had loaded all of Mrs. Pankhurst into his car and all the rest of the boxes and suitcases into Homer's Chrysler, he said, "Follow me," and drove ahead of them down the Polpis Road. There he pulled up in a familiar place among the weedy grass and sweet fern growing beside Alice Dove's mailbox. They all got out and walked along the driveway until Bob suddenly said, "In here," and ducked to one side into the undergrowth. There was a narrow path heading off to the right.

It led to the Hidden Forest. Mary and Homer found themselves standing in a mossy hollow among thick trunks and heavy branches mottled with patches of red light from the rising sun. The dappled shade was lucid and serene.

"It was here all the time," said Mary. "Think of that. Places

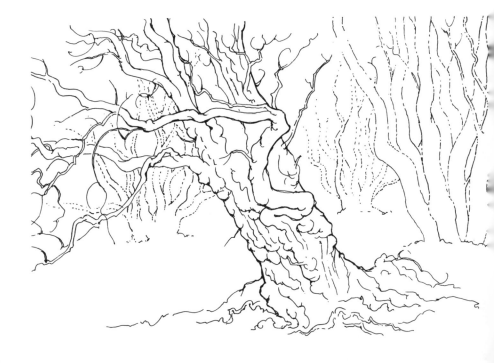

like this can make you feel foolish, the way they go on quietly existing while you're running around frantically somewhere else, warning everybody the sky is falling down."

"Well, maybe they go on existing, and then again maybe they don't," said Homer. "Isn't the Hidden Forest part of Helen Green's property? What in the hell is going to happen to it, Fern?"

Bob Fern grinned at Homer. "That's what I wanted to tell you." He turned and led them out of the grove of trees to the top of a hill from which they could look out over the moor. The risen sun shone pinkly on Bob's face and glittered on the polished leaves of the scrub oaks and made of every red-leaved shrub a burning bush as far as the eye could see. The fine hairs of the amber-colored grass gave back the color of the sky, and there were constellations and companies of asters and throngs of goldenrod, the scarlet hips of the rugosa rose sparkling among them like foreign stars. Far away on the horizon, a long low line was too blue and flat to be anything but the sea. "It doesn't have to go through probate court," said Bob. "Because the land wasn't Helen's to sell. It was Joe's all the time."

"What?" said Homer. "Joe's? But Helen inherited it!"

"That's what everybody thought. But they were wrong. The land was Joe's. He told me about it yesterday. He didn't know anything about it either, until he came to the island that first time to attend the funeral of his old Boatwright relative, and met Helen. Since he and Helen were the sole survivors, they went through all her grandfather's papers together, and they came upon this old deed that made it very plain that his side of the family had *bought out* her side a couple of generations back. The exchange had never been filed in the Registry, but the paper was legal, all right. So Helen had never owned the land at all. Well, when she understood that, she got to work on Joe and bowled him over and hogtied him and got the two sides of the family united in wedlock. So then, of course, they owned the land jointly. And then Joe wanted to put the land into a conservation trust that would keep it the way it was forever, but Helen didn't want any part of it. After a while he thought he had persuaded her, and she said she'd go along with the whole thing if he'd give her power of attorney, and she'd make it her special project and take care of the whole thing. And then of course she made this secret deal with Harmon. But she's gone, and the land is Joe's. So it's going to be all right! All this." Impulsively Bob reached down and broke off a milkweed pod from a dry stalk and blew at the gossamer seedlings that clung to it, ready for flight.

Mary caught one, then let it fly again. "Thank God," she said.

Homer gaped at Bob. "Jesus," he said. "No kidding? What's Joe going to do with it? I wonder if he's made up his mind."

The sunlight was shining through the floating wisps of thistle-down, catching on the finespun polished threads. One of the seedlings caught in Bob Fern's hair and glistened there like a sign of special favor. "Well, it just so happens," he said, "that I know what he's going to do with it. They asked me over for lunch, you see, yesterday, Joe and Kitty, there at Mr. Biddle's place. And Joe told me he's going to put the whole thing into a nature conser-vancy district. That means there won't even be any picnic tables or parking lots for tourists. Just jack rabbits and white-tailed deer and goldenrod and milkweed and—and me."

"You?" said Homer. "What do you mean, you?"

"They want me to be the caretaker. Joe's going to set up a fund to pay the caretaker's salary and finance any little researches he might like to make, and the caretaker is supposed to live there in Helen's house and be a host to people who might want to do studies on populations of grasses or quail or anything like that. Joe and Kitty want it to be a real Nantucket-run kind of place, they said, and that's why they asked me, instead of somebody from the mainland with a long string of degrees, which is the kind of person they really ought to have. But you'll notice I didn't say no."

"Oh, Bob," said Mary, "that's wonderful."

"Well, say, Bob," said Homer, "that relieves my mind. I didn't know what the hell you were going to do with yourself. That's just great."

They walked back to the cars. Mary crouched down and tried to fit herself into the front seat again between mounds of clothing and a box full of tennis shoes, half a loaf of bread, a jar of honey and a quart of milk. She looked soberly at the name DOVE on the mailbox beside the car, and leaned out the window. "What's going to happen to Alice now?" she said.

"Oh, don't worry about Alice," said Homer. "I don't think the district attorney is going to bother his head with Alice Dove. Right, Bob?"

"That's what I've heard," said Bob. "I hope it's true, because she'd be a big help with this new conservancy district. She knows more about the flora and fauna of Nantucket than anybody else on the island. She's still got her job at the Pacific National Bank, I know that. Dick Roper told me he didn't see any reason for firing her. Of course he knows now that she stole those papers from that safe deposit box of Helen's, right there in his own bank, but he's still so horrified by what Helen did that Alice's misbehavior doesn't hold a candle to it." Bob laughed. "I forgot to tell you about the last meeting of the Helen Green Society. They were really in a sweat. The first thing they did was change their name back to the Nantucket Protection Society so fast the gavel in Mr. Tillinghast's hand fairly smoked."

It was time to go. At Steamboat Wharf the boat was already swarming with passengers. Bob and Mary and Homer lugged Emmeline Pankhurst to the top deck, and then Mary sat down on the boxes while Homer drove the car on board. He rejoined his wife just as the boat whistle shrieked and the big crowded vessel began to slip away from its mooring. Together they stood at the railing waving at the diminishing figure of Bob Fern and looking up at the gray town rising beyond the wharf, rooftop above rooftop. The morning sun shone on the gold-domed cupola of the Old South tower and on the pointed steeple of the Congregational Church and cast an immense long shadow of the boat over the rows of houses behind the Brant Point light. One of the children at the railing shouted, "Look," and they turned to see cormorants perched on the end of the jetty, where pale green lights blinked on and off, and on and off, growing paler as the sun rose higher in the sky.

"Why, Mr. Kelly," said someone at Homer's elbow, "I don't believe you've introduced me to your wife."

It was Mrs. Magee.

Homer pinched his wife's arm and jerked her forward, eager to make amends for the terrible things he had thought about Wilhelmina Magee in the recent past. "Mrs. Magee, my wife! Mary, dear, Mrs. Magee!"

"Why, Mrs. Magee, I'm so pleased to meet you," said Mary, who was indeed delighted to get a good look at the notorious lady realtor.

"I think you know Arthur Bird," said Mrs. Magee, turning around to tuck her arm in the arm of someone who had been standing behind her, drawing him forward.

"Of course I know Arthur Bird," said Homer, glowering at him. "Destiny's right-hand man."

Arthur blushed, and beamed at Mrs. Magee. Mrs. Magee beamed at Arthur. "Arthur and I have a little announcement to make," she said.

"Surely, Mrs. Magee," said Homer, flabbergasted, "you don't mean . . . ?"

"A partnership." Mrs. Magee giggled. "Arthur and I are going forth together on a thrilling new adventure."

Christ, what a ghastly union! "You mean, you're going to . . . you two are going to . . . ?"

"No, no, we *three*." Mrs. Magee was beckoning to someone else, a tall stooped figure swathed in mufflers and sweaters and earmuffs and overcoats, an old man clinging to the railing looking out to sea. "Obed!" shrieked Mrs. Magee. "Obed Biddle! Oh, Mr. Biddle! Come here, Obed, I need you!"

Mary choked. Homer's mind reeled. Surely this was not the Obed Biddle who was Kitty's landlord. It couldn't possibly be the Obed Biddle who had stood up in Quaker Meeting and recited all those verses from Exodus. Surely it was utterly inconceivable that this was the Mr. Biddle who had stood like Moses upon the shore of the Red Sea and stretched out his hand over the enraptured congregation. But inconceivable or not, that was who it was. Mr. Biddle gaped toothlessly at Mrs. Magee, and at last he responded to her shouted introductions with a croaking gasp. "G'mawning." Then Mrs. Magee pulled him close to her and nestled one arm into his elbow and the other arm into Arthur Bird's and cuddled them to her in a cozy little threesome, a bizarre trinity, a three-headed monstrous disparate amalgamation, and explained her new adventure. "Arthur is putting his money into it and Obed is putting his land at Quidnet into it and I'm putting my know-how into it, and here we are all together on our way to Boston right this very minute to sign the franchise for the first Howard Johnson's Restaurant and Motel complex on Nantucket Island."

There was a stupefied silence. "You mean, *orange rooves?*" spluttered Homer. "On *Nantucket?* But what about the bylaw? The new zoning bylaw?"

"Oh, of course not orange rooves. Nothing vulgar like orange rooves. And as for the bylaw, we fully expect it to be overturned any day now, don't we, boys? I mean, the case on behalf of the bylaw was hardly advanced by the actions of its late supporter, Mrs. Green, was it, Mr. Kelly? But actually of course it doesn't matter anyway," said Mrs. Magee, patting Mr. Biddle's bony hand, "because Obed and I thought ahead, didn't we, Obed? We registered a plan for his property before the bylaw went into effect, didn't we, Obed? I said, *didn't we, Obed?*"

Mr. Biddle grinned vacantly and wobbled his head up and down.

Homer's jaw went slack. He couldn't think of anything to say. Mary politely gabbled something that sounded like "How nice!" and nodded her head up and down too, and the trio melted away to the railing once again and stood in a tightly knit triumvirate with elbows interlocked.

Homer wanted to go lie down. He leaned against his wife and quoted Melville. " 'Doesn't the devil live forever? Who ever heard that the devil was dead?' My God, it's all going to hell. All this time somebody should have been bolstering up Mr. Biddle, encouraging him, befriending him. But nobody thought—I mean, everybody thought she would at least wait until he was dead before she started gobbling up his property. Everybody thought she was just some kind of a vulture, but now it turns out she goes after living prey. Oh, why wasn't somebody more vigilant? Eternal vigilance, that's what it takes. Eternal vigilance is the price of an island."

Mary tried to comfort him. "Well, don't forget, Homer, at least you helped to save all that land of Helen Green's. Nothing can happen to that part of the island now, forever and ever."

"But damn it all, this is terrible. Poor old Mr. Biddle." Homer glanced at the old man again in anguished sympathy, and this time he was surprised to see that Mr. Biddle was beginning to look like Moses once again. His drooping sleeve was lifted up, he was stretching his arm out over the sea. Homer looked where his arm was pointing, half expecting to see the waters divided and the children of Israel walking across Nantucket Sound. What was he saying? He was croaking aloud, crying something in a hoarse fluting nasal shout. There was something in the water. He was shouting about something in the water. People were running over from the other side of the boat, crowding along the railing. "What did he say?" whimpered Homer. "I didn't hear what he said. What was that he said?"

"I think he said 'Finbacks,' " said Mary. She pointed too. Everyone was pointing. "It's a kind of whale, I think. Look, see them spouting!"

There was a whole school of them, small whales, finbacks, rolling over and over in the water. They were racing toward the boat, to the delight of all the passengers, who were clustered around Mr. Biddle like the descendants of Jacob around Moses in the Promised Land. Now the black backs of the whales were rising and falling under the outstretched patriarchal arm of Mr. Biddle. They were rolling in the water like chariot wheels, a manifest sign of God's whole and wondrous original creation.

On the morning of the day when Joe and Kitty were to leave Nantucket Island for good, Kitty finished her poem about the watery substances and humors of the body. She had started struggling with it on the day they met, so now that it was finished she gave it to Joe. The new part of the poem was about the salt tides of the blood, the breath steaming from the mouth, the words bursting from the lips in warm droplets on the air, and it was about the ocean depths of which they were proprietors.

> I behold you
> from this shore that I inhabit
> as another sea,
> an ocean walking,
> an undiscovered main
> within whose chartless depths
> move mammoth whales
> and glistening silver schools of little fish,
> while on the mile-deep sandy floor
> crawl eyeless nameless undiscovered creatures.
> A great shell settles,
> abandoned by its occupant.
> A sunken vessel rises and subsides.
> Wide tablelands and unascended mountains
> lie beneath the broad slow swells
> that roll from your horizon—
> but dolphins break your surface!
> You smile.
> The sun dazzles into ripples.

As servants of God, what land or estate we hold, we hold under him as his gift. . . . This gift is not absolute, but conditional, for us to occupy as dutiful children and not otherwise, for he alone is the true proprietor. "The world," saith he, "is mine, and the fulness thereof. . . ."

JOHN WOOLMAN, Quaker, 1770

Afterword

I wrote this book after witnessing the solar eclipse of March 7, 1970, from Nantucket Island, but neither the fictional eclipse nor the island in the book is in exact accord with its real counterpart. Weather conditions and tide levels and times have been changed. Houses have been picked up from one end of the island and set down at another. Patterns of land ownership are imaginary. Helen Green's zoning bylaw never existed, nor does her Boatwright Land Trust resemble any real land trust. There is no realtor like Wilhelmina Magee, and her Melville Estates and her marina at Monomoy are pure invention. So far as I know, Howard Johnson's does not plan to build a restaurant on Nantucket. There are no Ropers or Boatwrights among the old families of the island. Boozer Brown and his gas station are fictional. None of the articles attributed to the *Inquirer and Mirror* ever appeared in that paper.

I am especially eager to disentangle my often-befuddled Nantucket Protection Society from that worthier organization the Nantucket Conservation Foundation, which has been laboring so hard and so effectively under the leadership of its executive secretary, James Lentowski, to save the island from overuse and overdevelopment. Through the generosity of many people, this body has been able to accumulate land for conservation, until it is now the largest single landowner on Nantucket. In spite of its efforts, however, the great bulk of the island is still owned by private individuals and zoned for residential or limited commercial development. Thus, from the point of view of those who think Nantucket already overdeveloped, the larger part is still endangered —moor, field, wood, pond, salt marsh, dune and beach. The Nantucket Sound Islands Trust Bill, sponsored by Senators Kennedy and Brooke and Congressman Studds, may someday diminish the danger. The framers of the bill have not yet published in final form the map showing how the islands are to be classified, which parts are to be "open lands," where building will be forbidden, and which are to be "resource management lands," where it will be restricted. The ultimate fate of the bill may be determined by the Senate and House in 1975.

Several Nantucket people have helped with the writing of this book in ways large and small. Most of all I am thankful for the help and hospitality and friendship of Julie Perkins, which began with that first bowl of solar-eclipse split-pea soup. Especially valuable was the advice of naturalist Clinton Andrews of the University of Massachusetts Research Center at Quaise and his wife, ornithologist Edith Andrews, but I am anxious to say that they are not responsible for any blundering application of the information they gave me. I am also eager to thank Dr. Wesley Tiffney, Director of the University of Massachusetts Research Center; Chief Officer Wayne Tolbert of the U.S. Coast Guard and his crew, who took us to Great Point in the amphibious *Lark;* Chris Colberg and Gary Terrell, who demonstrated scalloping in Nantucket Harbor; Patrolmen Lionel Starr and Robert Kurcz of the Nantucket Police Department; Nantucket Fire Chief John Gaspie, Jr.; Louise R. Hussey, Librarian, Nantucket Historical Association; James Bartsch of "The Sunken Ship"; Henry Kehlenbeck of the Pacific National Bank; attorney Robert Mooney; and Wesley Fordyce, Clerk of the Superior Court.

Helpful friends and neighbors at home were Karoly Balogh, Elizabeth Hewitt, Alvin Levin, Emanuel Maier and Maryalice Thoma. Elizabeth A. Little of Lincoln and Nantucket read a manuscript that was a palimpsest requiring three sets of spectacles.

There really was a rainbow on the day of the eclipse.

J.L.

75 76 77 10 9 8 7 6 5 4 3 2

A BIRD'S EYE VIEW OF NANTUCKET ISLAND

GREAT POINT

THE MOON BEG
TO ECLIPSE THE SU
ONE HOU
BEFORE TOTAL

THE GAULS

COSKATA POND

WOODS

HALLOVER POND

HEAD OF TH

WYERS POINT

BASS POINT

HARBOR

NANTUCKET

FIVEFINGERED POINT

POCOMO HEAD

SOUND

THIRD POINT

THE JETTIES

SECOND POINT

POLPIS HA

JOE GREEN

QUAISE

FIRST POINT

ABRAMS POINT

FOLGERS MARSH

BRANT POINT

NANTUCKET

SHIMMO

FUDGE HILL

POLPIS ROAD

BOAT

STRAIGHT WHARF

HARBOR

SHAWKEMO HILLS

SA

TOWN OF NANTUCKET

MONOMOY

THE CREEKS